CW00508382

The Last Viking

Book 7 in the New World Series

By

Griff Hosker

The Last Viking

Published by Sword Books Ltd 2023

SWORD
BOOKS

Copyright ©Griff Hosker First Edition 2023

A CIP catalogue record for this title is available from the British Library.
Cover by Design for Writers

Contents

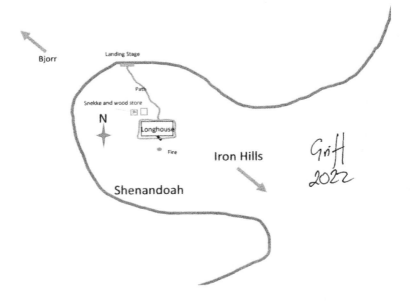

Prologue

I am Erik and I am the last Viking who still lives to the south of the Land of Ice and Fire. I am old now and weary beyond words. When the Moneton arrow slammed into my knee it left me with a wound I carry yet, and I cannot shake either the pain or the lack of movement. I carry other wounds but they do not keep me awake at night as I moan in my sleep. I know that I make such noises for my wife, Laughing Deer, mentions them when we rise. It is lucky that for the last few years, we have lived in peace. Since we defeated Eagle Claws and the men he led to try to take my magical weapons, the Clan of the Bear had prospered and grown. Although my friend Brave Eagle had not returned since our victory, some of his tribe, the tribe we had briefly joined, journeyed over the ridge of blue to our home Eagle Shadow, on the Shenandoah. When I found the grassy knoll, I had chosen it because it allowed us to grow and gave us safety from predators. Now our longhouse and storerooms almost filled it. We had grown so much that soon we would need to build a second longhouse. We would have to take more of the trees and cultivate more of the land by the ditch to provide food. We had added a ditch across a loop in the river to make a barrier against our enemies. It was a dry ditch for we had not broken through to the river. However, with the river, we had surrounded our home.

When I had slept in the dreamworld after the stone club had cracked my skull, the volva, Gytha, came to me in spirit form. She told me I was no longer needed as a warrior and I gave away my sword and my hand axe. I hoped that the spirit who had guided me since our time on Bear Island was right but I also knew that the Three Sisters spun their webs to entrap men. I was still vigilant. I made sure that one of the men from the clan walked around our land each day looking for signs of enemies. We had chosen our eyrie well and surveyed the valley below us. We knew the trails that enemies might use and the signs that they might leave. We were a small clan and that helped us to identify each other by the marks we left on the ground.

Chapter 1

The time after the battle was a good one. Laughing Deer and I spent more time together. Gytha was right and I did not need to be a warrior. I was still the best of sailors and I took the snekke out to fish whenever I could. I took with me those who were unfamiliar with the snekke and I taught them what I knew. Golden Bear and Brave Cub were the best sailors. The other snekke, *'Doe'*, was theirs and they fished too. When I was not fishing, I spent time with Laughing Deer. We were the elders of the clan and others took on the tasks that Laughing Deer had once called her own. When we sat on the two stumps at the top of the steep slope that led to the river, we could look west and see the virgin forest. We enjoyed each other's company. Of course, being Laughing Deer, she could not help but comment if a task was not performed properly. The two of us often acted as the carers of the young. When babies were no longer suckled, their mothers could take on more tasks and the two of us often sat playing with a clutch of toddlers. I would pull faces and make funny noises while Laughing Deer would tell them tales. She was the heart of the clan. The women would come to her to ask for advice and to help make decisions. I was unnecessary. We were not at war and we had no land to explore and so I was able to be the old man who watched the world slip by and his clan grow. Those were the best of times. They were the happiest time of our lives for we had peace and we had comfort.

My son Brave Cub and his wife Redbreast had just been delivered of a son, who they named Otter's Teeth, when the three sisters spun. Laughing Deer became ill. Her sickness came just the day after my grandson was born. She was still laughing at his name, because when he had suckled he had nipped his mother, when she suddenly gripped her middle and yelped in pain herself. Laughing Deer was the healer in the family and, until she was stricken, she was never sick. No matter what we did we could not ease her pain. She joked that she had cooked some bad fish. We knew it was not bad fish for we all ate from the same pot and no one else was ill. Had she been a warrior I would have said that there was some piece of metal within her body, for she held her right side as though it was a wound. It took a day for her to die and I never moved from her side the whole time. I held her hand while my family did all that they could for her. We used poultices, salves, and medicines all of which had cured before, but none of them worked. She gripped my hand tightly and our eyes locked. There were unspoken words between us as I held the hand of Laughing Deer. I was not a healer and others toiled to make her well. Little White Dove came into her own for she was a tower of strength. Even so, the pain became increasingly worse and forced involuntary tears from Laughing Deer's eyes.

I think she knew she was dying for there was one moment of clarity when the paroxysm of pain eased and she could talk. She whispered in my ear, "Do not mourn my death, Erik the Navigator, for my life since you took me from the Penobscot, has been a blessing. I never thought that you would outlive me but I am glad that you do for you are the heart of this clan. When I am gone…"

"We will cure this ill…"

"When I am gone, I shall return as Gytha does and bring you comfort. When you are in the steam hut and smoke the pipe filled with the dream leaf, close your eyes and I shall be there. We have brought up the children well and Little White Dove shall now be the matriarch. Kiss me, husband, while the pain abates."

I kissed her and she smiled. I began to hope that the ailment, whatever it was, had gone. Indeed. when Little White Dove came in and saw her mother with a smile on her face she thought the worst had passed. We were both wrong for within the time it takes to hoist the sail on a snekke it came back worse and the next hours saw her scream and arch her back. When she went still it was sad but a relieved sadness for she would no longer be in pain. I held her body to mine until Moos Blood and Brave Cub peeled me away.

"Our mother would not want this, Father. We have to bury her. The clan needs to say words and then we can begin to mourn."

Moos Blood, now a man grown and the next leader of the clan, was right. I obeyed him. The women of the clan laid Laughing Deer out in her best clothes, the ones she saved for special occasions, like the Winter Solstice. My sons dug her grave and we chose a spot where the evening sun would shine as it set in the west. It was close to the place where we had sat and enjoyed some peace. Now she would enjoy eternal peace. We had ever journeyed west and it seemed right to do so. Wrapped in a deerskin, for she was Laughing Deer, we put her in the ground and then each of us piled soil upon it. My sons and the other men of the clan had brought flat stones from the river and we placed those on the top before the last earth was placed there.

As we stood around, the family held hands to make a circle and they all looked to me to speak. The words almost choked as they rose in my

3

throat but I knew that I had a duty to speak and I did so. They were the hardest words I ever spoke.

"Laughing Deer, you always said that I saved you from the Penobscot but, in truth, you saved me. I think that without you, I would have died on Bear Island. My bones would lie there still, unmourned and without a marker. You gave me a family and a clan. You made sure that the blood of a Norseman would still flow through the bodies of those we brought into this world. You were my rock and my friend. I do not know how I will get through each day without you by my side. I will have to force myself to open my eyes each morning and take from the dreams that I know will be of you."

I dropped to my knees and prostrated myself on the earth. Tears came flooding from my eyes.

Moos Blood and Brave Cub lifted me to my feet. Little White Dove wiped the tears from my face saying, "This is not how our mother would want you to be, Father. Her spirit will live in this place, I know that. Her spirit will be in Otter's Teeth. The Allfather has brought one life into this world and taken another from it. You have a clan and a family who will need you to be as a mother and a father. This is meant to be, this is *wyrd*."

She was right but that did not take away the pain that I felt inside me.

My children were right and life went on. We were a small clan but we had young mouths to feed. When I had first come to the land on the Patawomke there had just been six of us in the clan. Now there were more than twenty of us. Moos Blood had three children and Little White Dove and Fears Water had two each. The three firstborn from Eagle's Shadow, two boys and a girl, had all seen more than six summers. They now worked with their mothers. They tended the crops and helped to pick the nuts and berries that the clan relied on. Soon the two eldest boys would learn to hunt and my grandson, Water Bird, would be introduced to the snekke. It is strange but only those of my blood were truly happy sailing the snekke. Fears Water had taken to sailing quite well but he was never as comfortable as Moos Blood, Brave Cub and Golden Bear. I wondered if any of Little White Dove's children would be sailors.

The two snekke were now old. *'Gytha'* did not have many voyages left in her. That spring, when we took the two snekke from their winter homes and examined them, I saw what my sons did not. *'Gytha'* was no longer sound. I saw that the timbers, despite the frequent painting of pine tar, were rotting. I let them put *'Doe'* in the river and fill her hull with ballast. When they returned to carry *'Gytha'* down the slope I shook my head. "*'Gytha'* is no longer whole. She will go on the water no more."

Golden Bear asked, "What do we do with her? Break her up for spares?" Golden Bear was eminently practical.

I shook my head, "No, my son, she deserves a better end." I stood, "When I die, then you will bury me in the snekke. I am the last Viking and it is fitting that I should have a Viking funeral."

Long Nose was close by, "A Viking funeral?"

I nodded, "When a chief dies he is placed in a snekke with his weapons around him. The sail is hoisted and the snekke is set on fire. It is the way I wish to be buried."

Moos Blood exchanged a look with Brave Cub, "Father, our mother would like you to look forward to life."

I smiled, "And I do. I do not intend to die any time soon." My hand went to the Hammer of Thor around my neck. "But the sisters spin and a man must plan. This makes me happy. I know that I shall have the funeral I want, no matter how far in the future that is. Place her back in the winter store for we must plan and build a new one. The clan is growing and we need two snekke."

They looked relieved and knew what I meant. When we had lived along the Patawomke we had devised a way to fish using a net hung between two snekke. It was a quick way to harvest the river. When the Shenandoah was full we used the same method. You could not do it with birch bark boats for they could easily capsize.

My sons had helped me to build *'Doe'* but the others had not. I gathered them around me to explain how it would be done. There would be ten of us and, in theory, it should have been easier. "The first thing we need is wood. This is good as we need to clear more land for crops. We need one tree that will have a natural curve. That will be the keel. It will be that tree that determines the length of the snekke. Then we need straight trees that we will hew and split. We will need to season them. We need a good, strong, sapling for the mast. When that is done we will need trenails. We have some but not enough. When we have found the trees then I will go with four of you and we will visit the cave of the bear to fetch iron. While we do that Brave Cub will show you all how to make pine tar. That is no bad thing for we can use the pine tar for other things too."

Moos Blood beamed, "This is better, Father."

I frowned, "Better?"

"For the first time since Mother was taken from us, you seem positive and happy. This is what she would wish."

The Last Viking

I nodded and smiled. What I had not said was that this snekke would be named *'Laughing Deer'*. Nor did I tell them that inside my heart still ached for my wife. At night my bed was lonely and I often found myself reaching out to put my arm around her but she was not there.

We had flint axes as well as some hatchets and hand axes made from iron. We would be able to work the wood better this time. We set off to examine the stand of trees that we would hew. I had decided to clear the land on the eastern side of the ditch. We could cultivate that land but, more importantly, it would give us a clear line of sight and prevent enemies from sneaking up to our ditch. In the years since the war we had lived in peace, but I knew that one day an enemy would come and we had to be prepared. The straight ones were easy to find but the curved one hid from us. Trees are living things and I did not mind that the tree was elusive. Golden Bear and Moos Blood came with me to head deeper into the forest while the others cut down the eight trees we had selected. The new men in the clan had yet to learn that making pine tar was far harder than hewing trees. That task would come next. When we found the wood for the keel, it was a hawk that showed us the way. It flew into the sky when we neared the branch he was using to look for prey. It drew my eye up and I saw the tree. When it had been young something had leaned against it, so that it grew not straight up but was bent like a bow. Had the curve been too extreme it would have been of no use, but whatever had bent it had not done so for long. It was perfect.

"Go and fetch axes, I will wait here."

In truth, the walk had made my knee ache. I would need the steam hut and the dream leaves to enable me to sleep. I sat on a large stone that lay close to the bottom of the tree. I wondered if it had been the stone that made the tree bend. I put my hand on the tree. "We are going to cut you, my friend, but we will not take you all. We will leave your stump. Perhaps you will begin to grow again. The part we take will live and fly across the water. I do not take your life, I just change it."

To give the tree a chance to regrow, I had my sons cut it at my chest height. It would never be as magnificent again but it would live and, as I had discovered after Laughing Deer had died, you looked for reasons to live. When the tree crashed to the ground it cut a swathe through lesser trees and there was more light. It gave me hope that the tree might regrow. The damaged trees could be harvested for kindling. We trimmed the smaller branches and left them in a pile. My grandchildren would be sent to fetch in the wood which would not be wasted, it would be firewood for the winter. It took all our efforts to drag it back to Eagle Shadow. The other timbers were there already.

6

That first day of work took it out of me and I went into the steam hut and lit my pipe. We had two kinds of leaves that we smoked. One I called the dream leaf and she had a strong smell. I used it judiciously and mainly when the pain was too severe. The smoking of the dream leaf normally coincided with a visitation by the spirits. I was alone and that day Laughing Deer and Gytha both came to me. Perhaps it was exhaustion, or maybe the spirit of the tree had spoken to them, but they came. They said not a word but both smiled at me. Their mere presence was enough and I was comforted with the thought that Laughing Deer and Gytha were together. It came to me, as they smiled, that I never saw Snorri with Gytha. I hoped he was in Valhalla. I was content and that night's sleep was one of the best I had enjoyed since my wife was taken from me.

While Golden Bear took the grandchildren to fetch the kindling, the rest of us spent the morning stripping the bark from the trees. The better pieces would be used to mend or make boats while the rest was collected to be dried as kindling. I marked the trees with a piece of charcoal and the others cut them all into the same lengths. Nothing would be wasted. We left them beneath *'Gytha's'* old sail to season and then returned to the stumps of the eight trees. While the keel was a birch tree, the others were mainly pine and the roots could be burned to make pine tar. Moos Blood and I showed them how to make the oven. That took all day. We had made pine pots while Laughing Deer was alive and we would use them to collect the pine tar. I set them to dig out the roots. That was backbreaking work and made the hewing of the trees seem like an easy task.

When we headed back to the longhouse I said, "Tomorrow I will take Golden Bear, Black Feather, Long Nose and Bjorr Tooth. We will take tools to dig the iron. Moos Blood, I leave you in charge of the village."

Brave Cub said, "Why do you have to go? We know where the cave is."

"And you know how to break down the iron but we need all the clan to know these things. When I am gone then you will have to pass these skills on. While I can still move let me be of some use to the clan, eh? Besides, I am still the chief and I decide these things."

Once more my sons exchanged looks and I wondered how long it would be before they challenged me.

We took not only tools and food but also weapons. We were moving far from the safety of the river. Thus far we had not encountered others close to our home but, since the attack by Eagle Claws, we were no longer hidden. One day someone would come and they might be belligerent. I took nothing for granted. I let the others bear most of the task of carrying, I had my bow and my seax along with my ale skin and a satchel with food. It had been many years earlier when I had found the cave in the place we called the Iron Hills. This would only be my third visit. Black Feather and Long Nose would have to be shown the way. This time I used my seax to mark the trees where we turned, with a rune. To any who did not know, the mark would have no significance but my clan would know and, long after I was gone, they would find their way to the bear cave on the blue ridge. I knew that the journey up to the cave would be easier than the one coming down. My bad knee hated coming down. I did not show my pain to the others but bore it stoically.

I was actually enjoying the peace of the forest. My son was a good tracker and knew that we were the only men to walk along this trail. We saw signs of other creatures, especially white-tailed deer, but ours were the only signs of humans. It was as if I had my own kingdom. I thought back to Orkneyjar. That had seemed relatively empty but within an hour of leaving our home, we would have found other homes. Even in the Land of Ice and Fire, we all lived on top of one another. Here there was room to move and to breathe. I knew that others had lived in the valley, but from the signs that I had found that had been many generations ago. Perhaps when my clan was no more the animals would reclaim their valley. I consoled myself with the thought that at least my spirit would still be here.

The last time I had visited the cave all that remained of the bear were a few gnawed bones. When we reached it I saw that the bones were gone and the stink of death had departed. I would not violate the cave by camping inside. Instead, we would use the campfire we had used on our first visit. It had led Eagle Claws to us and that was a sobering thought. It was too late to begin work when we arrived and so we set up a pot and lit a fire. We had brought enough food to make a hunter's stew and while I tended to the fire, the other four foraged for food. The cave was a peaceful place but also a sad one. The bear had been entombed in the cave and died a long and lingering death. I said a prayer to the bear's spirit as the flames licked the kindling. No creature deserved to die alone. The warmth of the fire was comforting.

After we had eaten and we lay in our sleeping blankets, we spoke. It was just Golden Bear and me at first but the others joined in. "When this iron is no more, Father, what then?"

"There will be other places where we can find it. I am not skilled enough to know where and it may well be that we rely on the three sisters to lead us there, but I am confident that there will be other places where it is found." I smiled, "And you and my other sons know how to recognise it. Soon," I waved a hand at the other three, "all of you will have that skill. I hope that you pass this knowledge on to your children too, for that is how the clan will survive."

Long Nose said, "It is a good land, Shaman of the Bear, but we are still few in number."

I nodded at Bjorr Tooth, "Willow Leaf and her family found us. There will be others. The world can be a cruel place, Long Nose. There are many men like Eagle Claws and not enough like Brave Eagle."

Black Feather had recently married Willow Leaf and he smiled, "My wife says that had you not found her then the four of them might have died. You gave them the chance of life."

"And I was happy to do so. I was saved on more than one occasion by another. The Allfather is always there for those in need."

"What of those who are not as lucky as we?"

I looked at Bjorr Tooth, "The Three Sisters can be wilful, Bjorr Tooth, and the Allfather sometimes loses the battle of wits with the Norns."

I had forgotten what hard, back-breaking work was involved in gathering the ore. We had brought large stone clubs to break down the rocks but it was the collecting of the rocks that made us have to work together and sweat and curse. We worked together to find large pieces which we would break up to make carrying them back easier. I had collected the smaller pieces on my first visit. I knew that the next time I came, if there was a next time, we would need more of us and we would have to spend more time here. By the end of the day, we had enough to make the trenails and a few axes. We now had more men who could learn the skill of shaping wood and they would need tools.

The hard day of work gave us all a healthy appetite. Bjorr Tooth's skill with a bow meant we had squirrel for our evening meal and the exercise allowed me to sleep almost pain and dream-free. I woke more refreshed than I might have expected. I was now an old man.

I was the first awake and as I made water I listened to the sounds of the forest. It was never totally silent. That morning I thought I heard something different from what I expected. I could not make it out but it jarred with me. Putting it to the back of my mind I woke the others and ate the remains of the stew. We had come prepared and I spread the weight of the ore between all the bags we had made. We tied the tools to the bags and carried our bows. It would be a much slower progress from the ridge and the Iron Hills than it was to get there. I led for I had done this journey the most and besides, I was the slowest.

9

We had travelled a mile when I heard the mewling from ahead. The others heard it too. I raised my hand for silence whilst stringing my bow and taking an arrow from the bag on my waist. The noise was coming from our right. I slipped off my ore bag and the others emulated me. I waved them to my left and right. Whatever was making the noise had to be investigated. Leaving something unknown within walking distance of Eagle's Shadow could be disastrous. It became clear that the mewling I had heard was not an animal but a baby. As we drew closer to the sound, we also heard an animal. It was a dog and it was growling.

We cleared some trees and saw a woman, in distress with a baby trying to feed at her breast. A rangy, mangy and ill-fed dog stood growling protectively before them. Black Feather raised his bow. Laying mine down I said, "Put your weapons down, the dog is protecting them. He does not deserve to die for doing his duty." Reaching into my satchel I took out a handful of dried venison. I proffered my open palm and the growling ceased but the dog still viewed me with suspicion. "There's a good boy. We mean you no harm." I know not why but I spoke in Norse. Hunger overcame his suspicion and he took the venison and swallowed it in one, "The rest of you stay back." I knelt next to the woman. She was alive, but only just. I did not recognise the clan markings nor the tribal artefacts and I knew she was not Moneton, Penobscot or Powhatan.

Her eyes opened and words burst forth like a torrent. I understood not one of them, "Does anyone recognise the words?"

"Just one or two, Shaman. I recognise the words baby and child. Her clothes do not look like any I have seen." Bjorr Tooth was Powhatan but had lived with the Moneton as a captive.

They looked to me to be more like the dress of the Mohawks, but they lived so far to the north that I dismissed the idea immediately. The baby was still trying to get milk but the woman's body was so emaciated as to suggest that the baby would go hungry. Having said that it was not a newborn. I now recognised the ages of children.

"Approach but do so slowly. I do not want the dog alarmed." The dog did appear to be calmer. Perhaps my gentleness had helped. I slipped my ale skin around and held the spout to her mouth. She drank some and tried to smile. She said something else. It had a more familiar sound to it and I thought she was giving me thanks.

Golden Bear had also given the dog some dried meat and was stroking the animal. Long Nose and Black Feather knelt next to the woman and it was Long Nose who noticed the wound. "Shaman, she has been hurt." He pointed to the tear in her side. The hide she wore had been cut and I saw an angry wound. Long Nose leaned in and sniffed, "There is badness there, Shaman." He shook his head.

"We will help you." I smiled as I said the words and I mimed helping her up. She shook her head and, instead, held the baby out to me. I took the swaddled bundle but the effort must have been too much for the woman. Her back arched and she fell back. Long Nose knelt next to her and shook his head. She was dead. The dog went to the woman and began to howl.

The baby began to cry and I instinctively did what I would have done with my grandchildren. I made soothing noises and holding the baby close to me patted its back. "You must bury her. She has chosen a quiet place to die. Fetch the bags and the tools. It will add time to our journey but it cannot be helped." Left alone I spoke to the dog, the baby and the dead woman. "The Allfather has sent you here to join my clan. I know not whence you have come but now you are part of the Clan of the Bear." Once more I spoke in Norse for I was speaking as much to the spirits as the three before me. Amazingly the dog ceased howling and the baby fell asleep. Perhaps the crying had wearied it.

Golden Bear managed to get the dog away from the body and the four of them dug a grave. They gently folded her arms and then they covered her first with rocks and then with soil. We took nothing from her. She would journey to the next world with her bracelets, necklets and hair fastenings in place. Whoever waited for her would recognise her.

"And now we journey home. Put your bags on your backs and then you, Golden Bear, can hold the child while I don mine."

"We can carry your share, Father."

"I want no one wearied to the point that they fall. I have been chosen to be the one to carry the child and I will do so."

When my bag was on my back, I took the sleeping baby and we headed back to the trail. I spoke to the dog. I used the Norse word for wolf, "Ulla, come." The dog obeyed and trotted at my side. I am not sure it was the words that made it obey. More likely it was protecting the child.

We stopped frequently. The baby woke once and I gave it some ale from the ale skin. Had we any milk I would have given the baby some but we had none and the baby clearly wanted liquid. It slept again. I knew that it would have soiled itself but I did not want to unfasten the swaddling. We had enough women in the clan for that to be dealt with more effectively at Eagle's Shadow. When we were close, I sent Bjorr Tooth to run ahead and warn them of our approach. I was weary beyond words. My knee had complained for the last five miles and I feared that it would not hold up on the climb up the path.

The light that glowed from the open door made me smile. It was like a beacon guiding us home. As we entered the longhouse Willow Leaf, now the oldest woman in the clan, came to take the baby from me. Ulla was still at my side. While the women took the baby to the fire where they could tend to it, Moos Blood and the others helped to take the bag from my back.

"Here is a tale, Father."

I nodded, "Aye, Moos Blood. Fetch the animal some water and food."

My eldest son shook his head, "You look ready to fall and yet all that you can think of is the needs of a mangy animal."

"Ulla here protected the dying woman and the child. He deserves to be treated like a hero. He is now part of the clan."

Willow Leaf called over, "And we have another girl in the clan. What did you name her, Shaman?"

"I did not."

Golden Bear said, "She is strong, as was her mother and her dog. Let us call her Iron Will, for surely she has iron in her."

It seemed right to name her thus.

Our late arrival and the need for food meant that we did not go to bed as early as we normally did. We had much to talk about. There was much speculation about the woman, the wound and the baby. We had two nursing mothers and between them, they ensured that Iron Will had milk and was put to sleep with the other babies. We sat and spoke. I largely listened. I knew that the spirits would talk to me either when I slept or in the steam hut. The spirits talking was a good thing for the clan.

"Did you notice that her mockasins were worn right through?"

"Aye, Bjorr Tooth. She had been walking for many days."

"The wound too was not a recent one. Where could she have come from?"

"I cannot see Brave Eagle or his clan letting her walk through their land in that condition."

Golden Bear suddenly banged the table, "The west. It is the only thing that makes sense. She has come from the West and that is why none of us recognised either her words or her clothes. We know the Moneton live to the north and the east but we have never explored the river to the west."

Moos Blood smiled, "Perhaps, little brother, when we have made our new snekke we should sail that way."

Fears Water shook his head, "Better not to poke the bear, Moos Blood. Let us stay hidden here."

Little White Dove smiled, "We are the Clan of the Bear, Fears Water. There may be others like Iron Will's mother. What do you say, Father?"

"I say that all that I have heard is good but Moos Blood is right. Until we have the new snekke we can do nothing and I had a mind to explore the land to the west of us before we made this discovery. Perhaps I have another voyage left in me, eh?"

Silence filled the longhouse, "Surely you will stay here, Father, and let me or one of the others take the snekke."

"Moos Blood, I am still Erik the Navigator. This task was clearly appointed for me but you are right, we build the boat first." I stood, "And now I will go to bed."

I had not smoked the dream leaf nor had I used the steam hut but that night I dreamed.

I saw, again, the roaring waterfall that had haunted my dreams before I had even met Laughing Deer. I saw the woman who had died and she was alive and laughing with other women of her tribe. They were washing clothes in the calmer waters below the waterfall. My dream grew dark and I slept.

Chapter 2

Ulla kept as close to Iron Will as he could. Willow Leaf decided that the dog was too smelly to be allowed inside and she ejected the animal. Each morning, when the door to the longhouse was opened, Ulla would be waiting. He would not move until he had seen Iron Will and we began to bring out the babe so that the dog could see she was well. He began to follow me around and gradually transferred his affection to me. He was still attentive, especially when Iron Will cried, but that was less frequent now that there were so many mothers around. Both the child and the dog began to put on weight and look healthier. To satisfy my daughter, Bjorr Tooth and I bathed the dog. Ulla was not happy about the bath and growled his disapproval, but the dried venison trick worked and he eventually submitted. His aroma became less pungent.

I began to organise the men and appointed them tasks in the making of the snekke. While we waited for the wood to season I had them, under Moos Blood's supervision, split the logs into planks. It would help with the seasoning and I knew that the new ones would make mistakes, so the task would not be completed as quickly had it been just me and my sons who were doing the work. Moos Blood had managed to make the pine tar and it was now in sealed pots awaiting the hull to be completed. I set to making the trenails and tools. Golden Bear liked the work as did Long Nose and Fears Water. They became my assistants as we first broke up the ore and then melted it. We had the moulds already made and over those first days melted and poured molten metal into them. I knew that what we produced would not be perfect. Only Golden Bear had a real skill in the process but mistakes could be born. The disasters with the axe heads became the trenails and arrowheads that we would use. The five of us had brought more ore back from the Iron Hills than I had anticipated. I did not see myself returning there any time soon. I made myself a hatchet to replace the axe I had given to my son. It was a test of my skill as a weaponsmith. I found I enjoyed making something that I could spend hours finishing. It turned out to be the best weapon I ever made. It was sharp and kept its edge well.

Once the tools and nails were finished, we used river sand to take some of the roughness from them and then began to sharpen them. It was time-consuming work. We also had animals to hunt and fish to catch. It made for full days and nights that saw us collapse into our beds. I did not dream again or, at least, I did not remember the dreams I had. I decided that after seven days of work, I would enter the dream world through the portal of the steam hut. The new arrivals and the hard work seemed to give me a new lease of life. I had not mentioned it to anyone for, now that Laughing Deer was gone, I had no one in which to confide, but I was looking forward to a journey to the West. I knew that the river flowed to the south and west. I would not leave the river and if that took me more to the south than to the west then so be it. I wondered how the woman had crossed the river. I knew that there were rapids and shallows but I did not think that a woman with a baby and a wound would either risk or be able to cross. As I sharpened the curved axe that would be used to shape the strakes of the snekke, I found myself smiling. I had come a long way since I had left Orkneyjar. When I thought of the voyage that I had made south, from the land of Ice and Fire, I had not known if I would find land. How much easier would it be sailing along a river with the land close enough to touch?

Golden Bear said, "It is good to see you smile again, Father. When Mother died, I thought you had died too."

"Part of me did die but new life, my grandchildren and the foundling have shown me that there is still a purpose for me. I am the last Viking in this land and the Allfather still sees a need for me. The day he tires of me, then he will let me join your mother and the rest of my clan." Golden Bear shook his head. He did not like what he saw as morbid thoughts. To me, they were not morbid. I knew that I was old and Laughing Deer's death had shown me that death could come in many forms.

The tools finished and the wood still to be seasoned, left us enough time to go on a hunt across the river for white-tailed deer and bjorr. The bjorr skins were for warmth, while the deer hide could be fashioned into many different clothes. The meat, of course, could be preserved as well as eaten fresh. I might have taken Ulla with us but for two things. I was not sure how he would take to crossing the river and he was still weak from his privations in the wild. Better to wait until he was stronger and better trained. This would also be the time when we took Water Bird and Brown Feather on the hunt. Last year had been, so my wife had said, too early. This time they would come and my task would be to see that they came to no harm. We paddled across the river and made sure that the boats were drawn up high above the waterline. Then Moos Blood led the men and boys of the clan towards the bjorr lodges. Although Brave Eagle and his clan called them beavers, we used my word for them, bjorr. If we had enjoyed the luxury of more metal, we might have attempted to make a trap for the bjorr, but I was not skilled enough a metal worker to do that. We had, instead some wooden traps we had made. Whilst not as effective, we would catch some and we would hunt others with arrows and spears. We allowed the youngest boys to help set the traps. Brown Feather had a soaking for his pains and learned a lesson. His father, Fears Water laughed at his son's discomfort.

Then we went to hunt the deer. We would use metal tipped arrows. They killed better and we could always recover them from the bodies and reuse them. Each arrow had been sharpened and if sent true would strike deep within the animal and make for a quick kill. This would also be one of the first hunts that I had not led. I had every confidence in my three sons. I knew the others were good hunters too, but I trusted my three boys to do things the right way. I smiled as I saw Moos Blood feel the air and lead us down the trail that would take us to smell the deer before they could smell us. The Allfather smiled on us that day for we found the trail of the deer and it was heading away from us. They would stop and graze frequently and that would allow us to close with them. When it had just been my boys, Humming Bird and Fears Water, it had been more difficult for we were fewer in number. The extra three, Bjorr Tooth, Long Nose and Black Feather, along with my grandson and foster grandson, meant we had more beaters to surround the animals. I stayed in the centre of our line with the two boys within grabbing distance. Moos Blood was ahead and when he stopped and nocked an arrow then I knew that we were close. I had no bow but a spear with a metal head on it. It could be thrown but I could use it both as a crutch and as a weapon to keep a beast at bay. There were bears in the forests although, as we had neither seen their sign nor smelled their stink, I was confident that we would not find any close by.

It was Brown Feather's foot that gave us away. He stepped on a branch that broke and the herd was close enough for us to see them and they first heard and then saw us. They started. My sons were the most experienced of hunters and their arrows flew. I barked, "Stay close to me." It was a command for the two young boys as a milling herd would have simply trampled them to death.

Herds of deer can be highly unpredictable and this one was no exception. The stag leading them suddenly whirled and instead of fleeing us, charged at us. It may not have been intentional, the young animal could merely have panicked, but that mattered not. The twenty or more animals simply charged at us.

"Behind me." The command and urgency in my voice made the boys obey instantly and I held the spear before me.

There was a tree close by and I edged nearer to it so that we had some protection. The others simply loosed an arrow and then sought cover themselves. As they did so, they formed a funnel into which the herd ran and it led directly to me. The stag veered towards the trail and that took him and the majority of the herd away from the boys and me but panicking deer behave even more irrationally and a young male, yet to grow his antlers tried to overtake the others and came directly for me. I could not evade him for fear of him striking the boys. I braced myself and used the tree itself to anchor the base of the spear. I did not have to thrust because, in his blind panic, the deer impaled himself on the spear. He drove so hard that his snout was less than an arm's length from me when it died. The boys had come close to death and I realised that I should have brought Ulla. A snarling dog might have made a deer back off while an old man with a stick did not.

I turned and saw that the boys were shaking. Water Bird had been spattered with the blood of the dead deer. I lowered the spear and putting my foot on the animal, pulled out the spear which made a sucking sound. I put my hand on the deer's head, "You were a brave one but foolish, graze in Valhalla, my friend."

I spoke in Norse and Water Bird asked me what I said and I told him. Although the words did not translate well, he understood why I had said them. All creatures were on this earth because of the Allfather and all needed respect, even in death.

Moos Blood looked over to his son and smiled when he saw that he lived, "Is anyone hurt?"

Black Feather shouted, "Long Nose has gashed his arm."

"It is nothing."

Black Feather laughed, "He is embarrassed for he did not get out of the way of the stag."

Brave Cub looked over, "It looks like the Shaman of the Bear has made the best and cleanest kill. I count two other dead animals.".

Golden Bear said, "Two more are hurt. We should follow them."

They all looked at me and I shrugged, "Moos Blood, this is your hunt. The boys and Long Nose can stay with me. I will tend to the wound."

"You are right. Follow me." The trail left by the herd was clear to be seen.

Taking out the honey and the bindings from my satchel I said, "Come here, Long Nose. You two watch what I do. Hunting skills are necessary but so are the skills of the healer."

17

The wound was bleeding and it was a deep one in his lower arm. I took a hide thong and tied it tightly above the wound to slow the bleeding. "Brown Feather, pour some of the ale on the wound." My foster grandson did so. It was a clean cut. I took some of the precious honey and smeared it along the wound before I took some moss from a nearby tree and sealed it. I bound the wound and then, after releasing the thong around his upper arm, fashioned a sling.

"I do not need this, Shaman."

"You do. Better to heal well than undo my work. Sit there and we will make stakes." I turned to Water Bird and Brown Feather. "You seek branches the height of Moos Blood and the thickness of my spear. When you find them begin to cut them. We will need at least five." Brown Feather was especially keen to make up for his mistake and we soon fashioned the poles that we would use to carry back the deer. After stripping them and sharpening the end we rammed them into the bodies of the three dead deer to help us carry them back.

Long Nose asked, "Do we gut them?"

Normally we would but I shook my head, "We now have a dog and while the guts might not serve us, they will feed Ulla."

The rest came back carrying one dead deer on a sapling. "There was just one wounded badly enough for us to catch." Moos Blood smiled, "And you have saved us a job. Thank you."

Even Long Nose and I had to help carry them back to the bjorr tarn. We were ready for a rest and for some food. I checked that Long Nose's wound was not leaking blood and then we checked the traps. We had managed to catch two bjorr. It was better than nothing and we could return over the next days to see if the other traps had yielded bounty. Brown Feather and Water Bird now acted as hunters too and each one carried a dead bjorr as we headed back to the boats. The catch meant we had to send the boats over with deer, bjorr and my sons first. We waited patiently for the return. My sons were the most comfortable on the water. That was no surprise for the voyage in *'Gytha'* from Bear Island had made them so. The two youngest members of the clan might turn out to be sailors, but until they voyaged down the Patawomke and ventured into the Great Sea they could not even dream of calling themselves that.

Once back at Eagle's Shadow, the whole clan had to help with the butchering of the dead animals. Preservation would begin immediately. Once they were gutted and the guts put on to cook for Ulla, the choice parts were stuck on wood and younger women of the clan supervised their cooking. They would be the hunter's treats. I was still the most skilled of skinners and I was given the stag I had killed to skin. My seax was the perfect tool. My skill would mean we had a better skin to use. Moos Blood and Brave Cub, along with Fears Water, were also competent skinners. Golden Bear and Black Feather were left with the bjorr to skin.

Little White Dove and the women pegged out the skins when we had finished. The pots filled with the water we made, would be poured over them to begin the process of preservation. We then began to joint and fillet the animals. Nothing would be wasted. The head and the bones would be boiled and that would give us soup. The bones could then be used. The smaller ones would make needles and the larger ones, weapons and tools. Willow Leaf and Little White Dove did the job my wife had done when she was alive. They sorted the meat into that which we would eat over the next three weeks and that which we would preserve. We had enough salt to ensure that we would not need to return to the sea for half a year. By then the new snekke would be ready. The butchery took two days and I had Moos Blood light the fire in the steam hut. I wanted to rid my body of the stink of animal blood and I needed to speak to the spirits.

We feasted on bjorr meat and, having drunk some freshly brewed ale, I took my pipe and entered the steam hut. I sat naked with my bad knee held out before me and I lit the pipe. The dream leaves had an aromatic smell and, allied to the meal and ale I had just consumed, put me in a good place. I was not even aware of others joining me for I had my eyes closed and, as it normally did, the spirit world opened up for me and I was oblivious to all that was around me.

I saw, for the first time since she had died, Laughing Deer. She looked to be happy, younger and pain-free. She was with Gytha and the two of them had linked arms. I had long ago learned not to speak when I was in the spirit world and I watched as they waved their arms and all went black. It was when the light came again that I saw the woman we had found and the baby along with Ulla. Shaven-headed warriors were attacking their camp and I saw clubs striking down on the heads of the warriors from the village. A warrior stood protectively before the woman and child. He used a war club and a shield to defend himself and his family. Ulla snapped and bit. It looked to me like the warrior would win and then a spear was rammed into his body. The woman stood and tried to flee. A knife entered her body but, even in his dying the warrior protected what I took to be his wife and child. His club smashed into the skull of his killer. All went black and then I saw the sun setting in the west. The woman, child and Ulla were at a river. I saw stones in the river and they gingerly made their

19

way across. As the sun set behind them they collapsed on the bank and all went black.

When I opened my eyes, I saw that I was alone. The pipe had fallen from my fingers and my leg was stiff. I shuffled towards the entrance and when I lifted it I was greeted with a wave of icily cold air. Two pairs of hands came down to help me to my feet. It was Moos Blood and Brave Cub.

"It is almost morning, Father. We know you dreamt for we heard your words." Moos Blood had been in the steam hut the most frequently and knew its effect.

I nodded and rubbed my aching knee. The steam hut had helped the pain but the position of the leg meant the leg felt stiff.

"What did you see?"

I smiled, "What the spirits wanted me to see, Brave Cub. I saw your mother with Gytha. They opened the world of the past to me and I saw Ulla with Iron Will and the dead woman. They were in a village to the west and north of here. I saw the sun setting behind them and they were crossing a river."

Brave Cub frowned, "I see the west, but the north?"

"The only river we have seen so far that flowed from the north was the Patawomke. All the rest seem to flow from the west to the east." I shrugged. I will have a better idea when we sail up the Shenandoah."

"You still wish to make that voyage?"

"I have to. The dream showed me warriors who were not like the Moneton or the Penobscot. They dressed differently. The woman fled east to escape them. What if they are like the Moneton and intent on conquering new lands and enslaving others?"

"We could return to Brave Eagle. With Eagle Claws gone, it would be a peaceful place to live."

"And if you wish then you can go, Brave Cub. For my part, I will stay here. It is where your mother is buried and I will not leave her until I go to the Otherworld."

"I will stay, Father, for I like this place. If enemies come then we can defend it. We did so against Eagle Claws and we now have a larger clan."

I looked at Moos Blood, "Each man must make his own choice. When I return from the voyage, we will hold a Thing." I smiled, "The snekke is not even begun so let us not get ahead of ourselves. We have much work to do and there are three new warriors who need to learn the skills of snekke building."

Chapter 3

We built the new snekke by the river. We had suffered the spring floods and now the level of the river was consistent. When we had searched for the wood needed for the snekke, I found six y-shaped sections that were as close to identical as possible. They would form the ribs of the ship with a thwart to give them strength. It took time to use the new tools to shape the wood and make each section identical. We spent a week fitting them to the seasoned keel. It took a week as I was trying to save us work in the future. We shaped the ribs so that they were both smooth and in the same position. I showed the others how to make the meginhufr, the L-shaped piece of wood that attached the ribs to the third strake from the gunwale. It was a vital piece of carpentry and necessary to give the snekke strength. I let Moos Blood and Brave Cub hammer in the nails and wooden dowels that joined the keel and the ribs. That was where the strength of the snekke would lie. The other men helped but were largely spectators. That was no bad thing for they were learning from a shipwright. Then began the hard work. The timber was split to make the strakes and they were immersed overnight in the river to make them more supple. We inverted the keel and then began to hammer in the nails that secured the strakes to the keel and the thwarts. Over the next week, the boat took shape. The soaking in the water had made the strakes more pliable and we had more strong arms to hold them in place while I hammered in the nails. Each strake overlapped the one below. I realised that this would be a much quicker process because we had more men working on it. Even the two youngest boys were able to help. Once the strakes were attached, I had the pine tar put on to heat. This task was for my sons and me. We needed to ensure that the hot tar completely covered the strakes. It would take at least two or even three coats and that took two more days. We had enough pine tar left to coat the inside when we turned her over.

Each night I went alone to work on the figurehead that I would attach to the prow. The face I carved was that of Laughing Deer. I loved the time I spent carving and cutting the wood for it brought my dead wife back to life each time I took another sliver of wood. I kept the wood hidden with a skin during the day. I wanted to be a magician who revealed my handiwork at the perfect time.

There was no rush to finish the snekke quickly. *'Doe'* was still a relatively new boat and I wanted my last snekke to be perfect. We began work on the mast and mast step. I let Brave Cub take Fears Water and Long Nose to make the planks for the deck. They would take time for they had to be shaped to fit the hull. Brave Cub knew that they would need to be sturdily constructed as a section would need to be removable for both cargo and to adjust the ballast. They were still working on that when I began to make the steering board. All the rest of the ship was important, but without a steering board sailing the snekke would be that much more difficult. Moos Blood watched my every move as I made the board and the withy that would help us to turn the lithe, little boat when she was built. The mast and yard were relatively easy to make and the youngest members of the clan were given the task of making them as smooth as possible.

Little White Dove had the old sail, made by her mother, as a template and the women sat and sewed and talked. When Laughing Deer had made *'Doe's'* sail there had just been the two of them and now the women of the clan chattered like so many roosting birds as their hands used the bone needles to make the sail. I knew that Laughing Deer would be happy and for the clan, it was as though each of us had a part of ourselves in the snekke.

Black Feather and Willow Leaf had married not long before Laughing Deer had died and the birth of their daughter, River's Breath, was a measure of the passage of time. The birth came just as we were preparing to finish the snekke. The birth of another member of the clan merited a day off work. In many ways it helped for it enabled us to reflect on our life. The men sat outside the longhouse and we smoked. The smoke from the burning leaves kept away the flies and the smell soothed us. The youngest in the clan played and the men watched the setting sun. The women were gathered in the longhouse to help with the birthing. Willow Leaf had given birth to Bjorr Tooth many years ago so we had all been delighted when she had fallen pregnant. Black Feather wanted a child but his love for Willow Leaf was so great that he was happy just to marry her and have Bjorr Tooth as a foster son.

The birth coincided with the evening and the silence of both the forest and the clan. The younger ones had tired of their playing and there was a peaceful and soothing silence. Brave Cub smiled, "All that you can hear is the breath of the river as it flows to the Patawomke and the sea."

It was as he said those words that there was the wail of a newborn and Little White Dove cried, "Black Feather, you have a daughter."

I nodded and smiled as I clasped his arm, "And I think you have the name, Black Feather."

He grinned, "River's Breath, it is a good name."

The birth energised the men. I knew that all the families in the clan were doing their best to make the clan stronger. Little White Dove and Sings Softly were with child again. The snekke was a way to feed the growing clan and we set to as soon as the sun had risen. I fitted the mast step first and then pine tar was heated to give another coat to the interior. While it was heating, I fitted the brace from the mast step to the keelson. Even as it began to dry, we put the deck in place. There was no ballast yet but we needed to make the hole for the mast. This was tricky work and only needed three of us. I sent the rest to fish on the river. We had meat but we needed to dry fish for the winter. Since we had been here the river had frozen twice and the land had been covered with snow. We were always prepared for the worst of the weather.

By the time they had returned with the fish, we had finished our work. Black Feather went to see his wife and child while the rest of us admired the snekke. Thanks to the tree we had procured for the keel, it was longer than *'Doe'* and would be able to carry more. The thwarts I had found gave it more strength than either of the first two snekke I had built. It told me that this was the place Gytha intended us to live. I would not move from here. No matter what I found to the north and west I would not leave this place. Eagle's Shadow would be my last home.

"What now, Shaman?"

"Tomorrow, we put her in the water and fill her with ballast. That will not be a quick job for we must balance her. Then we replace the deck and fit the mast. I will show you all how to fit the steering board and then," I smiled as I saw the anticipation on their faces, "And then we will have a day of rest so that I may look at our handiwork and see what improvements we can make."

My three sons knew what I was doing and they smiled. The others all looked disappointed.

That night I went to Laughing Deer's grave. I laid some flowers on the top. She had loved flowers and their smell. I wondered if you could smell in the Otherworld. "The snekke is nearly done, my love. I will take another voyage to a place I have never seen. I doubt that I will ever find a treasure such as you but the sisters spin so who knows? I know that I shall miss not having you with me. You were always a comfort and a strength. I did not tell you enough times how much you meant… mean to me and for that I am sorry. I hope that you know what was in my heart." I put my hands on the grave and I felt movement above my head, it could have been an owl or a bat but I chose to believe that it was Laughing Deer's spirit. I slept well that night.

The clan were all excited and even Willow Leaf with a nursing River's Breath came down to the wooden quay to see the launch. It took time to carry her, using rollers down the path to the wooden quay. With so many hands it was relatively easy to manoeuvre the snekke over the rollers and into the water. With ropes at the prow and the stern, she was secure. We all watched anxiously. Was she watertight? I knew within a heartbeat that she was sound as she bobbed in the water. I did not say anything. I was enjoying the anticipation from the others.

Satisfied, I nodded and pointed to the pile of stones, "This will be the clan's snekke and each of you should place a stone in the bottom. Choose your stone well and give it a message as you deposit it. Moos Blood…"

My son chose the largest rock and I saw his lips moving. A man's invocation was private. He went to the centre of the snekke and, leaning over, placed it close to the mast step. The others all followed suit. The men carried larger ones and they were placed in the centre. The women and the children used smaller stones and they were at the bow and the stern. I had not placed any stones and I would not do so. I was the master builder and I still had the prow to fit. When I was satisfied with the balance of the boat, the deck was fitted and I stepped back again to see that it was still well-balanced. A snekke is a fast little boat but it needed a good eye to see that all was in harmony. I spent the rest of the morning fitting the steering board. The women returned to their tasks and Moos Blood took the men to check the bjorr traps. I was left with Brown Feather and Water Bird. They were happy to sit in the snekke, the first passengers, and watch the Shaman of the Bear as he did what, to the two of them, was magic.

When it was done Water Bird said, "Can we sail her now, Grandfather?"

I shook my head, "There is no sail, but even if there were we have not yet fitted the prow nor named her. Until we do both those tasks, we keep her tied to the land. It is like the cord that joined Willow Leaf and River's Breath. It was not cut until the babe was born. So it is with this snekke. It is not named but it is alive." They looked disappointed. "What you can do is fetch the sheets and stays. I am too old to climb up a mast but you can do so." They both looked confused and I pointed to the pile of ropes we had made. "They are the sheets and the stays. We attach them to the prow and the stern so that the mast is supported."

They happily did as I asked.

That night I applied the last of the pine tar to the figurehead. I used charcoal, crushed beetles, marigold flowers and the blue tubers that I had dug up, to paint Laughing Deer's features. It had almost made me weep when I had done so for her face seemed so lifelike that I wondered if she lived. Perhaps her spirit would be in the snekke, I prayed so.

There was a decided air of excitement in the longhouse the next morning. The children chattered and everyone was keen to see the snekke fly. My sons carried the sail and, after taking off my boots and rolling up my breeks, I took the skin-wrapped prow down to the river. The two boys had greased the pulley on the yard and after it had been fitted the sail rose easily into position. The snekke was eager to move and pulled against the ropes that tethered her to the land. I looked at the sail. Little White Dove and the ladies had used dyes and thread to make a red-eyed bear on the sail. There was an audible 'aw' from the children when they saw it.

I nodded, "Laughing Deer would be proud. That is as fine a sail as I can remember. Now lower it please."

They did so and after placing my bundle on the quay and taking my stone hammer, I lowered myself into the water. It was cold but the immersion was necessary. The whole clan watched as I unwrapped the finished figurehead. I saw my daughter's hand go to her mouth as she recognised her mother. My sons touched their amulets. It was only the youngest who did not seem to recognise the face. I had tried out the figurehead before and knew that it fitted. I slipped it into place. It held but it would need the two wooden trenails hammering in before it was secure. Clambering from the water, I put the wooden dowels on the quay along with the hammer. I stood above the prow and took out my seax. I made a long cut down my right palm. I held my hand above the figurehead and let the blood flow down the back so as not to spoil the painted features.

"Laughing Deer, I name this snekke after you. You are the mother of this clan and this snekke will replace the old mother, Gytha. It is *wyrd*. I pray that my blood mixed with your spirit will bring the snekke and the clan, good fortune."

I knelt and hammered in the last two pieces of wood, completing the boat. All that needed to be done was to paint more pine tar on the joint and we would be able to sail her. As I looked at her, I thought back to the first snekke I had helped to build, '***Jötnar***', would my last one prove to be so sturdy?

The clan cheered and the children screamed. I put my hand in the river. The cold water slowed the flow of blood and it was good that my blood touched the hull too.

Little White Dove brought a cloth and some honey. She dried my hand and then gently smeared the honey on the wound. I saw the tears freshly falling down her cheeks, "That was more than well done, Father. You have built not only a boat but a clan. Mother will be smiling."

"And you are the new mother, you know that do you not, Little White Dove? Moos Blood will be the chief when I die, but it will be you that will see the clan prosper as your mother did."

"That is a heavy burden to bear."

I nodded, "But your mother and I brought you up well so that you can shoulder it. This is a good clan." I held up the hand she had just healed, "Good blood flows through its veins and all will be well." I smiled, "One day, far in the future, others will sail across the sea. Perhaps Fótr's clan will return. When they do there will be the blood of their kin here in this new world."

All the men and the boys in the clan were eager to sail in the new snekke. I chose Brown Feather and Water Bird. You would have thought I had given them the greatest weapon ever made by a weaponsmith. I confess that I was nervous as I asked them to raise the sail. Moos Blood and Brave Cub were in *'Doe'* in case of disaster, while Fears Water and Golden Bear were at the ropes tying us to the land. I felt *'Laughing Deer'* tug against the ropes and knew that she was ready to fly. The wind was opposed to the flow of the river and so I went with the wind knowing that I could turn and tack back easily with the river. I needed to get to know the new snekke. Moos Blood and Brave Cub would follow me.

"Let her go." The ropes were released and the snekke was born.

She leapt as the wind took her. I would teach the boys how to adjust the sheets and stays later. I used the steering board. She was lithe and responsive to the touch and far quicker, despite being bigger, than *'Doe'*. I knew that we had at least two miles of deep water ahead of us and the snekke was shallow-draughted enough to sail much further. The two boys were excited and they gripped the gunwales as though their lives depended upon it. They had yet to sail the maelstrom that was the confluence of the Shenandoah and the Patawomke. When they did, they would truly know fear.

A good navigator keeps his eyes to the side, the bow and the stern. I searched for white-specked water that would warn of danger. I looked to see if the sail was taking all the advantage that it could from the wind. When I glanced astern, I saw that Moos Blood was struggling to

26

keep up with me. It was joyous for *'Laughing Deer'* seemed not only to be flying but also singing. I knew that it was just the air passing the sheets and stays but I chose to believe that the boat was alive. When I spied the bend in the river ahead, I said, "Watch out boys, we are going to come about. You two will need to pull on that sheet on the steerboard side." They both turned and I held up my right hand. They nodded. "Now!" Not only was she fast she was responsive to the touch and we spun around. I had to adjust my turn for we threatened to dip the gunwale into the river. I had been too cocky. The boys held on to the sheet until I said, "You can let go now. Water Bird, go to the larboard side." He looked and I held up my left hand. When he was in position I said, "When I call your name, pull on your sheet until I say to stop."

"Grandfather, if we go as fast as we did before we might fall overboard."

I laughed, "And we shall learn if you can swim but fear not. Our journey back will be quite sedate in comparison to the wild ride we have just enjoyed." I had been going to say, like riding a wild pony but realised that they had never seen a horse.

Moos Blood had turned *'Doe'* when he saw our move. He shook his head, "I thought we were fast. What have we built, Father?"

"The best boat I have ever constructed." I patted the gunwale, "And the last. The next one will be the one you boys build."

By the time we reached the quay, the two boys had learned how to respond quickly. If nothing else they knew the difference between steerboard and larboard. They would be able to crew.

As we tied them up, with their sails reefed, I said, "Tomorrow we fish. The sky looks set to be fair. We can cure and dry the fish ready for winter."

"We could do it now, grandfather."

I shook my head, "No, Water Bird. She needs to catch her breath. Let her become used to the river. *'Laughing Deer'* is a living creature. She has tasted my blood but needs time to adjust to being alive. We took the trees and did not kill them but changed them. She is like River's Breath. At the moment all is new to her. We must teach her."

"Can we come with you when you fish?"

"Perhaps, but we will need Brave Cub and Fears Water too for the catch may be too heavy for you two to lift." I let them clamber out. "One thing more, learn to swim. You cannot guarantee that you will not be doused in the river. A dousing is one thing but drowning? That is quite another."

The longhouse was quite crowded and while we all got on well, I knew that any conflict could quickly escalate. We had no sooner finished the snekke when I spoke to the clan. "Tomorrow, we begin work on a second longhouse." Their faces, even the younger ones, all turned to me. "Iron Will was a sign that we have not stopped growing. If we lived in Brave Eagle's camp then each family would have their own yehakin. Here we live as my ancestors did."

Moos Blood said, "Where?"

"Now that we have cleared more trees to the east of the path we can move the wood and snekke store. They occupy a large area and if we built the next longhouse at right angles to this one, then we would make it a stronger place to defend. One house could butt against another."

Brave Cub said, "The leaves will soon be falling and winter will be upon us before we know it."

I nodded, "And it will mean more work, I know, but we have shown with the building of the snekke that when we all work together, we can achieve much in a short space of time. When we move the snekke and wood store, half the work will be done already, for the holes for some of the timber posts are there and the ground is flat."

Little White Dove shook her head, "This is not right, Father, you should be enjoying a quiet life. You should be dangling babies from your knee and passing on wisdom to the young."

"I can pass on wisdom whilst we work and that is where I differ from every other man I have met in this new world, I am of Norse blood and we work until we can work no longer. I am content that when I go to meet your mother, I will leave the clan stronger." I looked at their faces and saw concern. "We will still do all the tasks that are needed. The work on the longhouse will be done after the sun has reached its height. In the morning we will fish the river and, in the afternoon, move the wood and snekke store. We do one task at a time. The next morning we fish again and harvest the river and, later, cut the timber." I smiled, "While I am still the chief then I will make these decisions. Now I am so hungry that my stomach thinks my throat has been cut. Let us eat."

There was the usual hum of conversation as we ate but I noticed that my children kept glancing at me. They were worried. This was where I missed Laughing Deer more than ever. Such mealtimes had been the chance for us to talk and catch up on the day the other had enjoyed. Now I sat at the head of the table and I was almost alone. I knew that they did not see the loneliness but I felt it. I had grown up with my brothers and cousins around me and when they had been taken from me, Laughing Deer had come into my life. This was the most isolated I had ever been.

When I rolled into my bed that night it was as though I was going home. When I closed my eyes and slept I knew that I might enter the

28

dream world and Laughing Deer would come to me. I might see my brother and cousins. Perhaps Gytha would show herself. When they did, I was no longer Erik Shaman of the Bear, I was Erik the Navigator.

I always woke up first these days. I was most often the one who saw the sun rise in the east. I knew that it was the same sun that would rise over Fótr and the rest of the clan who had fled the new world. That gave me comfort as I stood in the chill of the early morning.

The men and boys of the clan were eager to fish. We would all be involved. We had perfected the method on the Patawomke. The birch bark boats would be needed to collect the bounty the snekke gathered. Brave Cub and Fears Water were both eager to sail in the new snekke. There was much more room than on either of the others. We headed downstream towards the shallows. Once there we turned our snekke and lowered the sails and dropped the stone anchors. We held a net between us and when the birch bark boats were in position, we lowered it. The Shenandoah was not as fruitful as the Patawomke. The fish we caught were slightly smaller and there was not the variety but we still caught enough on that first netting to make the six of us who hauled on the nets struggle. The boats came between us and we dropped the catch into Humming Bird's. He and Long Nose headed back to the shore where we had a large keep net in which the fish could be held. We wanted them as fresh as possible. Four catches later we had enough fish and we dropped the last catch onto the deck of *'Laughing Deer'*. We sailed to the side and hauled the keep net clear of the water. It took every one of us, boys included, to do so and we dropped half onto our deck and half onto Moos Blood's.

"A good catch and now we can sail upstream."

The ones in the birch bark boats shook their heads, "Aye, and we shall have to paddle while you use the wind."

We did not beat them back by much. Bird Song, Little White Dove's daughter, had been keeping watch and the women were waiting by the quay when we arrived. They had woven baskets for the fish and while we spent the afternoon moving the wood store they would gut and prepare the fish for preservation. We would enjoy a hearty fish stew from the heads, bones and guts for our evening meal while we would eat raw some of the smaller fish as a noonday treat.

The next day we started work on the new longhouse. Having only built the wood and snekke store a few years earlier it was relatively easy to shift it. The hardest part was moving the wood that would keep us warm in the winter. As evening approached, we had the space for the new longhouse. The second day was almost the same as the first. The fish were caught and brought back. We had learned from that first day.

We had enough, I estimated, so that we would not need another harvest. Some of the fish were already smoking while some were salted and others were brined in ale. It gave us variety. Some might be ruined but that was to be expected. Ulla had now grown back to what I thought would be his normal size. He was like a wolf and would eat anything. He was adept at cleaning up when anything remotely resembling food fell to the floor. Always, though, he kept one eye on Iron Will. He had shown an attachment to me and when we went hunting, he would lope alongside me. He had been well-trained by someone.

It meant that by the third day, while the fish were preserved, we took to the trees that lay close to the river. We would cut down a stand of them and dig up the roots to make pine tar. The cleared ground would be ready, by the spring, to plant crops. When the river flooded, it deposited its bounty on the land. We had used stakes to protect the banks and to hold in any deposits from the river. Our fields were fruitful. We had enough stone, iron and flint axes for all the men to use them. The boys had hand axes and they chopped the branches from the trees to go into the wood store. By the end of the third day, we had the wood for the longhouse. The fourth day would be spent working the wood with smaller axes so that the timbers were all the same size.

It took a week to have the ground and timber prepared and we were all exhausted at the end of each day but it was a satisfying exhaustion for we saw the fruits of our labours. The erection of the longhouse was a longer process. My sons knew how we had built the first one but for the others, it was a learning experience. They had to learn how to pack river stones evenly around each timber so that it was vertical. The split timbers had to be nailed to the frame. The roof needed every single man and boy to hold the wood in place and then the cutting of the turf from the cleared area by the river, was backbreaking work, but three weeks after we had begun, the building was finished. It was not yet ready for habitation as the floor needed work and a chimney for the fire had to be built. Moos Blood, Brave Cub and I were the ones who showed the others how to build a chimney using clay and river sand as mortar. When the fire was in operation it would harden the clay and sand mixture. As we had discovered with the first longhouse, we had to keep the mixture maintained but it gave us warmth in the winter. The turf on the roof and stacked along the side of the house meant it was warmer and better protected against the weather. When the summer sun dried out the soil, we might need to replace some turves but it would be worth the effort.

By the time we were finished, it was almost time to put the two snekke in their store for the winter. We went for one last fish but this time went upstream and we did not use a net but spears, lines and bows for we sought the larger fish. We wanted the smaller fish to grow and breed. The larger ones were more of a challenge.

We had learned each year since we had stored the snekke that this was a momentous time. We had to remove the steering boards and masts and then it took all the warriors to lift the snekke and carry them up the slope. The carrying of the snekke up the hill was almost like a religious ceremony. They were like the bears that hibernated for the winter. We had enlarged the store so that all three snekke fitted snugly. *'Gytha'* would not leave the store until I died and I made sure that she was tucked safely up.

That done, we prepared for winter as the days grew shorter and the air colder. Each day saw us up at dawn and working until the sun set in the far west. We hunted once more and we gathered food. The berries of autumn were bountiful. The furs of the animals we had hunted had been prepared and divided between the two longhouses. We would all be warm.

Moos Blood and Little White Dove had chosen to stay in the first longhouse, the one referred to as the Shaman's. Golden Bear and Fears Water as well as Bjorr Tooth had stayed as well. All the rest were in the new longhouse. We always called it that. Brave Cub and Redbreast were the ones who sat at the head of that table. Black Feather and Willow Leaf seemed quite content to defer to my second son. I knew that Moos Blood and Little White Dove wanted to stay with me because they were worried about me. They had no need to be but I did not mind. It meant my eldest grandchildren and foster grandchild were all with me. Like the animals of the forest, we prepared to close up for the winter. We had done all that we could to ready ourselves for whatever was thrown our way but one could never dismiss the Three Sisters. They spun and they wove.

Chapter 4

This would be the first winter solstice without Laughing Deer. She had always made it a special occasion. Despite the larger numbers of the clan, it was a quieter one as we celebrated in our two longhouses. In mine, the talk was all about Laughing Deer as we remembered her. It was good to talk about her as it made her seem alive once more. The one it seemed to have the greatest effect on was Golden Bear. He had been our youngest child and had been closer to his mother than any of the other three.

I found him, the day after the shortest day, at his mother's grave. He looked up when I approached, "I miss her more than I have words, Father. I think back to all the things I could have said when she was alive and I did not. I thought that she would always be there."

"You cannot change the past, Golden Bear. You learn from it. I too think of things I might have said. Luckily there are few of them for having been close to the Otherworld I, more than anyone, know how thin are the threads that bind us to this life. None of us know how long we have left in this world. My brother sparkled like a star in the sky and then was gone. He had children and that is a blessing for it means his blood went on. He never saw his children become husbands and fathers though."

He nodded, "Is Corn Tassel too young to be married?"

I looked at my son and realised that he had grown into a man without me knowing. "You have desires?"

He shrugged, "When Brave Cub married her sister, I envied him and began looking at Corn Tassel. I had thought of her as a child but when I looked with fresh eyes, I saw that she was becoming a woman and," he looked down, clearly embarrassed, "I felt urges."

"You need to speak to her. We are not Moneton or Penobscot. We do not simply take women. I know some of my people, across the seas, did so but it was never the way of my family and clan. The clan was guided by Gytha and we honoured women. Speak to her and then to Willow Leaf but to answer your question, she is a young woman and if she says that she is ready then she is."

Corn Tassel, it turned out, was also ready. More, she had been looking at Golden Bear with the new eyes of a woman. When Willow

Leaf quickly gave her blessing then we knew that we had something to celebrate. We could begin to heal the pain and loss of Laughing Deer. The night before the ceremony my sons and I used the steam hut. Outside the ground was covered in snow but that seemed to make the hut even more effective and we sat within and smoked our pipes. We used the dream leaves. I had a disturbed dream which I did not understand. My mind might have been on the marriage of my last child, I know not but it was not a continuous flow of a dream, it was like lightning flashes. They came and disappeared in a heartbeat. I saw Arne falling at the falls. I saw Fótr at the helm of a drekar. I saw a battle between Norse warriors and men led by my brother Fótr and they were fighting alongside the Dragonheart's clan, led by Sámr Ship Killer. All went black and then I saw a bear, at least as big as the one I had killed on Bear Island and it was coming for Iron Will. I could do nothing to stop it and then I woke.

Golden Bear was moaning in his dream. That was to be expected. My other two sons looked, by comparison, peaceful. I put more water on the fire to make more steam and fanned the fire to make it hotter. I relit my pipe and waited for the others to come back from the dream world. Moos Blood and Brave Cub did so first and they were both smiling.

"I saw our mother."

"As did I."

Moos Blood picked up his pipe to refill it, "She said not a word with her mouth but her eyes and her face showed her joy. She is happy, Father. Did you dream of her?"

I shook my head, "I had a dream that was…well, strange. I saw the past and what I thought was the present. My brother Fótr was going to war but I think I saw the future. I think that the Norns were here tonight and I cannot untangle the order of their threads. That is their way."

They both clutched their hammers of Thor.

It was then that Golden Bear awoke and he had upon his face such a look of terror that I knew he had not dreamed of his mother. His eyes were wild and he said, "A bear. A bear is coming."

Moos Blood looked at his little brother and shook his head, "You talk wildly, brother. What bear? When?"

I said, quietly, "I dreamed of a bear too and it was coming for Iron Will."

Golden Bear had a mixture of terror and relief on his face, "I saw that as well but I saw the bear and it killed bear cubs. It was huge and had terrible claws. I tried to run away but it was as though my feet were trapped in mud and I could not move."

I put my arm around my son, "It did not catch you."

He shook his head, "No, but I felt the heat of its breath upon my head." I knew that was when I lit my pipe for it had been close to his head. "It is coming, what can we do?"

Brave Cub said, "A bear, in winter? Do they not hibernate?"

"They do. I am taking these two dreams seriously. Tomorrow, we take some warriors and we look for signs of this bear."

"But, Father, it could be anywhere."

"I know, Moos Blood, but we have to try. Golden Bear, I saw the bear close to the longhouse. You saw dead cubs. Did you have any clue as to where they were?"

He picked up a twig and put it on the fire. He was thinking. "The sun was rising and the slope led up to the sunrise."

"Good, then it is to the east of us and that makes sense. We found the dead bear in the cave of the iron. That gives us a start."

"Is it not dangerous to hunt a bear, Father?"

"It is, Brave Cub, but I did not say we hunt it. I said we look for signs of it. My dream was of the future. This has not yet come to pass. It may be that the four of us will be able to change the future."

"The four of us?"

"Yes, Golden Bear. I am the Shaman of the Bear and I have hunted a bear before now. We leave the other men of the clan to guard our home and we seek the bear. We get ready to defend ourselves but I would not harm it unless it threatened us."

"This seems like madness to me, Father."

"It seemed like madness, Moos Blood, when I set sail in a snekke from the Land of Ice and Fire to seek a new home and yet here I am with a family and a clan. It is in our blood. If we do nothing then the dream might come true and the bear might strike at the clan and those who cannot defend themselves. Iron Will is a new member of the clan without parents and we must defend her. Your mother would have wished us to undertake this task. She would not be happy about the danger but your mother was a wise woman and knew that you cannot hide from danger, you face it."

"You are right and I suppose this is a lesson to me for when I lead the clan."

"It is."

"Aye, not all decisions are easy ones or those that we might choose."

"We cannot escape the threads of the Norns."

We planned the expedition well. We would take the three metal-headed spears. My sons had the sword and the metal axe and hatchet I had given them and we each had a blanket as well as a fur. We had seal skin capes that would keep us dry and freshly preserved fish and venison. I told the other warriors what we would be doing and made sure that they understood their duties. We would leave at first light.

The Norns were spinning. It was the wind that woke me. We had picked a home that rose above the land and while there had been trees that gave us some shelter our recent work had thinned them a little. The sturdy longhouse did not shake but the wind howled like a wolf. I rose from my furs and headed across the longhouse. The air was not as cold as it would normally be. I went to one of the arrow slits and moved the deer hide that stopped the wind from whipping through and looked out on a white world of snow. It was a blizzard. Whilst nowhere near as frequent as they had been in the Land of Ice and Fire, they did strike the valley, sometimes. I replaced and fastened the deer hide and went to the corner to make water in the pot we kept there. Its contents would be used to tan hides. I snuggled back under my furs and fell asleep wondering about the Norns and their webs.

The blizzard still raged at what passed for dawn. When we peered out all that we could see was snow and the outline of the other longhouse. The place we used to cook and bake bread was clearly unusable that day and we would be forced to cook using the fire in the longhouse. Someone would have to go to the building we stored our food and fetch it. I had been the first up and dressed. I put my seal-skin hat and cloak on and with seal-skin boots upon my feet, I prepared to leave the longhouse. Little White Dove was nursing and I said, "Tell the others that there is a blizzard. We will be longhouse bound this day. I will brave the elements and fetch food."

"Father, you are chief, let another do this."

"And I am up and dressed. It is my appointed task." We had a bar on the inside of the door but we also had a latch to ensure the door stayed closed and the interior warm. I closed it and turned. The snow drove into my face. It was coming from the north. *Wyrd*, had it travelled all the way from the Land of Ice and Fire? It had been a heavy fall of snow and the three snekke and wood store were large rounded mounds as was the bread oven and kitchen. I headed for the food store. It was raised above the ground but the snow had filled the gap. I was grateful for the lined seal skin. It not only kept me dry but it stopped the wind from scything through me. I cleared the snow from the door and regretted not wearing my squirrel mittens. The snow was like a dagger. The wood had swollen slightly and I had to pull hard to open it. I took out enough food for the two longhouses and headed for Brave Cub's. As I approached, my feet crunching in the freshly fallen snow, the door opened and my son stood there.

35

He shook his head, "Father, you are the oldest in the clan. There are others who could do this."

I shook my head, "You sound like your sister. While I can then I will. Here, I have brought you food. It goes without saying that we will not be seeking the bear this day."

He took the food and shook his head, "The Norns are spinning." Just then the wind howled and screeched particularly loudly, "And laughing at us."

I smiled, "Of course, for we are their playthings and it amuses them to see what we do with the problems they pose for us."

I turned and headed back to my longhouse. Despite my protective clothing, I was still chilled to the bone. The women took the food from me and went to prepare it. I hung my cape and hat from the hook behind the door. They would drain and make a puddle behind the door but that could not be helped. Others would need to leave during the day. The pots with the ale and mead were without and wood was in the wood store. The storm had set my mind to work. I would need to finish the bjorr skin cape that I would wear beneath my seal skin cape. I had thought to wear my deer hide coat but I now had time to finish sewing the bjorr cape. The work would stop my mind from dwelling on the Norns.

The women made the maize porridge that would form the staple of the breakfast. When I had lived on Orkneyjar it had been made from oats. It had been the Mi'kmaq who had introduced me to the new world version. With berries dried from the summer and a spoon of honey, it warmed and sustained everyone. I only had one skin left to add to the cape to ensure that the upper half of my body would be warm. I had not had time to finish it. I needed it for the storm and the storm stopped me from leaving. Which was the cause and which was the effect? I shook my head. I was thinking too much. Laughing Deer had told me it was my biggest fault. Perhaps she was right. I should just get on with life and stop worrying about the future. I had all day and I used small stitches to ensure a good fit. The younger members of the clan came over to see what I was doing.

I nodded at the pile of offcuts. There had not been much waste but there were pieces of the bjorr I had used left over. I nodded to the eldest three, "There are bone needles, thread and spare fur. Make mittens for yourselves."

Bird Song frowned, "But we do not know how, Grandfather."

I held up the needle and cape, "Then watch this old man. I did not know how to do this but I learned."

"But we might make mistakes."

36

I smiled at my eldest granddaughter, "Then you unpick and start again. We learn as much from our mistakes as from our success."

That seemed to satisfy them and they struggled to thread the needles and choose their fur. As they did, they spoke to me. It was warm and cosy inside the longhouse with the wind howling outside. "You have never made mistakes though grandfather." Although they were close in age, my first grandson always seemed the most mature of the three. I knew that I was closer to him than any others. I had thought that when Laughing Deer died I would have grown closer to my granddaughter, Bird Song, but it was Water Bird who was closer.

I laughed, "Water Bird, I have made many mistakes and the Clan of the Fox, when I lived with them, made many more. We thought that the Land of Ice and Fire was the one that we were intended to find but we were wrong. Had we not found that place then we might never have discovered Bear Island and I would not be here." I nodded at them, "You would not be here."

Brown Feather stopped, "We would not be here? But I am not of your blood."

"No, but your father was pulled from the river by me. Had I not been on the Patawomke that day and spied the floating branch with the arm draped from it, then who knows? It is unlikely that he would have met your mother." I saw them all digesting that. It was a hard idea to grasp. It had been Laughing Deer who had voiced the concept the first night that we had slept at Eagle's Shadow. She had been a clever one. Her time as a slave of the Penobscot had given her the ability to think things through.

The three of them then questioned me at length about Orkneyjar, the Land of Ice and Fire, and Bear Island. I did not mind telling them the stories for that was how they would learn about themselves and their place in this world.

"Grandfather, your people used to sing songs about what they did. Sing us one now."

"Brown Feather does not speak Norse and you only have a few of the words."

Water Bird smiled, and I saw his father in that smile, "It matters not, for the words, though we do not understand them, will speak to us. Sing, Grandfather."

I nodded and thought back to the voyage from Larswick across the sea we thought was endless. We had chanted and sung this one more than enough. I started.

The clan of the fox has no king

37

The Last Viking

We will not bow nor kiss a ring
We fled our home to start anew
We are strong in heart though we are few

Lars the jarl fears no foe
He sailed the ship from Finehair's woe
Drekar came to end our quest
Erik the Navigator proved the best
When Danes appeared to thwart our start
The clan of the fox showed their heart
While we healed the sad and the sick
We built our home, Larswick

The clan of the fox has no king
We will not bow nor kiss a ring
We fled our home to start anew
We are strong in heart though we are few

When Halfdan came with warriors armed
The clan of the fox was not alarmed
We had our jarl, a mighty man
But the Norns they spun they had a plan
When the jarl slew Halfdan the Dane
His last few blows caused great pain
With heart and arm he raised his hand
'The clan of the fox is a mighty band!'

The clan of the fox has no king
We will not bow nor kiss a ring
We fled our home to start anew
We are strong in heart though we are few

When I finished there was silence in the longhouse and I realised that the others, whilst still working, were all wrapt, listening to the song of the Clan of the Fox. It made me smile for it was as though the clan was still alive. The deaths we had endured had not happened because they were alive in the song, my father lived once more. The children all worked away happily after that. I heard Water Bird humming and I knew he was singing a song in his head. It was not the song of the clan but the song had stirred him.

They had heard names and they asked me of the people I had sung about. The day passed and the three of them learned. I taught them more

Norse words. It was important that they understood them. Even though Brown Feather had no Norse blood in him, we used my words when sailing the snekke. He needed the language.

The storm raged all day and well into the night. I confess that I wondered if this was not the work of the Norns but the Allfather. Was he protecting us by forcing us to stay at Eagle's Shadow? I debated with myself. Should we cancel? That night my dream was of a bear scratching and tearing at the door of our longhouse. It made me wake suddenly as though it was real. All that I heard, in the cosily warm longhouse, was the sound of sleeping and the wailing of the wind. No creature was stirring outside. It had been but a dream. The dream had been sent to tell me that we had to seek the bear. If I did not then it would seek us.

Chapter 5

When the storm finally abated, we stepped out onto a white world that had made our land full of soft bumps and humps. There were no tracks in the pristine snow, not even birds. Brave Cub came from his longhouse and shook his head, "We have plenty of work ahead of us, Father, even before we can contemplate seeking the bear."

"Aye, let us clear a path."

All the men and the children, well wrapped against the cold, cleared paths to connect the longhouses as well as the food and the wood store. When that was done and while we cleared a path to the quay to check on the birch bark boats, the women collected food from the store and wood for the fires. The boats were merely covered by snow. They lay on the quay and had not been blown into the river. We removed all the snow and ensured that they were still tethered and then returned to the longhouses for hot food.

As we trudged up the hill, Moos Blood said, "We still seek the bear." I looked at him. He shrugged, "I had a bad dream and the bear came for Blue Feather."

That confirmed my decision for me. We had both dreamed a similar dream. "We still hunt, although it may be harder to find the bear for the snow will have covered his tracks."

"His tracks?"

I nodded to Golden Bear, "Your brother thought it was a male bear and, in my dreams, it was a male."

Moos Blood said, "And in mine too."

"Golden Bear thought it was on the way to the Iron Hills. We know that we can be there in a day if we leave early and that the cave offers shelter."

"Unless the bear is there too."

"And if it is we are meant to find it." I sighed as we stopped outside my longhouse, "This is a thread, and it ties us to the bear, we cannot escape this task. Let us go prepared for anything. When we find the tracks of this animal then I will know what to do."

We ate well that night and I woke before dawn. The air outside was so cold that it hurt my face as my breath appeared before me. There was a clear sky and there would be no snow. More importantly, we would not need to use the snowshoes we had made for the ground was frozen hard and like a rock. I went to Brave Cub's longhouse and roused him. The sun was just peeping over the hills to the east when we set off. We wore layer upon layer of clothes and looked huge as we set off down the trail. Golden Bear insisted upon leading as it was his dream which had set us on this path. I brought up the rear. I did not mind being in the position for it was my sons who would be leading the clan when I had gone. They would need me when we neared the bear. Until then I was baggage and happy to be so.

Despite the cold, our layers, and the speed with which Golden Bear took us down the trail meant that we were soon sweating and my knee was complaining. The Moneton arrow had hurt me in such a dramatic way that had I not had the spear as a staff, I might have struggled more than I did. As it was, being at the rear meant that no one saw my pain and my struggle to keep up. I did not want my sons to have to worry about their father. When we stopped, in the small clearing we always used, I almost wept with relief. I adopted a smile and said, "We have done well."

Moos Blood frowned, "You have done well, Father, for I can see by your face that you found this harder than we." He turned to his brother, "Golden Bear, you went too fast."

My youngest son looked distraught as he saw my face, "I am sorry, I should have…"

I was using my right hand to lean on the spear and I used my left hand to waft the words away. The cold made our foggy breath appear before us, "It is no matter. We have made good time and I am sure that we will reach the cave by dark. That is what we want, is it not, Moos Blood? The last thing we need is to approach in the dark and risk the wrath of a bear we cannot see."

"Perhaps, but eat and drink, Father, and I will be at the rear from now on. While our speedy little brother leads, Brave Cub and I will be your guardians."

We moved more slowly after that. It was not just their concern for me but the slope became steeper and slippery. In addition, we were getting closer with each step to the place Golden Bear had dreamed. We looked for signs. It was good that we did for when my youngest son stopped and held his spear defensively, we knew he had seen something. We joined him and he pointed his metal tipped spear at the ground. There, freshly made, were the tracks of a large bear. It had to be the same size as the dead one I had found all those years ago. The fact that they were clearly visible in the snow told us that the bear had been outside since the blizzard. It was not hibernating.

I nodded, "Well at least we know that the bear is real."

Brave Cub asked, "Real?"

I shrugged, "It could have been a ghost bear. That would have been equally dangerous but far harder to deal with." I leaned in closer and pointed at the tracks. "It seems to me that it came from the north and then headed across the slope to the south." I looked up at the sky. "Do we follow the trail or find shelter and track it in the morning?" I knew my answer but this was as much about my sons learning to lead as anything else.

Moos Blood looked at the sky, "It is still clear and there are no signs of clouds. That means no snow and the ground will remain frozen. The tracks are not going anywhere and if we near the cave and find that they are there then we have an answer, do we not?"

My answer was a smile and a nod. Brave Cub gave his assent, "I can find no fault in your words, brother. Lead on, Golden Bear, but keep your sharp eyes looking for signs."

All we would see were the tracks made by Golden Bear. It was his eyes that would spot the tracks and we were reliant on him. What I did not like was that while there was little breeze, what there was came from behind us. The track we followed twisted and turned up through the trees and the bushes that, in the spring, would be laden with berries but now were just spiky barriers hemming us in.

The cave was just a thousand steps ahead when the bear burst from behind the bushes. We had not caught a whiff of its smell and it had used cunning to ambush us. A bear can move very quickly when it wishes. Despite my age, I was the first one to react as it raced to attack the first in the line, Golden Bear. Holding my spear before me I ran at its side. Poor Golden Bear looked frozen with fear as the bear raised its mighty claws to slash down at his head. I knew that if the blow succeeded then even a helmet-protected head would not save my son and all that he had was his bjorr skin hat and the hood of his cloak. My spear drove up under the bear's armpit. Not a mortal blow, it was a painful one and arrested the downward swing. The bear turned his reddened eyes to me and began to swing his left claw at me. I managed to swing the haft of the spear around but the blow shattered the wood in two and knocked me to the ground. I fell on my back and the bear towered over me. I held the two broken halves of the spear and made a cross like the White Christ above me. I was the shaman of the bear and it was fitting that I should die at the claws of such a huge bear. This was the third such bear to enter my life and I would be able to do nothing about it when it ripped its claws across my head and stomach. I wore no mail byrnie and I had no sword. I would not have a Viking death. As its claw came down to eviscerate me, I wondered if this death in combat would afford me a place in Valhalla.

My sons were not going to let the bear have his own way and even as the blow was being struck the three spears struck simultaneously. They drove their heads deep into the body of the mighty beast. Even in its dying, it fought on and one claw smashed Moos Blood's spear in two. While my other two sons stabbed again, Moos Blood drew my sword and drove it up through the bear's neck and into his skull. The bear fell and there was just one place left for it to fall. It crashed onto my body. My sons surrounded me and I was in no position to move away. I barely managed to move my head to the side as the animal's body covered me.

I heard Golden Bear shout, "Father!"

Although the danger was that I would be suffocated, I could feel its weight crushing me. The bear was huge and even though my sons were strong, it was still a mammoth task to move the bear. It felt as though my bones would break and the weight seemed to grow. I forced myself to stay calm. My face was touching the frozen ground but already the heat from the bear was warming it up. The fur was so close to my nose that I was in danger of drowning in fur. I used my mouth to breathe and I did so slowly as I heard my sons struggling to remove the carcass that was crushing and suffocating me. My chest felt as though it was being forced through to my back and even breathing slowly was becoming too difficult. I felt my eyes closing as darkness enfolded me. Was this my death? I would not even be able to utter Laughing Deer's name for it was as though I was slipping beneath the waves and entering darkness. I prepared to enter the Otherworld. It would not be Valhalla and I would not see Arne and my father.

Suddenly the weight was moved and I sucked in air. My eyes were still closed but when I opened them, I saw the terrified faces of my sons and behind them the most glorious sunset I had seen in a long time. The red, purple and yellow would have been a fitting epitaph had I died. As it was, they made me smile.

"He lives. We thought you dead, Father."

He and Brave Cub lifted me to my feet. My chest and back hurt but I said nothing of the pain. Instead, I nodded. It took me some moments but eventually, I was able to voice my thoughts, "As did I but the Allfather, it seems, is not done with me yet." I looked down at the bear. It was enormous, but now that I looked more closely at it in the last light from the sun slipping down in the west, I could see that it was gaunt. It should have slept and instead had still prowled. I wondered why.

"Let us get to the cave before dark. The bear will be going nowhere."

I nodded, "My spear."

Golden Bear handed me the two broken halves. "I owe you a life, Father. Your blow saved me and almost cost you yours."

"And that would have been a good trade, Golden Bear, for I have lived my life and yours has a course yet to run."

By the time we reached the cave the last rays of the setting sun illuminated the cave and we saw the reason for the bear's behaviour. There was a dead female and two young, dead cubs. Golden Bear's dream had misled us. The bear had not killed the cubs, their mother had died and they had starved to death. The cave was an unlucky one. The stink of death in the cave meant that if we were to use it then we would have to shift the carcasses. My sons decided that I had to sit and watch while they dragged them from the cave and then collected dead wood to make a fire. The animals had been dead too long to be of any use to us and, once they were outside and a fire lit to warm us, I said, "Before we leave this place we will build up the fire and let it send these three to whatever Otherworld the Allfather has for them."

As the flames flickered, Golden Bear shivered, "I know we had to kill the bear but I understand why it did what it did. If Corn Tassel and my unborn child died then I know now how I might react."

I ached from the fall and breathing was difficult. I spoke merely to take my mind off my injuries, "The bear had a good end. He fought four warriors and almost ended the life of one of them."

Moos Blood suddenly stood, "And we have not yet looked at your wounds. The fire is warming the cave and the food will soon be ready. Strip to the waist so that we may see what ails you."

I shook my head and it hurt me. Every breath I took seemed to send waves of pain through my body. I knew I was hurt but feared to know what the wound was.

He smiled, "That was not a request, Father. We cannot lose you and we know not the hurt you have suffered."

I sighed and the pain came again. I nodded. Once I was stripped to the waist the three of them examined me. Moos Blood touched my side and it was as though someone had stuck a seax in me. "You have broken ribs."

Golden Bear asked, "How do we heal them?"

Moos Blood shook his head, "We do not. Father will have to endure the pain when we descend."

I said, a little more angrily than I intended, "And I will not be carried on a litter."

Moos Blood shook his head, "You are stubborn."

I smiled to take the sting from my reaction, "We have a bear skin and bear meat to carry back. If we take it slowly then we might make Eagle's Shadow by dark and the meat will feed the clan. I have endured worse." While we had been talking, Brave Cub had been dressing me and I sat down.

Moos Blood said, "I still do not know how you survived the Moneton arrow and were still able to fight off your enemies."

"That is simple, my son, I do not want to die yet. I have another voyage left in me and I would see my grandchildren grow. Your mother is patient and she will wait for me." I smiled, "Now is that food ready?"

The food and the fire helped. I was so weary that once we had eaten and I had made water, albeit painfully, I rolled into my fur and I slept. The boys must have fed the fire for when I woke it was still burning. I used my left hand to throw wood on the fire for it was the ribs on my right side that were broken. My sleep had been fitful as when I rolled onto my right side it woke me up. With an injured right knee and ribs there too, I would not be much use to anyone.

I walked out of the cave to make water. It was less painful than it had been the previous night. I had worried that something else had been damaged by the falling bear. As the sun came up behind the cave, I saw the three dead animals. They, like the bear who had been buried alive, had suffered an end I would not wish on an enemy.

"How are you this morning?"

I turned as Moos Blood spoke, "Alive and realising that I will be of little help to you this day."

"You need to do nothing, Father, to be of help to the clan. You inspire us. It was you who had the wit to save Golden Bear. Had you not been here then he would have died. I wonder about the people that made you. You are different to any man I have ever met. We have your blood but there is something different about you that marks you as special."

I laughed and regretted it immediately for it hurt, "For one thing I am the last Norseman in this land. All the rest live across the seas from here. I believe that someday my people will return, but not in my lifetime."

When the others woke, we built up the fire and dragged the carcasses to it. Then we headed down the trail to the dead bear. The animals would have a lonely funeral. The fire would take all day to burn the flesh and leave just charred bones but they would not be disturbed by carrion. The rats would not feast on them. If there was an animal Otherworld then they might be whole when they reached it.

While I would be of little use carrying the meat and the skin I could, at least, help with the skinning and the butchery. I had done this before and under my guidance and the judicious use of my seax, we had the skin from the bear, with the head intact. We rolled it up and I sat on it for even that little effort had tired me and my breathing was laboured. I told them how to butcher it. We could not carry all of it home and so I had them take the legs and the choicest meat. Golden Bear took the offal back to the cave and put it on the funeral pyre.

"They are burning well. When next we come here there will be nothing but bones left."

I shook my head, "I shall never return here. I may journey by river to the west but I will see this cave and ridge no more."

My sons were laden and I insisted upon carrying one of the bear's legs. I used the broken spear as a walking stick in my right hand and carried the leg over my left shoulder. We made our way down and my sons made me walk behind Moos Blood who led the way. It was hard going and we had to stop many times. It became clear that we would not reach Eagle's Shadow before dark.

It was Golden Bear who came up with the solution. "Moos Blood, if you stop here, I can leave my burden with you and run to Eagle's Shadow. There are four warriors there and they can carry our father back."

Moos Blood held up his hand as I began to object, "You may not wish to be carried, Father, but I for one do not wish to spend a night here on the trail and we are not going to leave you. A good plan, Golden Bear."

I was somewhat relieved as I knew I could not walk much further. I sat on the bearskin and we waited. The sun had set when we saw, through the trees, the lighted brands of the rescue party. How they had made a litter so quickly I will never know but as soon as they reached us, I was put on to the crude litter and Fears Water and Black Feather carried me home. With the extra hands, we made much better time but it still took a couple of hours to reach Eagle's Shadow. As they struggled up the slope with me, I realised how much harder it would have been for me to climb up. I would not have made it. It was at that moment I realised that I had become old. Few of my family had enjoyed old age. Snorri Long Fingers, my uncle, had been the only one who was even close to my age.

Little White Dove's face was tearful as I was carried in. All the women of the clan were gathered in my longhouse and I saw that they had made up my bed.

Willow Leaf said, "Golden Bear told us about your ribs, Shaman. We will undress you."

"There is nothing to be done about ribs that are broken."

"Undress my father." Little White Dove's voice was firm and commanding, "We can bind them. It will hurt at first but it will allow you to sleep. You warriors know war but we women know how to heal and you, Father, will not stir from this bed until we deem you to be fit. We cannot afford to lose you so soon after our mother." There was iron in her voice and she reminded me of her mother, once more.

I was in no condition to argue and I obeyed. She was right and I almost cried out in pain as the tight bindings were wrapped around me but the honey ale they gave me, with some concoction inside, put me to sleep and I slept well that night. In fact, I did not wake but I did dream.

Gytha and Laughing Deer came to me to tend to my wounds. They picked me up and we seemed to fly through the air. I looked down and saw the Shenandoah below me. I saw my snekke with me at the helm. I could not see who was with me. They came down lower and I saw a camp with a fire and warriors painted for war. Some had shaved heads and they had feathers and bones hanging from their hair. There were prisoners who were bound. Suddenly I was whisked into the air. Just before I was dropped and began to spin to earth Gytha said, "You have more to save."
"And add to the clan."

Laughing Deer's words were the last I heard until my eyes opened and I was in Eagle's Shadow once more.

Chapter 6

I did not stir from the longhouse for a month. I used the clay pot to make water and emptied my bowels in another and I was fed like a baby. I healed. My healing was helped by the visits of my family and the clan. Each day I had them all visit until either Willow Leaf or Little White Dove shooed them out. I was touched by their affection. My grandchildren and foster grandson were all growing as were the younger ones. All of them wished to see me and speak to me at least once every day. More babies had been born and even Iron Will was beginning to toddle.

When I was allowed to walk out beyond the door, I saw that the snow had long gone and while spring was still a month or two away, the land was beginning to emerge from its own hibernation. The bear's skin had been dried and cured. As I saw the size of it Moos Blood said, "We have taken the head and it will be on a pole in the middle of the houses. It tells the world that we are the Clan of the Bear. The skin will be your cloak to wear." He smiled, "To keep you warm. We do not need to have Erik the Ulfheonar anymore."

The wound in my side had also kept me from exercising my injured knee and I struggled to walk. When I returned to the long house, I had my grandson fetch me my broken spear. I could see the younger ones curious about what I was doing. The men were all hunting or fishing and the women were tending the fields. Only Water Bird and Brown Feather had been left to keep me company. The bear had not smashed the haft evenly in two. The end with the head was longer. I began to take off the bindings that secured the head and when it was off, I gave it to Water Bird to put in my chest. The chest was the one that I had sat on when I had sailed the drekar. It was now old and I wondered how much longer it would last. I could not bear to be rid of it. There were too many memories in it.

"What are you doing, grandfather?"

"This is a good piece of wood. It came from close to Bear Island and is older than even your father's. It has served me well. I now need a stick to help me walk until I am recovered. I will smooth this haft to make it more comfortable. Find me a rock, the size of your hand, Brown Feather."

He hurried outside and I took out my seax.

"Water Bird, give me my whetstone." While we waited for Brown Feather, I showed him how to use a whetstone and a seax. By the time I had the stone, the seax was as sharp as it needed to be. I stripped the bark from the wood and was pleased that it was smooth. The end, however, was not. There was a hole where the spear had been. I used the seax to remove the worst of the roughness and then patiently worked the stone over the rest. It took time but eventually, the wood was smooth. I stood and tested the stick. It worked.

Brown Feather looked at the seax, "Shaman, the knife you used is a strange one and looks nothing like the other knives you have made."

"This comes from across the seas. A people called the Saxons use such weapons and they gave their name to it. With just one edge it is a slashing weapon but I use it more as a tool. The Saxons are good weaponsmiths and the metal in this blade is superior to any that I can make here in this land."

"But one day we might be able to make such weapons."

I shook my head, "No, Water Bird, we will not. The last ore we took from the Iron Hills was not as good as the first we found. It was good enough for nails and for small axes but the metal will not last as long as this. Your fathers watched me make the metal but they will never know what I know from watching weaponsmiths. I am a pale copy of those men and by the time you try to work metal…" I shrugged.

"Then eventually we will be the same as all the other tribes, but fewer in number."

"That is not true, Water Bird. You will always have better weapons and you have the snekke. As for numbers…the clan is growing. It will continue to grow. The heart of this clan is strong and we all help each other. That is something that makes a people survive."

Unbeknown to us my granddaughter, Bird Song, had entered and had been listening, "You must be sad, grandfather."

I patted the bed and she climbed up, "Why so?"

"You are the last of your people and Laughing Deer has gone. You must be lonely."

I hugged her close to me, "I still have the memories of the ones who are gone in my head and my heart, and I have new memories now. I have the young of my blood and the clan to watch and that pleases me. Perhaps the bear did me a favour for I have been able to watch all of you in a way that would have been impossible if I was busy with your fathers, hunting and fishing."

"But they will need you when they launch the snekke again."

"You are right, Water Bird, but you are all growing and as you become older so you will help and I will be able to watch you closely."

Bird Song shook her head, "But not me, for I shall be with the women, grandfather."

"If you wish to come on the snekke there is no reason why you should not. Your mother knows how to sail the snekke and she helped me to sail all the way from Bear Island to the Patawomke."

When her face broke into a smile my heart melted. I missed Laughing Deer but I was not yet ready to go to the Otherworld.

The stick helped and as my ribs healed, I was able to walk about more. I now had three to help me. Bird Song joined the other two and as I busied myself with the tasks I set myself, so they aided me. We had already picked out a replacement haft and while I was talking we were fashioning the wood into a spear shaft. They hurled question after question at me. Everything I did was questioned and scrutinised. They asked me about my homes on Orkneyjar, Larswick, the Land of Ice and Fire, Bear Island and Brave Eagle's camp. It was as I spoke to them that I realised I was passing on my story, Erik's story. My sons and daughter knew part of it but they had never interrogated me like these three. They were learning about the world of the Vikings and Norsemen.

I was not allowed to participate in the carrying of the snekke down to the quay. The warriors did that. I ensured that it was I who supervised the fitting of the mast, yard, sail and steerboard on the two boats but I was not permitted to step aboard. It was as though I was a naughty child being punished. The clan and especially my children were taking away that which I loved.

My children were ever watchful and I had to use cunning to do more than just observe the clan. The younger ones aided me. Their parents thought that they were taking the burden from me when, in fact, they were merely sharing it. When my snekke was not being used by the warriors I would take the three of them with me and sneakily take the newly built boat on the river. I felt more alive when I had a steering board in my hand. I was also teaching the three of them how to sail. Bird Song was more delighted than any for she was being treated like her cousins. They were fast learners and although we just sailed around the loop of the river, they became skilled. We were undone when we were spotted by Humming Bird who had been downriver in a birch bark boat to look for signs of any strangers. That evening I had to endure the wrath of my four children.

"Father, you are still not fully healed. We cannot afford to lose you. Why did you sail the snekke?"

"Because I need to test my body. If I am to sail upstream and seek the village of Iron Will, then I must know if my body can do this."

"Perhaps it is a bad idea for you to sail upstream. Another can do this."

"Moos Blood, as skilled as my sons are, I am still the Navigator. This task is mine and as it may well be my last voyage, before the great one, let me do this my way."

Silence greeted my words. Bird Song said, "The three of us ensure that he does not try to do too much, Uncle, and we are learning. We shall have three more sailors when grandfather has done with us."

The three of them had manoeuvred themselves before me like a shield wall and I could not help but smile. They were challenging their parents in their defence of me.

Little White Dove shook her head, "You are a cunning old man, Father. You have used your magic to weave a spell and enchant the three of them."

"I am not a galdramenn, daughter. I just do with these three what I did with you four. I am teaching you the skills to sail. That is what will mark this clan as different when I am no longer here to lead you."

They knew when they were defeated and the four of us used *'Laughing Deer'* to sail further and further upstream each day. One day we passed beyond the tree I had identified as the furthest point upstream that we had travelled. There must have been rain at the headwaters for the river was full and swift. I risked sailing further upstream and was rewarded when the river split into two branches and I saw that one of them headed north. This made sense. Iron Will's mother and Ulla, along with other companions who must have fallen, could have followed the river south. Knowing that, we turned and with the river aiding us had a wild ride back to Eagle's Shadow. The three children glowed with excitement. All three were confident sailors but the journey had been so exciting that they had gripped the gunwale tightly as we had bounced along the white-speckled water.

As we tied up, they were chattering and laughing with each other. I was planning the voyage. I knew that I would have to take Ulla with me and that meant taking the dog with us the next time I sailed. Once we came to a new land, I could take the dog and, hopefully, he would remember his home and lead us to it. The journey in the snekke would not be anywhere near as long as one taken on foot, especially in winter. I was guessing that the family had trekked from somewhere within thirty or forty miles of us. To them, it would have seemed like a huge journey but *'Laughing Deer'* could easily make it in one sailing with a good crew. I had not noticed any shallows on the journey although it did not mean that there might not be some on this new branch. The other question I had in my head was who to take. My original plan had been to take two of my sons but I now saw that would be wrong. They had families. I needed just two people and they had to be those without ties. That left me with one warrior, Bjorr Tooth, but he had little sailing experience. He would need to sail with me first. The other name that came into my head was Water Bird. Bird Song and Brown Feather would be disappointed not to be chosen but Water Bird was of my blood and while Bird Song had shown skill, the most natural sailor was my grandson. I also felt closer to him than any other. I loved all my grandchildren but Water Bird was special.

I used my stick to walk up the slope. I did not need it as much as I had but I had become used to it and took it with me whenever I walked. Nearing the longhouses, I saw Bjorr Tooth playing with Iron Will. Ulla was lying down but his wary eyes were fixed on the toddler. My three crew left me and I watched Bjorr Tooth play with his foster sister. The more I thought about it the more it made sense and I saw the threads that bound us. Bjorr Tooth and Iron Will were close. Bjorr Tooth seemed to regard me as his grandfather. It just remained to see if he was willing to risk a ride into the unknown and into danger.

Willow Leaf came out and said, "Bjorr Tooth, Iron Will is filthy. Come here Iron Will and I shall clean you up." The toddler was quite happy to be muddy but Willow Leaf was not a woman to be argued with. She went and faithful Ulla rose and followed.

"Bjorr Tooth, I would ask you a question and before I ask it, I want you to know that whatever answer you give me will be the right one."

I could see he was intrigued, "Ask anything, Shaman."

"When I sail upstream to find where Iron Will came from, I will need a crew for the snekke. Would you be part of that crew?"

His face broke into a surprised smile, "I would be honoured but am I skilled enough?"

I nodded, "A good answer and to make certain, when I sail tomorrow you shall come with me."

"Who else will we take?"

"I will decide that later." In my heart, I knew that it would be Water Bird but I needed to speak to my son first.

The opportunity came sooner than I thought. That evening, as we ate in my longhouse, Moos Blood said, "Some of the fish we stored have gone bad. We will need the two snekke tomorrow." It was a polite way of telling me that I could not indulge myself with the three youngsters.

I nodded, "I will steer *'Laughing Deer'* and for my crew, I will have you, Moos Blood, Bjorr Tooth and Water Bird."

As I had expected Brown Feather and Bird Song were disappointed but Moos Blood seemed happy enough. He would be sailing with his son and his father. As far as he was concerned, it was a perfect arrangement. I did not like manipulating my family like this but I suppose with age comes cunning and I did not want to upset my family. The incident with the bear seemed to have made them think that I was in danger of dying and they were trying to protect me.

"Father, should we risk the Patawomke?"

I shook my head, "Whilst we could guarantee a large catch the risk is too great. The next time we sail to the Patawomke will be when we go to the Great Sea for salt. The river upstream of here will do. If the winds are right, we can tow the birch bark boats. Today the river was high and the shallows should not be a problem."

It seemed to me that the Norns had been spinning again. I would be able to watch Bjorr Tooth and Water Bird and see if they were able to work together. I knew, all too well, what problems could be generated if two crewmen did not get on.

The warriors all enjoyed the fishing expeditions for it brought a bounty that we could guarantee. Fishing and hunting with spears and bows were less predictable. Using the nets the women had woven and with the strength of the two snekke, we could fish and know that not only were we safe but that we would return with laden holds.

As we headed up the river with the birch bark boats being towed behind us I said, "Today we will not offload the catch to the boats until our hold is full. That way we can take more back."

"We will not use the keep nets?"

I shook my head, "We can work quicker this way and our journey back to Eagle's Shadow will be faster for we will have the current with us."

He nodded his agreement and then, while I steered, shouted the orders back to Brave Cub in *'Doe'*.

I knew exactly where we were going to fish, in the confluence of the two branches of the river. There would be twice the numbers from one river and the water would be calmer and deeper. With the birch bark boats at the side, we ran out the net. We dropped our sails and threw out an anchor to hold us steady against the current. I gave Water Bird the task of holding the snekke's steering board into the current. I saw that Brave Cub was also using Brown Feather. It allowed the stronger warriors to be there to haul the catch aboard.

The Allfather, or perhaps Ran, smiled on us that morning for the first catch almost filled *'Doe'*. By the third catch, both snekke were full and the last catch was offloaded onto the birch bark boats. We hauled in the anchors and while Brave Cub and I turned the two snekke around, the sails were lowered and we flew, as I knew we would, down the river. It was as we headed back that I broached the subject of the expedition, "The two young ones work well together, do they not, Moos Blood?"

He beamed, "Aye, Father. You have trained my son well and Bjorr Tooth did better than I might have expected, for he has not sailed as often."

I nodded, "And I am pleased too, for I would have these two come with me when I explore the upper reaches of the north branch of the Shenandoah."

The other two had been listening and they looked to see Moos Blood's reaction.

He saw no cunning in my words and just responded to the basic idea, "You are still intent on this voyage?"

My dream came back to me. I had not spoken of it to the clan but I knew that there were shaven-headed warriors and that they were a threat to the clan. "It must be done. Iron Will's mother was cut and she had fled. We need to find the reason. We know that the land to the south and east is safe, for Brave Eagle's people rule that land. We know that to the north and east lies the dangerous Moneton but we are protected by the rapids. We must know what is north and west of us. I can explore the river and then, when I return, others can cross our river and head north."

There was silence as Moos Blood, whom I knew to be both reasonable and intelligent, considered my words.

"Moos Blood, the bear and the injury it caused told me that I am no longer a young man. I might have died. Let me do this one thing and then I will do as you all wish and fade away in Eagle's Shadow."

He laughed, "That you will never do." He nodded, "Very well, I give you permission to take my son with you. I will deal with the wrath of his mother."

The look of joy on Water Bird's face was enough to tell Moos Blood that he had made the right decision.

"Say nothing, Water Bird, until I have spoken to your mother."

"Of course, Father."

We reached Eagle's Shadow in the middle of the afternoon. Someone must have been watching from the longhouses for the women and children were there already. The babes were swaddled in slings so that their mothers could use both hands. As soon as the catch was offloaded then they began their preparation. The fish were gutted. The guts were thrown into the river and there they would feed the shellfish that we could gather at our leisure. The heads and bones were dropped into a pot that would make soup and the bodies were put in another pot.

It took us time to tie up and by the time we did so, we were able to send a pot back up to the longhouses. Willow Leaf went with her son and Iron Will to begin the salting and brining.

Once the fish were unloaded, we cleaned the decks of the two snekke and by the time the sun was starting to set we had the boats cleaned and the fish prepared for preservation. I stayed with Bjorr Tooth and Water Bird to scrub the deck of our new snekke. Our meal was one of raw fish. It was delicious and tastier for knowing that the preserved fish would mean we could have a few lazy days. The river's bounty had come to our aid once more.

The women spent the next day preserving and cooking fish. Ulla was happy to be cast the scraps. The warriors prepared for a hunt. We had not culled the deer on our side of the river for the last hunt had been close to the bjorr water. They had a day sharpening weapons and making more arrows. That left Water Bird and me to go over *'Laughing Deer'* to ensure that she was in perfect condition. She would not be needed for fishing again before our expedition and this was an opportunity for me to grease the moving parts and check the ropes and sheets. We had spares and this was a new snekke but my voyages had taught me that you could never prepare too much.

Water Bird was fascinated by the thought of a ship as big as a drekar. "And you could fit the whole clan on one?"

I shook my head, "We had a knarr and a snekke when we sailed west. As for when they left..." I shrugged, "I did not see them go. They thought me dead and by then we had lost many of the clan. When we sailed to Eagle's Shadow, we fitted the whole clan on two snekke. If we had to move again then we could all fit on the two of them but it would be a tight fit and we would need all the birch bark boats. I do not think we would have to move again."

"Why not, Grandfather?"

"For one thing, we were guided here by Gytha and it is as perfect a place as one can find. This is why we must go, with Bjorr Tooth, to discover if there is danger close by. We cannot flee for the only place left to us would be Brave Eagle's camp and I would not risk the Moneton. They know the snekke and they would try to destroy us. I am not afraid of a fight but neither do I seek one. When we sail up the river, we will be armed but those weapons will be just for our protection."

Chapter 7

We left Eagle's Shadow on the eve of the Summer Solstice. The days would be as long as they were going to get. They would be nowhere near as long as the ones on Orkneyjar or the almost endless ones of the Land of Ice and Fire, but as the level of the river was lower, I wanted as much light as we could get. The clan all came to see us off. The new bearskin was in my chest at the steering board along with my compass. I knew I should not need it but old habits die hard and it gave me comfort to know that they were in my chest. This time there would be neither a helmet nor a sword. I still had my seax and a hatchet made with the last of the ore. I had my bow and my new spear. Water Bird had the knife I had made for him and it was Bjorr Tooth who would be the warrior on the boat. He was well armed with a bow, arrows, seax, spear and a hand axe. He would be at the prow while it would be Water Bird who worked the sails. I adjusted the ballast to accommodate the crew. We had taken Ulla along the river to allow the animal to become used to the snekke. He seemed comfortable. If he showed signs of distress when we left Eagle's Shadow then I would return and leave him.

I sat at the steering board while the other two bade farewell to their mothers. Moos Blood came to the stern, "How long will you be away?"

I smiled, "Moos Blood, you of all people know that is an impossible thing to answer. I know not. It may be a week but it may well be longer. At the first sign of smoke, we will stop and hide the boat. I have no death wish especially with my grandson with me. We must discover if there are people living close. When Iron Will and Ulla came to us, I knew that there were people living close enough to walk to our home. They may be like our clan and peaceful but, then again, they may not."

He nodded and pointed to the dog, "And Ulla?"

"We need Ulla for if we find Iron Will's people then he is evidence that we mean them no harm."

Bjorr Tooth nodded as he took his place and, after hugging his mother, Water Bird sat by the mast.

"Raise the sail." As Water Bird hauled on the rope that raised the sail, I felt the snekke tugging. "Let go." The two ropes were thrown aboard. I caught one and dropped it to the deck while Bjorr Tooth caught the other and began to coil it. As we began to pull into the centre of the river Ulla began to moan. Water Bird began to stroke the dog which, whilst never taking its eyes from the quay, did at least calm a little.

We turned the bend and all that we saw of our home was the smoke rising from the fires. We used dry wood for the fires and the tendril of smoke was thin. The first part of the journey, until the fork, would be familiar land but I had impressed upon Bjorr Tooth that he needed to keep a good watch on the banks, both of them.

"Water Bird, put out a couple of fishing lines. We will augment our dried food with fresh."

It was more to keep my grandson occupied than anything. He moved easily down the snekke and dropped the two lines with the baited hooks on the larboard side so as not to foul the steering board.

The winds were gentle and while that made for a more comfortable voyage, we were not as swift as we had been on the previous journeys. The sun was setting slowly ahead of us when I saw the fork in the river.

"Bjorr Tooth, keep your eyes open for somewhere to land."

"Will we not keep sailing at night?"

"I am too old to lose sleep these days. We will land and have a cold camp."

We passed the slower water where the two rivers met and entered the narrower channel which was the unexplored river. Here the waters were more turbulent as they raced to the confluence. It was still more than wide enough to accommodate the snekke. Bjorr Tooth held up his hand and pointed to the shore. I saw the gap between the overhanging trees. It looked to be a perfect place to land.

"Reef the sail." Water Bird did as I ordered and we began to slow against the current. This river was not as powerful as the one we had left and we nudged gently into the bank as the sail was lowered. Bjorr Tooth leapt over the side with the rope and was tying us to a tree when I said, "Ulla," and pointed to the shore. The dog leapt over the side and cocked his leg to relieve himself. He looked around and I pointed. He ran off. Bjorr Tooth took his spear and ran off after him. Water Bird climbed to the bank and I handed him the rope. Secured fore and after I took the fish we had caught and climbed ashore. I ached and was stiff. As if I needed it this was confirmation that I was getting old. I handed the fish to my grandson along with my seax, "Gut them."

I opened my chest and took out the bear's skin. It would be both my bed and blanket but, until Bjorr Tooth returned, I would not prepare my bed. I dropped my breeks and made water. The sun had just dropped behind the hills to the west when Bjorr Tooth and Ulla returned.

"I could smell no smoke, Shaman, and I only saw the tracks of an animal. There are many white-tailed deer here. This is good land to hunt." In explanation, he added, "Ulla smelled them and began to chase them. He came back when I commanded." Both Bjorr Tooth and Water Bird were able to command Ulla. It was as though the animal had chosen who to follow. Iron Will was at the top of the list followed by me and then my crewmen. He also had a soft spot for Little White Dove and Willow Leaf but I think that was because they fed him.

We shared the fish which we ate raw. Ulla ate the heads, guts, and some dried venison. I wanted the dog fed for he would be our sentry. It was another reason for his inclusion. He would growl if there was danger. We had no fire and we slept close together. Water Bird was between Ulla and me while Bjorr Tooth used Ulla as a backrest. The bear skin was warm and would serve as a blanket for both my grandson and me.

When I woke there was a mist along the river. The trees were shrouded in grey. It must have been a cold night but I had not noticed the cold. The bear's skin had served me well. It was still dark and I slipped from the bearskin and covered Water Bird with my side of it. I was making water when I spied a movement. Before I could reach for my seax the white-tailed deer fled. Bjorr Tooth was right. This was a good hunting ground. If the deer approached as close as that one had then it suggested they had few encounters with men.

I was ready to sail by the time the other two woke up. I had disturbed Ulla who went into the undergrowth. He seemed to have learned to use the time ashore to his advantage quickly. We had finished the fish the night before and I ate some venison and drank some ale. While they made water and ate, I went to the snekke. The mist would still be there for some time. Once boarded, we headed upriver. There was little breeze and I wondered if we might have to use the paddles we had brought to maintain our progress. When the sun did come out it not only burnt away the mist but gave us a little more breeze so that, by tacking back and forth across the river, we made better progress.

We had our routine now and Water Bird put the lines out without being told. We did not speak for I wanted to listen to the land and until we knew that the land was peaceful, I would not announce our presence loudly. The land looked similar to that around Eagle's Shadow. There were plenty of trees and that suggested that few people lived here or else they would have cleared them close to the river for crops. It came to me, as we headed ever north and west, that this land might not belong to any one clan but was, perhaps, used for hunting by clans that lived some way away. I had already decided that we would harvest the bounty of the white-tailed deer. We would allow the herds close to our land to prosper and increase. As the clan grew so we would need to find more food.

We saw no one on that second day and when we tied up for the night, it was on the larboard side of the snekke where there was an open area. This time the trees had been cut down. While Bjorr Tooth and Ulla scouted, I examined the tree stumps. The cut marks were old and made by a crude stone axe but they were evidence that someone had cut them. This was the first indication that there were people who might have lived close by at some time in the past. With no smell of woodsmoke, I risked our own fire. The mist the previous night had told me that the nights might be cold and hot fish was something to be savoured. Water Bird caught some crustaceans and they would also be cooked. We ate well that night but I did not feed the fire. Once the food had cooked, I let it die down naturally.

"How much further upriver do we travel, Shaman?"

"We have only travelled for two days and the journey back will be faster for it will be downriver. This land has the mark of man. Tomorrow, we keep an even better watch on the river. Water Bird, you can sit with Bjorr Tooth at the prow. We watch both sides of the river."

There was no mist on that third day of the voyage. I was actually enjoying myself. I liked the company of my grandson, Bjorr Tooth and Ulla. We got on well and reminded me of that long voyage from the Land of Ice and Fire in the snekke. Those companions were now dead but they lived still in my mind. As far as I knew, only Fótr lived and, perhaps, my wife Ada. I knew not. I did not think that Fótr was dead. He had not visited me in the dream world and we were so close that if he were dead then I know he would have come. I had seen Arne and the others although as I had witnessed their deaths, I needed no confirmation from the spirit world.

We saw the thin spiral of smoke in the far west as the sun began to set. It was a camp and it was on the larboard side of the snekke. When Bjorr Tooth and Ulla set off, Water Bird and I remained on the snekke in case we had to make a hasty departure.

I breathed a sigh of relief when the two returned and Bjorr Tooth appeared unperturbed, "The camp is not close by but I did see signs of man. Wood had been taken for timber and the bushes and trees have been stripped of fruit, berries and nuts. There are people close by."

"Then tonight it is cold fare and tomorrow we will sail just a little way up the river and investigate the camp, on foot."

It was while we were eating that Water Bird said, "What if the people we find are aggressive and wish to harm us?"

"You and Ulla will guard the snekke when we land and Bjorr Tooth will be cautious and approach the camp as though it is a nervous herd of white-tailed deer." He looked disappointed, "When you are a man grown, Water Bird, then I will let you risk your life, but we need the snekke to be protected. If anything happens to Bjorr Tooth and me then you can take the news back to your father. Even without the sail, the snekke can be steered down the river and I know that you can steer."

He was not happy about my decision but he nodded.

I woke early. I knew that we were in the Norns' web but we could do nothing about it. What would be, would be. I made water and then sharpened both my seax and hatchet. The spear had been sharpened before we had left and would be as sharp as any weapon in this land. We ate and then set off. You could feel the nervousness on the snekke. Even Ulla seemed affected and sniffed the air with his ears pricked as we headed down the river. The smell from the wood fire determined where we would stop. I found a place where trees had been cut and this time, I swung the snekke around so that it was facing downstream. If we had to leave quickly then we could and as my intention on this voyage was to discover people, then we need to go no further upstream. We just tied it by the stern so that if we had to leave hurriedly it would be easy to do so.

Bjorr Tooth and I left the snekke. He had his bow and I had my spear. Ulla made to come and I held up a hand and said, "Ulla, stay." The dog sat down again. "Water Bird, if we are not back by the time the sun has reached the top of the sky, then leave and give the news to your father." He looked to argue and I held up my hand, "I am your grandfather, the chief and the Shaman. Obey."

He nodded, "Yes, Grandfather."

I followed Bjorr Tooth. He was younger and his senses would be more acute than mine. We headed along the trail that led to the river. It was narrow and there was a risk we might meet someone but I gambled that the visits to the river would have been more likely in the morning and, as there were no signs of nets by the river, I was hopeful that we would not encounter anyone.

The smell of woodsmoke grew stronger but there was not the noise I expected of a large village. The wind was blowing the smell of the smoke towards us and I guessed any noise that we might make would not be heard. Bjorr Tooth raised his arm and then nocked an arrow. I moved next to him and peered towards the clearing just forty paces from us. There were just three yehakins. It hardly justified being called a camp. We waited and watched. I saw an old man and woman, two younger women and five children. That was all. I tapped Bjorr Tooth on the shoulder and signed for him to put his bow down. To confirm my command I rammed my spear into the ground. The people posed no threat and I did not want to frighten them. However, I knew that my face might do so and I signalled for Bjorr Tooth to head along the trail first. We were both silent and when we emerged no one noticed us at first. When they did and the woman screamed, the old man grabbed a flint-tipped spear. It was not even a real head. We both held up our hands.

Bjorr Tooth spoke, "We come in peace and mean you no harm."

What I dreaded was that these people spoke the same language as Iron Will's mother. To my relief, I understood most of the old man's words when he spoke. The children sheltered behind the two women and the older woman who held a stone knife in her hand. The man with the spear held his weapon before him but he did not seem ready to use it. I let Bjorr Tooth speak.

"We have come from the river to the east of you." He pointed as he said the words slowly. "We are of the Clan of the Bear. I am Bjorr Tooth and this is our chief and Shaman, Erik."

I am not sure how many words they all understood but the old man's eyes and nod took in that he had understood most.

He spoke and did so slowly. I saw that the head of the spear was now touching the ground. Unless we did something stupid there would be no violence. Even the old woman had lowered her knife.

"I am Lost Wolf and my son was chief of this clan, the Clan of the Dog." I found that I could understand most of his words and he spoke so slowly that I was able to deduce the others. "What you see are all that remains of the clan."

I nodded, "We too are a small clan."

He put down his spear and said, "There will be no weapons. Let me clasp your arm so that I may know that you are real and that I am not in the Dreamworld." I walked over and held out my arm. We clasped arms and he nodded. "Let us sit. We have little to share but…"

"Bjorr Tooth, go to the snekke and fetch Water Bird, Ulla, food and ale."

He nodded and trotted off. With the warrior gone the others visibly relaxed, especially when I sat down. Lost Wolf said, "I did not understand all the words you said, Shaman of the Bear, and your name, Erik, seems strange."

I smiled, "I come from another land, beyond the Great Sea to the east. I am the last of my people to live in this land."

His face broke into a smile and he turned to the older woman, "See, I told you the dream would come true."

"Aye, you did and I doubted you. I am sorry, husband."

"This is my wife, Grey Shadow."

"Your dream?" Dreams always intrigued me.

"Long ago I had a dream of a man who came to this camp on a water bird. He wore a bear about him and carried a shiny stick. He defeated our enemies and kept us safe. When the Shawnee came the last time, I thought that the spirits had deceived me."

"I have a bear skin and I sail on a boat that looks like a bird. This is *wyrd*." He frowned at the word and I said, "Strange."

He nodded, "And you have a shiny stick?"

"I do, my son has it now for I am old."

He smiled, "No older than me and I am guessing that we have both seen the same number of summers. We have a tale to tell you but we will wait until your companion returns. Until then I pray you tell me how you came across this Great Sea. I have not seen such a sea but I have heard of others who passed through and they claimed to have seen a sea so big that it went further than the eye could see."

I began to tell him my story, of Orkneyjar, Larswick, the Land of Ice and Fire, Bear Island, Brave Eagle and finally the Shenandoah. I had to simplify it mainly because of the Norse words but all of them were wrapt as I told the story."

"If I had not dreamed and if you did not look so different from any other man I have ever seen, then I might have judged you to be speaking untruths, but I believe you."

Just then Ulla bounded into the camp. He ran straight up to Lost Wolf and jumped up at him. He began to lick the old man.

The woman's face cracked into a smile that was riven with tears, "It is true, Shaman of the Bear, you are truly welcome."

"You know Ulla?"

Lost Wolf said, "I know the dog, it is Howls in the Night and was my son's, the chief. You did not tell us this part of the tale."

My grandson and Bjorr Tooth walked into the camp. "No, for I did not know the thread bound us. Water Bird, Bjorr Tooth, share out the food."

"Water Bird? He is a boat?"

I laughed, "He is my grandson and Water Bird is his name. The boat that is like a water bird is called *'Laughing Deer'* and we shall show it to you when we have eaten." The food was distributed and I said, "I will tell you how we found Ulla and Iron Will."

I told them the story. At one point one of the younger women tried to interrupt but Grey Shadow intervened. When I had finished, he nodded. "All now makes sense. You talk of threads, Shaman, and they are strong ones. My son, Wolf's Tooth, was a good chief and a kind one. We lived in peace. One day he found a woman. She was not of our people but came from the north. She and my son had eyes only for each other and they wed. She was called Walks Far by my people for she had come a long way. She told us of a people called the Shawnee. They were, she said, a cruel people who raided lands to take women and children. They lived many days travel to the north. She had lived in a land by a large waterfall and had been taken as a child. She fled because she was to be married to a man who was even crueller than most. She warned us that they would follow her. We shifted our camp and came here, further south and closer to this river. We lived peacefully. When Walks Far had her child, we had not even named her, we heard of attacks to the next clan. It was the Shawnee. My son decided that he would not bring danger to the clan and he took his wife and child and they fled to the river."

Grey Shadow said, "We said we would defend them for all the clan liked them. My son feared for our lives and he left."

"We waited for an attack but it did not come. At least not for a while and we wondered if my son's flight was necessary." He shook his head, "They came but it was when I was out hunting with Blue Jay, Red Wing and Silent Stone." He pointed to the three youths as he spoke. "It saved our lives but the rest of the clan were either taken or slain." I looked at the two young women. He smiled, "My wife managed to take my daughter, Moon Calf and the wife of my second son, Wind Talker to safety."

Grey Shadow patted her knife, "The Shawnee who tried to take us learned that I might have white hair but I know how to use a knife."

"That was almost a year ago and we were preparing to flee again when you came."

"Flee?"

"They will come again. Walks Far told us that each year they travel further and further. Their chief is ambitious. We have moved but we know that they will find us."

I had finished my food and my mind had been working. The Norns had been spinning. "This is what I think happened. Your son and his family were pursued. I think that your son gave his life so that Walks Far would live. They must have crossed the river but Walks Far was hurt. We were meant to find them."

"Yes, I can see that."

"Come with me and I will show you how we reached here and then listen to my words." He stood but the rest remained seated. "No, all of you. It is important that you see this."

I led them, having retrieved my spear, and Lost Wolf walked next to me. Ulla never left his side. I was forgotten for the dog had been reunited with his clan. Bjorr Tooth walked at the rear. When we reached the river, I heard the gasp from them all.

Lost Wolf said, "This is how I dreamed it but it had white wings."

I nodded, "Water Bird, raise the sail." He climbed aboard and hauled on the rope. The snekke was secured to the bank but when the wind caught the sails they billowed. The women, Grey Shadow apart, recoiled. "Lower it now." He did so. "And so you see how I crossed the Great Sea and how I came here."

"This is meant to be but the Shawnee will come."

"Hear my words. I think our clans are tied as is our fate. I would take you from here to Eagle's Shadow. You can join our clan for we have warriors and weapons that the Shawnee have never seen. I have fought enemies before and always have I been outnumbered. I know that I am old but I am a warrior and I know how to fight."

Lost Wolf said, "It is a good idea but unless you have another two of these magic boats I cannot see how we can do this."

I patted one of the trees that lined the river, "We hew trees and tie them together to make a raft. We will tow you."

"Tow?"

"Pull you through the water."

He shook his head, "It will take many days to cut down the trees and the Shawnee are coming. We would have left the day after tomorrow had you not found us."

"It is getting on to dark. I will leave Bjorr Tooth here to watch our boat and Water Bird and I will come to your camp. By this time tomorrow, we will be ready to leave." He looked dubious, "Trust me, Lost Wolf. I was sent here and I know that we can do this."

Grey Shadow nodded, "And I believe you. I have watched your eyes and heard your words. You mean what you say, I always wondered about my husband's dream. Now I see that it is our salvation." She took her husband's hand, "And I would see our granddaughter too."

"Then we are in your hands, Shaman."

Chapter 8

I took my bear's skin back and rather than imposing on the clan and sharing a yehakin, Water Bird and I slept in the open under the skin. There was a happy atmosphere in the camp. I am not sure they understood what I had in mind but they now had hope that there was a life free from the threat of the Shawnee. As we snuggled beneath the skin Water Bird said, "You have often spoken of these three sisters, Grandfather, but it is only now that I truly understand them. When Ulla left us to bound off I wondered why, but when I saw him with Lost Wolf then all became clear." He was silent and then said, "Will the Shawnee pursue them? Will we be putting our clan in danger?"

"Perhaps but we travelled for many days to reach here. Perhaps we are too far from the Shawnee homeland, I cannot say but we cannot leave these here, can we?"

"No, it is clear we have to save them but it will disrupt our lives." He suddenly stopped and then said, "We will need a new longhouse!"

"And we shall build one and it will make us stronger."

"How so?"

"The three of them along with the snekke and the wood store will make a," I struggled for the Powhatan word and I could not think of a word. I was thinking of a fort such as the ones built by the Romans, "will make a stronghold. We will have walls and a ditch around us. You were too young to remember but when Eagle Claws came for vengeance, even the one longhouse was too strong for him. Three of them will stop the Shawnee."

My words sounded confident but my heart still feared for my family.

The next morning I had the clan fetch everything. "You will not need to stay here again. We will make a raft that is big enough for all of you and your belongings. Leave nothing here."

It took some time and the sun was burning brightly as we neared the river. We could hear the sound of Bjorr Tooth's axe. "Your warrior is working already."

"He knows what to do."

When we reached the river Lost Wolf could not believe what he saw. Bjorr Tooth must have begun at dawn for three trees were hewn already and he was sharpening the axe.

"How can this be?"

I took my hatchet from my belt and handed it to him. "We make metal. This is not like stone for we can sharpen it. You can use your stone axe but we have three metal tools that will make the work easier. Have the boys gather vines to bind the logs."

We piled their belongings by the river and began to clear another six trees. With three of us working it did not take long. We soon stripped all the branches from them and left just the sturdy trunks. They were all roughly the same length. The boys came back with the vines and I set the rest to binding them into a raft. I went off with the axe and the hatchet.

I heard Lost Wolf ask Water Bird, "Where does the Shaman go?"

"He goes to make a steering board." I knew that Lost Wolf would not have any idea what that was. Water Bird did though, "My grandfather is a Shaman. He knows the magic of the water. You will see."

I went to the branches we had trimmed and chose the best pieces. I first split them and then used the hatchet to shape them. We had axes back at Eagle's Shadow that would have been perfect but my hatchet would have to do. All I needed was a crude device to enable Bjorr Tooth to steer the raft. It still took most of the next day to construct it and the raft was ready long before I had finished. Lost Wolf, Bjorr Tooth and Water Bird came to join me as Grey Shadow and the others prepared food. We had run lines in the river and would enjoy a hot meal. With Bjorr Tooth to aid me, the work went much more quickly and just before the sun dropped below the hills in the west, we were able to go back and I used some of the nails we had in *'Laughing Deer'* to attach the steering board to the raft.

"You will steer the raft, Bjorr Tooth. All you will need to do is to make sure it points in the same direction as mine."

"I can do that, Shaman." The young warrior was growing in confidence each day.

Lost Wolf stood in wonder, looking at the raft. He shook his head, "I have never seen such a thing. Your grandson is right. You are a magician. You turned trees into this."

I nodded. The others had left us and I said, "But we have also left a sign for the Shawnee. We cannot disguise what we have done here. We left a clear trail from your camp and the fire will remain a blackened mark for many months. They will see the stumps of the trees and wonder where they are. If you are right and they are coming ever south then one day they will cross the river and look for signs of you. It may take them years but they will find us just as we found you."

Smiling he said, "But by then my grandsons and yours will be warriors. We may be long dead but if we are not then we can show these Shawnees that they cannot simply take over the whole of this land. Someone will stop them."

"Aye, you are right. A man can only run so far before he makes a stand and says, this much and no more."

All were excited as we loaded the snekke and the raft. The two young girls, Moon Calf and Doe's Milk, were the most fearful and they were placed with the softer belongings in the middle of the raft where their mothers and grandmother could watch them. The heavier belongings were placed in the snekke and I asked Blue Jay and Red Wing to sail with me. They could act as lookouts and Water Bird could teach them how to sail. It was noon when we were ready. The one called Silent Stone would be with the others on the raft. I had used a good rope to attach to the raft. The two youths were ready to untie the snekke and jump aboard. Lost Wolf was by the vine that secured the raft to the land.

I spoke to those on the raft, "Keep seated when we sail. We have tied your belongings well. Hang on to the vines if you are fearful. The waters may become choppy but we will not sink."

They nodded, the women and the two young girls looked fearful. Grey Shadow said, "This will be an adventure. We go to a new life and just as birth can be both exciting and dangerous, it is necessary for life. Trust this Shaman and his magic."

"Let go. Water Bird, hoist the sail."

Once free of the land the current and the slight breeze took us. There was a tug as the raft slowed us a little and then Bjorr Tooth turned the steering board and we were off. It was slower than it would have been without the raft but we had to hurry. Slow and gentle would be better than the ride we had first had along this river.

"Water Bird, have the two boys watch ahead for danger. When you can, look astern and ensure that the raft is behaving itself. I must concentrate on steering the safest course."

"Aye, Grandfather." He took the two youths to the prow and placed them on either side of the figurehead. I saw him pointing to the water and they nodded. He came back and stood by the mast to look astern. He waved and then sat down. "They are all happy, Grandfather."

"Then give us a little more sail."

He took out a reef and we moved a little faster. I would not risk sailing in the dark and when I spotted the place we had camped on the way north, I headed to the shore. We tied up and stepped ashore. I smiled as the Clan of the Dog tried to walk on land after being on the water. We risked a fire and cooked the fish we had caught on the river.

I sat with Lost Wolf and we spoke of the journey. "This is easy, Shaman."

"My name is Erik and you are right."

"Your people must be powerful. You say that the boat you came on held many people?"

"More than five times the number who are aboard here."

"You could rule the world if you wished."

I shook my head and told him of my brother Arne. When I had finished, I said, "We could still be living peacefully at Bear Island but here," I patted my head, "he had a vision of himself as ruler of this land. It killed him and most of my family and friends. I think that the need for such power is a worm that eats into a man and changes him. The secret for me is living with a family and a clan that you care for. You protect them but you do not provoke danger."

"My son tried that and look what happened."

I shrugged, "I did not say that it always worked out, but if he had not done what he did then we would not be here and what would have happened to the Clan of the Dog?"

He had clearly not thought of that and he said, "You are wise. I am looking forward to seeing this Eagle's Shadow."

It was the next day that the Clan of the Dog saw the wilder side of the river. We joined the other branch of the Shenandoah. We bumped and bobbed through the combined waters until we reached the flatter, calmer and wider side. There were squeals both of fear and excitement until we serenely sailed down the much more powerful river.

The river was stronger than it had been and we moved much more quickly. I knew that we would only need one more camp before we reached my home. Even the wind was in our favour and Water Bird was able to use the full power of the sail. The Clan of the Dog could not see the bear on the sail but if they had it would have impressed them. It was a magnificent achievement and made the snekke more like a living being.

That night we camped on the side of the river with which I was more familiar. I was more confident about a fire. As we ate, Grey Shadow and Lost Wolf asked me more about my clan. I knew why. They would be outsiders.

"We will build you a longhouse."

"Longhouse?"

"Yes, Lost Wolf, a house made of timber and with turf upon it. There will be a fire within and all your people will share the same roof.

It will take time to build but with both clans working together then we should finish it within a week."

Grey Shadow said, "And will we be welcomed?"

I nodded, "We have taken in others before."

Lost Wolf gestured with his finger at Bjorr Tooth, "Already the clans are growing closer look."

Bjorr Tooth was laughing with Moon Calf, Lost Wolf's eldest daughter. They were seated close together and seemed oblivious to the rest of the camp.

"Such things are meant to be."

Water Bird rarely left my side and he said, "And my grandfather can make iron tools that will make your clan stronger."

"You made those axes?"

I nodded, "It is not easy but yes, we can. The shiny stick you saw in your dream is a sword that was made by someone far more skilled than I am. It is a sharp and strong weapon. Mine are pale shadows and someone will have to fetch more ore."

"Ore?"

"The rocks we melt to make the iron."

Lost Wolf shook his head, "You can melt rocks? I think I must still be in the Dreamworld."

There was both trepidation and excitement from the Clan of the Dog as we left our last camp and headed for Eagle's Shadow. We turned a bend and saw *'Doe'* and the birch bark boats on the water. Moos Blood had brought the warriors to fish but as we were still a couple of miles from our home, I suspected that he was looking for me.

"Lower the sail, Water Bird. The current can take us."

We drifted next to the snekke. The other warriors paddled their birch bark boats to join us. The joy on their faces was clear. We had been away from home for some days and I was no longer a young man.

"Well, Father, I see you have found more mouths to feed." My son was grinning when he said it. They would be welcomed.

"This is the Clan of the Dog and Iron Will is of their people. Ulla belongs to this clan."

My son's hand went to the metal symbol he wore around his neck. It was a crude version of the Hammer of Thor, "*Wyrd*."

"It is and we will need to build another longhouse."

"Of course. We will sail ahead and warn the others. Little White Dove and Willow Leaf will want to make a good impression."

'Doe' looked magnificent as she turned and with the sail billowing flew down the river, the birch bark boats paddling for all that they were

worth like ducklings after their mother. Had we not had the laden raft in tow then we would have beaten her.

"Raise the sail. We are almost there."

By the time we reached Eagle's Shadow, the snekke and the boats were tied to the bank. They had left the quay clear for us to tie up. The women were not there. They would be waiting at the top of the slope. Moos Blood greeted the clan as they disembarked. "Welcome. Bjorr Tooth and Water Bird, take our guests to the village. We will bring your belongings."

"We can help." I heard the pride in Lost Wolf's voice.

Moos Blood shook his head, "The women are anxious to see you and Iron Will needs to see her family. All is well."

Lost Wolf turned to me, "Your son?" I nodded. "I can tell. You are good people." He followed with his wife linking his arm.

I knew that his words had filled my son with pride.

I nodded to the raft, "I will stay here with Brave Cub and Golden Bear. The raft gives us some timber for the longhouse and it is right that we use the wood from the land of the clan. When you have taken their belongings, return and we will carry the timber up. That way you can moor the snekke and the boats."

It took the rest of the afternoon to cut the ropes and vines from the raft and take the timber up to the top of the slope. I stayed at the river. It was not laziness, it was just easier on my knee. I waited until all the boats were secured against the bank and then I ascended with Moos Blood. As we climbed, I told them the tale of Walks Far and the Shawnee.

We stopped just shy of the houses, "Then they will come here."

"As sure as the leaves will drop after the harvest, but it will not be for some time. It took some days to sail here and the Shawnee will not know which way we went. I assume that they would think downriver but there are two branches. We have time. Someone will need to fetch more ore before winter."

"Not you."

"Not me."

"Then we cannot expect the quality to be as high."

"It does not need to be. Even poor ore makes better tools and weapons than stone. Arrows will be the secret to victory. We make iron arrowheads."

"It is good to have you home. We worried."

"Yet it was right that I went. Lost Wolf also dreamed and I was his dream. The Norns have woven a web that is truly spectacular."

As we entered the open area between the longhouses, both clans were there and they all ululated and shouted, "Erik, Shaman of the Bear." I now had a much bigger clan to lead and my work was not yet done. The Allfather still had plans for me. The women got on and that was the most important thing. Grey Shadow was the matriarch of her clan but she saw, immediately, that Willow Leaf and my daughter were kind and thoughtful women. Lost Wolf, for his part, was pleased that he no longer had the sole responsibility for the young of his clan. They would be trained by Moos Blood and my sons.

The longhouse took less than seven days to build thanks to the timber of the raft. The vision I had of the finished camp materialised and we had a secure and solid home that could be easily defended. Ten days after we had begun it was ready for the Clan of the Dog to occupy. Bjorr Tooth left my longhouse for he and Moon Calf married. He had been ready for a wife and Looks Far was happy that her daughter had such a good husband. He had impressed all of them on the journey downriver. I was pleased. Bjorr Tooth was like another son to me and his happiness was clear to see.

As the harvest approached, both clans worked hard to gather all that we could for the winter. The three extra youths helped us with the fishing and the hunting while the four females were desperate to show that they could share the load. As soon as the harvest was in, Brave Cub would take six men and boys with him to gather ore from the cave. I would stay with the others. We had arrows to make as well as bjorr traps. With more mouths to feed, we would have one last hunt before winter. It was, for me, an easy task as we did not have to move from the working area close to the fire. My knee did not need to object to constant movement. I was able to talk with Lost Wolf and the others. The Clan of the Dog had bows but they were not as good as ours. We had made ours from yew and they were longer. Our arrows were also longer. It was when we fitted the metal arrowheads that Lost Wolf and Red Wing became fascinated.

"You made these, Shaman?"

"My clan made them but I was the first on this side of the water to make such things. They can go through the hide of even the oldest deer." I wondered what they would have made of the wild pigs and boars we had hunted close to Larswick. "You will see when we cross the river and hunt both the white-tailed deer and the bjorr."

"After the Shawnee took our warriors, I only had my two grandsons and Silent Stone to accompany me on the hunt. Using our bows and the handful of arrows we were lucky to bring down a squirrel."

I pointed to one of the oak trees that grew nearby. We encouraged their growth by using mostly beech and birch for our needs. "The oak grows from something that is smaller than my thumb. Your clan will grow. Bjorr Tooth's blood will mix. Blue Jay and Doe's Milk, not to mention you, Red Wing, will marry and have children. A clan does not grow overnight. I just hope that I live long enough to see it."

"As do I Erik, as do I."

While the two boys had been animated while we had worked, Silent Stone lived up to his name and said nothing. When the boys took the arrows we had made to be stored safely I asked, when the two of us were alone, "Silent Stone, tell me about him."

"We named him for even when he was born, he said little. Now he speaks even less and it seems the name we gave him might have been a curse. His mother died giving birth to him and he was nursed by all the women in the tribe. They all felt attached to him. His father was a great warrior and my son's best friend. When we returned to the camp after the hunt we saw that the Shawnee warriors had despoiled their bodies badly." He saw my look and said, "It is their way of honouring bravery. Silent Stone has not spoken a word since that time. Perhaps one day he will."

"He can talk then?"

"Yes, but his words are like snow in early summer, they are very rare and to be treasured when they come."

It was important that the clans became one and I did not want my clan to think that Silent Stone was putting on an act. I spoke to my grandchildren and my sons to let them know his tale. "Involve him in what you do. Even if he does not speak back to you do not take offence at that. He is now the only orphan in the clan. Iron Will has her grandparents. Silent Stone now has our clan. I will take him the next time we go fishing, Water Bird."

"And I will do my best, Grandfather."

With so many more mouths to feed and so few warriors added to the clan, we had to hunt and fish more, in that time after the harvest, than was normal. I did not want another harsh winter. First, however, we needed to have more ore. Brave Cub and Golden Bear chose their miners carefully. As well as Bjorr Tooth and Black Feather they also asked Brown Feather, Red Wing and Blue Jay to go with them. That suited me as I was able to take Water Bird and Silent Stone to the river to fish. It was mainly a way to teach Silent Stone how to sail. The two boys were of a similar age but the privations of their lives meant that, as Ulla had been, Silent Stone was underweight. I had them both sit close to the mast. We still used my Norse words for many of the parts of the boat and the instructions I gave. It had helped Fears Water and I when we had been forced to sail north on the river with Eagle Claws' killers.

As we prepared to cast off, I said, "Water Bird, make sure that you repeat all the words to Silent Stone. He may not reply but this will be like the action of water on a stone. Gradually, it will have an effect. We will sail downriver towards the sea."

Water Bird chattered happily to Silent Stone as he passed on my orders. Where there might be confusion, he took Silent Stone's hands and put them on the rope or the timber that he needed him to use. Silent Stone listened and was a quick learner. The two of them worked well together and, on one occasion, I even saw a smile on the orphan's face. It was a start. I looked up into the sky when he smiled for I knew that Laughing Deer would have approved. She had the kindest heart of anyone I ever knew.

We had two kinds of net that we used. One was the larger one we strung between two snekke and we had a smaller one that we used when fishing with just one boat. When we neared the shallows, I stopped the snekke and we lowered the sail. Water Bird showed Silent Stone how to throw out the two anchors to hold us against the current. That done I shifted down to the mast. Normally, I would have helped but this time I would just be on hand. I let Water Bird give the instructions. It made him more confident and helped to bond the two of them. The art was to keep hold of the cord that was attached to the lower part of the net whilst hooking the upper part onto the gunwale. Water Bird was patient as he gave his instructions. They lowered the net and waited. It was a matter of feel and touch. Water Bird would know when fish became entangled and it was all about the judgement of pulling up at the right time.

He kept up a commentary for Silent Stone, "Can you feel the fish as they strike the net?" Silent Stone nodded. "When I say *'now'* we pull up as one. Today, Silent Stone, we become twins working as one." There was another nod. After a couple of heartbeats, he said, "Now!" Silent Stone had made the mistake of using his weaker arm to hold the lower part of the net and the weight of the catch was too much. They were in danger of losing the catch and whilst not a disaster might make the orphan even less confident. I reached over and helped him to pull. My arm made the difference and the six large fish tumbled, wriggling and writhing, onto the deck.

"Well done, boys. That is a mighty catch." The two grinned. "Next time, Silent Stone, use your stronger arm. I will deal with these fish while you try again." As I used a stone club to kill the fish, the two threw the net overboard again. I knew that I would not be needed again but I was close, just in case. In the end, we caught eighteen large fish. There were five smaller ones that I threw overboard to grow. We were like farmers and encouraged our fishy crops for the future.

Silent Stone's smile remained all the way back upriver to Eagle's Shadow. He heeded all of Water Bird's instructions and proved to be just as natural a sailor as my grandson. I let the two of them string the fish on the pole and they laboured under the heavy weight as they ascended the slope. I secured the snekke.

By the time I reached the camp, the two of them were busily gutting the fish under the smiling but watchful gaze of Water Bird's mother, Blue Feather.

Grey Shadow came over to me as I washed the fish scales from my hands, "You are truly a magician, Shaman."

"How so?"

"Silent Stone walked into camp with a smile on his face. Since we found his father, I have never seen him smile and even before that smiles were rare. What did you do?"

"I made him part of my crew and gave him purpose."

Lost Wolf had been listening and he said, "Your boat, a snekke?" I nodded. "It is special in many ways. I can see how your people could travel so far across endless seas. I should like to see this sea."

"Perhaps you shall, Lost Wolf."

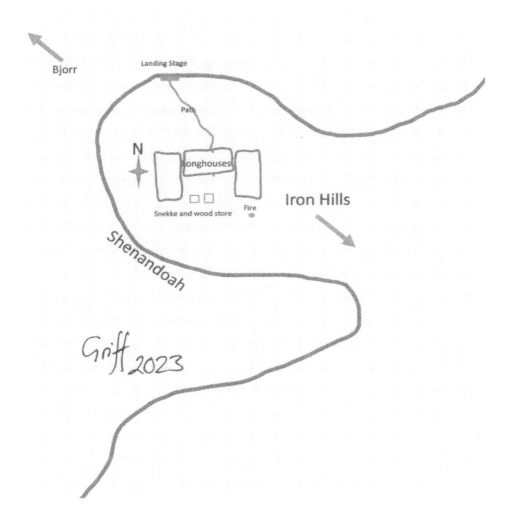

Chapter 9

When the ore was fetched, we stored it. The hunt and the catching of the fish were the priorities. We could make the iron when the cold came. Lost Wolf and Ulla joined the hunt and I stayed in the camp to be the guardian of Eagle's Shadow. My knee might slow down the hunt and besides I wanted Moos Blood to be seen as the chief of the clan. They came back laden with meat. I enjoyed my day with the women and the young children. I got to know Lost Wolf's granddaughters. Moon Calf and Bjorr Tooth had married and now her cousin, Doe's Milk, was beginning to realise that she was almost a woman. There were no suitable young men and it was as I spoke with her that I realised the clan still had some growing to do.

A few days later we went downriver for the last fishing hunt and I had my crew of Silent Stone and Water Bird, but I asked Lost Wolf to sail too. He had not been on the snekke when we had left his home and I had seen his envious looks. He was a passenger but Silent Stone helped him. He even uttered some words as he warned Lost Wolf when the old warrior tried to stand. It was but a couple of words and yet it was a beginning. When we held the nets between the snekke, it was my voice that issued commands. The fishing was a success and we headed back to what was now a village with smiles on our faces. Water Bird, joker that he was, even made Silent Stone and Lost Wolf reel with laughter as he used a fish head to talk. I had seen his trick before but it still made me smile. When we docked, the four of us let others take our catch while we cleaned the snekke. We would soon be storing the two boats for winter and you could tell that none of the three of them wanted the day to end. It was a start.

Once we had stored the snekke, we went into the forest to gather the wood we knew would keep us warm in winter. The women had deer and fish to salt and so it was the men and boys who entered the forest. Each boy had a stone axe. My grandson and foster grandson both had a small iron hatchet and the others looked enviously at them. It was as the boys began to trim the branches we had taken that I saw the closeness of Water Bird and Silent Stone. Water Bird let the orphan use the metal hatchet. They were becoming as close as I had been to Siggi, my cousin. My brother Arne and I had never been as close. I was happy that my grandson and the new member of the clan were forming a bond. It was *wyrd*.

The weather changed, as it always did, about three weeks before the Winter Solstice. The wood store was full and the larder we had built bulged under the weight of food. That was the province of Willow Leaf and Little White Dove who would manage it and ensure that food was eaten before it went bad. The harvest had been a good one and had provided, we hoped, enough to last even through a harsh winter. It was time to make iron. As the fire was lit and the bellows fetched, I was acutely aware of the passage of time. I was not certain exactly of my age but I knew that I had seen more than fifty winter solstices and soon would have seen sixty. I was ancient beyond words. I had to pass my skills on to my sons and the rest of the clan.

I would let Water Bird and Silent Stone work the bellows. It would help to make them stronger and make them even closer than they were. I explained everything that I was doing to the rest of the warriors. When I was gone, I hoped that they would be able to do as I was doing. My sons had seen me do this before but the repetition would not hurt.

I had them take the stones from the Land of Ice and Fire as well as the ones we had found by the cave and helped them to make the oven we would use. They packed it with mud. I had Long Nose light the fire and then let the two bellows' boys start to pump.

"We need the fire to be so hot that the stones will glow. Now you may begin to break up the ore. The smaller the pieces, the quicker we can make it."

While they did that I showed Lost Wolf how to clean out the moulds we had made. The sand we had first used had become hardened with the heat from the molten metal but small pieces of iron remained. We picked them out and dropped them in the precious iron pot that had been brought from Orkneyjar and I had salvaged from Bear Island. What we would do when it broke, I dreaded to think. It was as we waited for the fire to heat that I thought of that moment. It would probably be my sons and grandson who had that problem. How would they deal with it? The thought came to me that when this pot died, then the ability to make metal might die with it. The clan would then be like every other tribe and clan in this land. Until my people came west again, perhaps to seek me, then it would be as though we had never set foot on this land. When the metal pot died and the tools were broken, then the only evidence of the last Viking in this new world would be his bloodline. I found myself looking at my sons and grandson. Laughing Deer and I had done all that we could do to make them strong. The rest would be up to them.

The two boys were sweating both from the exertion and the heat of the fire by the time the pot was half filled and ready to use. We would have two firings. One this day and one the next. As the stone began to melt, the Clan of the Dog peered into it. My clan had already viewed the magic of stone becoming liquid. When I began to shave charcoal into it Lost Wolf said, "Why do you put the blackened wood in the pot, Erik?"

I tapped my seax, "Back in my homeland the weaponsmith did so. I do not know why but I believe it makes the iron stronger. The problem is the amount I put in is guesswork. When my sons make their own iron, they will need to make that judgement."

The pot was always so hot that had any of us attempted to touch it with bare hands we would have been badly burned. We had fashioned two large mitts made from three layers of deer hide. With two poles to lift the pot, my task was to tip the molten iron into the moulds. We had to work quickly and I had laid out the moulds on the ground.

"Stand back. Now!" Moos Blood and Brave Cub lifted the pot and I used my seax, held in my mittened hands to tip the pot. The metal hissed and steamed as it poured. My sons had done this enough to know when to move to the next one. We made the tools and weapons first and then, with the last of it, poured it all into the arrowhead moulds. As the now empty pot was placed on the ground, the warriors all watched the magic as the molten metal settled into the moulds. The arrowheads would solidify quickly while the axe and hatchets would take much longer to cool.

I smiled and applauded my sons, grandson and Silent Stone. "You have all done well and the meal this night will be well earned."

We all crammed into my longhouse. The beds were moved and the room cleared so that we could all squeeze close together. We had made a fresh batch of ale. Lost Wolf had been most impressed by the quality of the beer and the mead we made. We did not have enough bees to make large quantities of mead but that night we broached some and everyone was happy.

Golden Bear said, "Father, the newcomers have never heard you sing. Give them a saga."

Lost World frowned at the new word. He had picked up some of my words but not this one, "Saga?"

"A song of my people. It is the way we pass on our history."

He nodded, "Like our Wapapyaki."

"Just so, but this will be in my language and you will not understand the words."

"I would like to hear it, if you would not mind, Erik, Shaman of the Bear."

I nodded, "This one is the tale of how we hunted a sea beast. It is so large that it could have swallowed four of our snekke. It lives in the Great Sea." I began.

> *Lars and Snorri had five fine heirs*
> *They hunted enemies in all their lairs*
> *Wolf or fish, dragon or bears*
> *They could not be taken unawares*
> *From Bear Island the five set sail*
> *Hunting the monstrous big black whale*
> *The whale that came from Ran's deep home*
> *Rose like a monster through sea and foam.*
> *The clan feared no black-skinned beast*
> *On its flesh, the clan would feast*
> *Njörðr flew like a hunting bird*
> *Waiting for Ebbe to give the word*
> *Lars and Snorri had five fine heirs*
> *They hunted enemies in all their lairs*
> *Wolf or fish, dragon or bears*
> *They could not be taken unawares*
> *Longer than a drekar and foiled with teeth*
> *The whale was like a black-skinned reef*
> *None was dismayed as the creatures rose*
> *Arne and Siggi were the hunters chose*
> *And two spears hung in mid-air*
> *Waiting to strike at flesh laid bare*
> *Arne hurt first and struck down fast*
> *While Siggi's spear made a hole so vast*
> *The beast it dived down to Ran's seabed*
> *Erik Navigator kept his head*
> *As Njörðr fought her own hard battle*
> *The whale rose and gave a deadly rattle*
> *The clan had fought and the clan had won*
> *Their great sea battle was over and won.*
> *Lars and Snorri had five fine heirs*
> *They hunted enemies in all their lairs*
> *Wolf or fish, dragon or bears*
> *They could not be taken unawares*

They did not understand the words but they liked the sounds. I was asked to explain to them what my words meant and I did so. My sons understood them all. Then I was asked to sing again.

At the end of it, they all sat in silence. To my amazement, the only words came from Silent Stone, "I should like to see a sea beast."

Grey Shadow's hand went to her mouth and Lost Wolf smiled at me, "Your magic has worked again, Erik."

It was not the undamming of a river but it was the beginning and Silent Stone spoke more each day from that day.

We used the shorter days to work outside on the new weapons and tools. The crude metal needed to be worked and shaped using stones from our river. When we had cast the iron, I also made a metal tripod to hold the pot. I had an idea that we could speed up the collection of salt that way. The scraps of metal that fell as we worked, even the tiniest of them, were retained in a jar. The iron was more precious to us than gold for what would we use gold to buy? Handles had to be fitted to axes, hatchets and seaxes. When they had been roughly worked, we sharpened them. I showed them how to use a whetstone. As I had always done, I ensured that every warrior had a tool or a weapon. Even Grey Shadow was given a gutting knife to replace the stone one she used. The last task was to fit the arrowheads to the shafts we had made. Fletched with the feathers of birds brought down by stones, each of us used unique feathers that would mark our arrows as our own. Finally, after shaking the nails in a bag of sand, they were stored until they were needed. There would always be a bag of them aboard the snekke when we sailed for we would be able to repair any minor damage to our most valuable assets.

The feast that solstice was a merry one. We finished off the last of the mead for it seemed a fitting time to do so. The children and babies were given honey cakes made with the fruit we had dried at harvest and, to them, that was a great treat as they craved the sweetness. Once more packed into one longhouse it was a cosy atmosphere. I was asked to sing the song of the Clan of the Fox and I did so. It was when I finished that Long Nose said, "Shaman, perhaps we should change our name for the last bear almost killed you. Should we not be the Clan of Iron?"

Silence, save for the giggling of the babies and young children, gripped the longhouse and every eye swivelled to me. I shook my head and my hand went to my hammer of Thor, "You mean well, Long Nose, but such words should never be uttered. You risk the wrath of the Norns and bring bad luck. We did not choose our name, it was chosen for us by the bear on Bear Island. That was in a time before any of you, except perhaps Grey Shadow and Lost Wolf, were born. Our destinies are inexplicably bound to the bear. But for the bear dying in the Iron Hills, we would never have found the ore that you wish to be the name of the clan. We will always be the Clan of the Bear. We are like the bear. We only attack when we are threatened but when we are then we fight ferociously and fear not our enemies. We value family above all else and we do not take more than we need. We care for our world and when we are gone there will be no mark left to mark our time in this land."

Bjorr Tooth said, "What about the trees we have hewn and the fields we have sown?"

"It might take years but the turf and the wood of the longhouses will rot and decay. The trees will sow seeds and colonise the land once more." I had enjoyed the mead and it made me reminisce, "Back across the seas we lived close to the Land of the Wolf. There had been a mighty people who had conquered the land. They built in stone and made trails that were dry all winter and wide enough for eight men to march up them, yet even those would change if man did not maintain them. Nature has a way, if man allows, of reclaiming what was here before man made his mark." I pointed north, I always knew where the north lay, "In the Land of Ice and Fire there are pools of molten rock that are spewed forth and spread over the land. They melt solid ice and when they harden become new land. The land on which we live is a living thing. There are powers just below the surface that we can only dream of." I smiled, "At sea, there are islands of ice which are higher than the hill upon which Eagle's Shadow lies."

Lost Wolf shook his head, "Truly, Erik, you have seen more of this world than any other man. You have lived a wondrous life and you continue to touch the lives of others. I was always happy to follow you from the land threatened by the Shawnee, but now I see that even without that threat we were meant to come here."

I nodded, "I do not often think about it but you are right. My brother and my first wife and son live on the other side of the Great Sea and when I stayed here it was as though my life was split in twain. My blood will still live close to the Land of the Wolf and yet my body and the rest of my blood live here."

I saw the fathers all nodding as they took that in. Lost Wolf's sons were dead but his daughter and grandchildren still lived.

"And one thing more, Lost Wolf, the threat of the Shawnee is not over. It may not be in our lifetime, but one day the Clan of the Bear will have to defend this land from the predators from the north."

It was a sombre way to end the night but we did and all departed for their beds when my words were spoken. I knew that all of them would dream of my words as would I.

The cold and ice came not long after the shortest day of the year and snow followed but this was not the blizzard of the previous year. It was a dusting that coated everything in white and when it froze made a crunching path beneath our feet. It inconvenienced us, that was all. The wood we had collected before winter kept us warm and we had enough food so that none went hungry.

Lost Wolf and I, as the two elders of the clan, often had little to do other than talk of our lives in the past and the changes in the present whilst speaking of the hopes for the future. It was as we did so that I realised we were like the Norns but without the power to change. We could see all three times, the past, present and could dream of the future but knew that there was nothing we could do to change the past. All that we could do was try to predict the future just as Skuld determined our future. The difference was that when we made changes, we would have no way of knowing their effect. We sat and talked, watching the two clans as they became one. The new children had all been born into the Clan of the Bear. There were others who still had memories of the Clan of the Dog.

"You know, Erik, I thought that we had prepared well in our camp but people went hungry in the winter. Often people who were our age died from the cold and lack of food. Here we eat as well as we did in summer. You are right, if the Shawnee heard of a people who lived as well as this, they would come to take it."

I nodded and puffed out the smoke from my pipe, "And yet in trying to take it they would destroy it. If the Shawnee wanted to live as we do then they could just copy us." I pointed the stem of my pipe to the south, "Brave Eagle and his clan have learned from my time with his clan. They do not live in longhouses and they have no snekke but they know how to preserve food with salt. They, like us, will have fewer deaths this winter."

"Aye, salt, it is powerful is it not? A tiny amount added to food changes the taste. We never had enough."

I nodded, "And we do not either. Little White Dove told me that the last fish we preserved used up most of our stock. Someone will have to fetch more."

"Fetch more? Where from?"

"The Great Sea." I shook my head and tapped out the embers from my pipe, "It is a journey fraught with danger for we have to risk the Moneton who live at the mouth of the Shenandoah and then the tribes who live close to the sea. They seem to think that the sea belongs to them, as though the sea could be owned by anyone."

Lost Wolf suddenly sat up, "Then you would go to the Great Sea?"

I looked at my sons who were carving bones to make hooks and I thought about Lost Wolf's question, "Someone will have to go and sail a snekke. It will need to be in summer and the long days mean that the snekke will be seen. The tribes who live along the river are not all friendly and they know the snekke. The boat might make the sea but the voyage back would be slower and filled with danger. I cannot ask my sons to risk that. Better that I go."

He gave me a sly look, "But you would not go alone."

Keeping my face as a stone I said, "I can sail, *'Laughing Deer'* alone and I can collect the salt by myself."

"But you would not go alone, would you, Erik?"

"No, I would not go alone. However, the choice of those I will take with me requires much thought and consideration." He nodded, "And I do not need to be pestered by questions from those who wish to come with me so I would appreciate it if our words were kept between us, Lost Wolf."

He put his hand on his heart and said, "You have my word and all that I will say is that I would like to see this Great Sea before I die."

"Even if the sight of it brought about your death?"

"I have lived longer than I should. A man should not outlive his sons. I was saved from the Shawnee and now I see why. It was to save the rest of the clan. Well, I have done that now. If my time on this earth is over then I would like to enjoy just a part of that which you have, Erik. I would see the Great Sea and, if it is meant to be, the great sea beast that you hunted on your dragonship. I know that I can never see a dragonship but to see a beast that is as big as you say, would be a wondrous thing."

I nodded, "You are right, Lost Wolf, and I have much to be grateful for."

His words set in motion thoughts and plans that continued while I slept. I knew that I had one last voyage in me. I would sail to the Salt Islands and let Lost Wolf see a sea beast. The questions in my head were who else would I risk on a voyage that might result in my death and therefore theirs?

I decided to use the steam hut. I needed the help of the dream world and the spirits. I had Moos Blood prepare it. Lost Wolf had seen us use it before and he asked if he could join me.

"You may see things that you do not wish to see, Lost Wolf. It is not like looking in a river and seeing a reflection. You see only that which the spirits wish you to see."

"I am content."

Once the hut was hot enough, we entered and we lit our pipes using the special leaves that helped to enter the world. I knew I was ready when all went black and I heard the voice of Laughing Deer in my head.

'Your time, my love, is almost done. Soon you will see Valhalla. The clan is strong and that is thanks to you but a task awaits Erik the Bear.'
I saw the sea and the waves were white tipped.
It was Gytha's voice that came to me, 'This may be the last time I shall speak to you. I see that your work is almost done. When it is time for you to go to the Otherworld then take my hand and I will lead you to Valhalla.'
Her voice faded and I found myself on the new snekke. Water Bird was by the mast and Lost Wolf by the prow. Silent Stone held a spear and ahead of us, I saw the great sea beast.
All went black and when the light came again, I was at Eagle's Shadow and there were wild warriors trying to get at my family. I realised that I was wearing the bear's skin and I laid about me with a hatchet and seax. I saw the stone-tipped spear that came for me but I was old and could not move out of its way. All that I could do was to try to take the warriors who surrounded me, with me.
All went black.

I opened my eyes and the fire was dying. Lost Spear was still in the dreamworld and I waited. He opened his eyes and they were wide, immediately. "I saw the sea." I nodded. "And a sea beast." He frowned, "The Shawnee came."

"I know, and I have dreamed my death. Keep these thoughts to yourself, Lost Wolf, they cannot aid any save our enemies."

He nodded, "I know and this is powerful magic, Erik. I am not sure if I like it."

"This is my world and my life, I did not choose it. I just have to accept it. I saw my wife and I am content. As for the rest? Let us see."

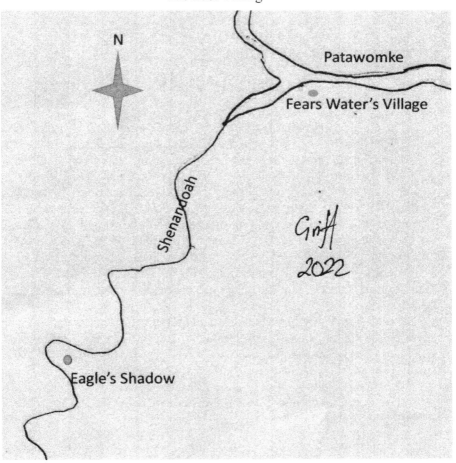

Chapter 10

The thaw came earlier than we expected. Sometimes it was like that. One year might have a winter that refused to let go of its grip on the land and then at others, the green shoots of spring would come before you were expecting them. This was one such year. The ground by the river flooded with the thaw and we lost two birch bark boats. That was not such a disaster as the ones we lost were two that we had brought from Brave Eagle's camp and they were old. While the young warriors went for the first hunt of the year, Lost Wolf and I, along with the boys of the clan, made a pair of new boats. My method of building was different from Lost Wolf's and that was because I always had the building of a snekke in mind. The ones we made were a mixture of our ideas.

By the time the hunters had returned and the meat had been butchered, we had almost finished them. Little White Dove, Willow Leaf and Grey Shadow came to see me, "Father, we have used the last of the salt. Someone must go to the sea to find more."

"You know that the voyage is perilous, daughter."

"I do but unless you know of somewhere else that we can find some then I can think of no other way."

Lost Wolf volunteered, "I have heard of tribes, many miles from here, that dig salt from the ground."

Grey Shadow shook her head, "Husband, you might as well say that there is salt on the moon, for it is as insubstantial as the idea that there is a cave with salt and all we have to do is to find it."

I smiled as Lost Wolf subsided. Laughing Deer had the same ability to cut to the quick. "Then *'Laughing Deer'* will have to brave the Patawomke and the voyage to the sea." I pointed at the skies, "This early spring may be a trick of the Norns. We will wait for a month before I risk the voyage."

It took a moment for that to sink in and when it did Little White Dove said, "I did not mean for you to risk the river. My brothers could go."

I smiled, "And their lives are less valuable than mine?"

"You have done so much already. You should enjoy the time you…"

I finished the sentence for her, "Have left before I die."

"I did not say that."

"But that is what you meant. Let me make it clear to the whole clan, I shall live the last years of my life as I have lived it so far. I was meant to be a navigator and I think I have one more voyage left in me. The clan needs me to do this and when it is done then Moos Blood, who will be the chief, can make the decision of who will risk the river. Until then it is my decision, now we have two boats to finish."

They left us and we continued to work. I knew that when they returned to the village, they would seek out my sons and try to use them to dissuade me. I could not help but smile as I walked into the enclosed heart of the village for the warriors were gathered there, all with serious looks on their faces.

"I see that you have been told of my decision."

Brave Cub said, "Father, I have been to the Salt Islands and I can sail a snekke. I will go and Golden Bear will come with me."

"It is true that you have been to the sea and both of you could do this." I saw the relief on their faces as they took in what they wanted to hear. "When I go, I will not go alone but I will take others who have never seen the Great Sea." I gestured to Lost Wolf, "Lost Wolf wishes to go with me. I will also take two others who have never seen the Great Sea so that when I am with your mother, Brave Cub, there will be more than my sons who know how to sail to the sea. I promise that this will be my last voyage on *'Laughing Deer'*, my last voyage of all will be on *'Gytha'*.

"But if you do not return then…"

"Little White Dove, if I thought I would not return then I would not go. I go because I am meant to go. The spirits have spoken to me and I trust your mother. Do you?"

They had no arguments left and they accepted my decision. Knowing that I would not be taking my sons meant that every other warrior and boy pestered me to accompany me. That some, like Fears Water, did so purely out of duty, did not upset me. The ones who really wanted to come were those who rarely sailed on the snekke. Water Bird and Silent Stone came to me together, after the first rush and clamour of volunteers.

"Grandfather, Silent Stone and I would like to be your crew. We wish to be your crew for we have sailed with you and we work well together. We both think that this is meant to be. That it will be dangerous, we understand and we are both willing to risk death." He smiled, "I do not think that you are yet marked for death, Grandfather."

I was intrigued, "Why do you say that?"

He looked at me and stared into my eyes, "At night I dream. Sometimes I cannot remember my dreams and often I cannot remember any of the words but there is a woman who comes to me and she is not dressed like my mother or the other women in the tribe. She has white hair and long fingers." I felt the hairs on the back of my neck prickle. He was describing Gytha. "She came to me after the feast on the shortest day and her words were clear. She said that you would die at Eagle's Shadow and I had to be on hand when you did. I am happy for you to take this journey for I know that you will not die. When you are here, in this place of safety, then you are in danger." He nodded to Silent Stone and held up his palm. There was a scar there, and Silent Stone did the same, "We have sworn a blood oath and we are now blood brothers. We will stay by your side while you are at Eagle's Shadow and protect your life with ours."

I shuddered for I remembered the blood on the blade of that first oath I had sworn with Siggi and Arne. I knew the power of such an oath and that it could not be undone. Ours had only ended with the deaths of Siggi and Arne. That oath had led me to Eagle's Shadow. Where would it take Silent Stone and Water Bird?

"I will consider what you say, although if your dream is true then I could take anyone, even your sister, and I would be safe."

Water Bird said brightly, "And if Apple Blossom or my cousin Bird Song could sail the snekke then I might believe you. But you, Grandfather, are a sailor, and you will want two with you who can sail. That is Silent Stone and your eldest grandson."

He was clever and used good arguments. I had already decided to take him but having Gytha's approval made it an easier decision to make.

I was watched carefully by the whole clan as the month progressed. I think that they feared I would just depart without letting them know. What I did do in that time was to have sacks prepared to store the salt. We had used pots the last time but the weight of the pots was unnecessary. If the salt became wet on the voyage north then we could simply dry it. The summers were so hot that it would soon dry out. The women wove the sacks for me. I also had the boys of the clan carve as many hooks as they could. Some would be small for the river fish, but others had to be bigger in case we had the chance to hunt the red-fleshed fishes that were as long as a small child. While the snekke was out of the water I gave her hull another coat of pine tar and had more ropes made. A snekke could never have too many ropes.

As the time to my departure grew close so I was questioned more closely, especially by Moos Blood. "I know you will not be taking your sons, but you should know that we are all more than a little interested in who you do take. I know that you have made your decision, tell me, as your heir."

"I have decided on my crew. I will take two of the young with me as well as Lost Wolf. I just need to speak to the father."

"And who is that?"

"You." He looked stunned. "Water Bird has dreamed and he has skills but if you say no then I will not take him."

He shook his head, "His mother will not wish it and I fear it but I must accept your choice for if I do not then I drive a wedge between my son and me. I would not do that." I nodded, "He dreamed?"

"Gytha came to him."

"Yet he said nothing to me."

"Do not be upset, Moos Blood. The young often confide in grandparents. We are seen, I think, as safer somehow. You may tell him yourself if you wish."

"Thank you and who is the other?"

"His blood brother, Silent Stone."

"I did not know that either."

I smiled, "Then the two of you will have much to speak about. I will tell Silent Stone."

When Silent Stone was not with Water Bird he was to be found playing with Ulla. I found him grooming the dog. Ulla was getting old. He moved now as slowly as I did. His life had been hard and his body was now paying the price. That he was loved by the clan gave what would probably be the end of his life, some joy.

"Silent Stone."

"Yes, Shaman." Silent Stone still spoke rarely and most of his words were reserved for me or my grandson.

"I would have you and Water Bird as my crew."

He knelt, grabbed my hand and kissed the back of it, "I will not let you down and I thank you for this honour."

It was the most words he had ever spoken in a single utterance and I was touched. Raising him to his feet I said, "You will need a blanket, a hat, spare shoes and weapons. You have your sling and bow?" He nodded, "Gather round stones for we may need them. This journey will be filled with peril from both man and nature."

Once the crew became known then the two youths were pestered by those not going. Lost Wolf was not a sailor and I spent more time with him preparing for the voyage than the younger ones. They could sail and he could not. We prepared our weapons. I took my metal spear as well as my bow and metal tipped arrows. Lost Wolf also had some metal tipped arrows but most of his were flint. I had made him a hatchet as well as a knife. What none of my crew had that I did were the sealskin boots and cape. I rarely wore either on the river but I knew that in the estuary they would be vital. I also packed the bear's skin in my chest as I wanted to be as warm as I could be, especially on the island and the skin would be large enough to cover all four of us. The women brewed fresh ale and we put most of it in a large jar. We would top up our skins from it and when it turned to vinegar, as I knew it would, then we could use it for the ailments and injuries we encountered. Laughing Deer had taught Little White Dove how to make the salve that would soothe chafed hands and I packed that in my chest. The packing of the chest was like a ritual and prepared me for the voyage. This time we also filled the hold with kindling. I had learned the lesson. There would be little available on Salt Island and we had plenty. We packed the hold with all that we could and had a few faggots on the deck too.

The night before we left, I ate with my family. Silent Stone and Lost Wolf dined with the Clan of the Dog. We were saying goodbye. I was confident we would return but the Norns could spin and it was better to say what was needed while we could than regret it. I had not bidden farewell to Ada, Fótr or the rest of the clan. I would not make that mistake again.

Before we ate I took the hands of Moos Blood on one side and Little White Dove on the other, "Take hands everyone and let us make a circle of blood." They did as I asked, "None of us can know the future. We did not know that Laughing Deer would be torn from us. Let no one take for granted that we will meet again. You all know that you are my family and are more precious to me than anything. I hope that you all know that I love you but I do not say that enough and I say it now. If the Norns spin and I am not meant to come back then know that I will be happy with those who have died before and I know that the clan will grow strong." I let go of my children's hands and said, "And now, no more sadness and melancholy. Let us celebrate being alive and having this fine food to eat."

They ate in silence. I later wondered if that was because they feared to speak. None wished to weep and sometimes words can make tears flow.

Eventually, Moos Blood said, "Will you visit with Brave Eagle?"

I nodded, "Aye, but on the way back. My aim is to make the voyage downstream as secretly as we can. I still fear the Moneton. We have hurt them and they may still seek to do us harm."

Blue Feather said, "Then tell my family that I am well."

"And mine also," added Humming Bird.

The Last Viking

"Of course. This will be the last time I sail down the Patawomke and
Brave Eagle and I were close. You cannot pull a man from the sea and
not have a bond that ties no matter how far apart."

We did not leave early on the morning we sailed. By the time the
snekke was loaded, it was getting close to noon. The other snekke and
the boats would come with us as we would need to portage the snekke
over the shallows. I knew that the risk to the keel was small but using
wooden rollers would make certain that we had a whole hull for the
voyage to the sea. We disembarked and as the rollers were laid on the
ground I pointed to the water, "Unless I am mistaken, Moos Blood,
either the water is higher or the rocks are not as high."

"You are right but now is not the time to test that theory. We will
still pull you across the ground. We have many warriors. It is coming
back that the four of you will struggle."

With the rollers in place, we pulled and soon had the snekke in the
water. The others boarded and I stood apart with my eldest. "We will
leave the rollers in place." I nodded. "Take care of yourself, Father, and
bring back my son. He is my firstborn and..."

"I would not take him if I thought I would not bring him back. There
will be danger but as with you and your brothers, navigating that danger
makes you better warriors and better men. My adventures have
hardened me."

"I know and we can only hope that we are as tough when we are as
old as you."

I climbed aboard the snekke and said, "Just half the sail, Water Bird,
we want to sneak down the Patawomke." We waved our farewells and
we left the safety of the Shenandoah for the perils of the Patawomke.

By the time we reached the mighty waterway, the sun was setting
behind us and as the moon had yet to rise, we were sailing into
darkness. I looked up at the bluffs to steerboard. That was where Fears
Water and his clan had lived. It was where Eagle Claws' killers had
been butchered by the Moneton. I said, quietly, "From now on we do
not speak until I do so again. We will sail south through the night. You
can sleep if you wish. I will find somewhere to hold up during the day.
If you want my attention then wave to me."

I saw the fear in their eyes. The two youths were excited but the
excitement was fuelled by fear. It was like entering a huge black cave. I
knew that the river was wide and the channel more than deep enough
for the snekke but they did not and they had to trust me. In the last light
of the day, I found the middle of the river and settled into the stern. I
was gambling that any Moneton would be in their yehakins. I had not
heard of them using the river at night. During the day the river would be

filled with boats taking the harvest of fish but at night the river belonged to navigators like me, and as far as I knew I was the only one to the west of the Great Sea. One day, I knew, others would tire of the Land of Ice and Fire and sail south. If they did not stop until the Mi'kmaqs then they might find a welcome, but if they landed before then the greeting would be a warlike one.

Lost Wolf lay at the prow, peering into the dark. He was getting his last adventure and I wondered what thoughts would fill his head. For me, this was familiar territory. I had often taken a watch on the drekar when we had sought this land, and when I had fled with Brave Eagle and my family from the Penobscot I had frequently gone without sleep. To steerboard the forest came alive with the animals of the night as they hunted one another. Owls swooped and the predators prowled. Man was rare in their forest home and night was the time when he hid in his villages. With a sail only half raised, we were as close to invisible as it was possible for us to be. The image of the bear was hidden and the folds in the sail made it appear darker. It was the current that shifted us. The voyage upstream would be harder. The two youths fought sleep but the easy motion of *'Laughing Deer'* soon rocked them and Lost Wolf to sleep. I was alone with the creature that, to me, lived; the snekke.

I became more alert when false dawn appeared. I knew where I sought. When I had been injured and crawled through the forest it had been close to this point that I was rescued by my son. Here there was a tangle of trees some of which were submerged. I was looking for it. It was the change of direction as I headed to shore that woke my crew. As the snekke heeled a little then they were rolled and came to quickly. I said, quietly, "Keep a good watch to steerboard and ahead. Water Bird, lower the sail, we will let the river do the work. Silent Stone, take an oar and fend off any branches that threaten us."

They both raised their hands. I saw the place I sought ahead. The river curved beyond it. *'Laughing Deer'* was bigger than *'Doe'* and *'Gytha'* but I found a channel that took us into the tumble of trees. I stopped when a branch threatened to take the top of the mast.

"Lost Wolf, slip ashore and cut some undergrowth to disguise us. Water Bird and Silent Stone, secure us to two of the trees. This shall be our nest for the day."

By the time the sun rose we were as hidden as we were likely to be. I had made water and eaten a little while the others had disguised the snekke. If anyone approached within a few paces then they would see us but I could not see why they would do that.

"I need some sleep. Lost Wolf, you are in command of the watch. Do not fear if you see boats on the river. They will only see us if we move and I will be beneath my bear's skin. You may wake me if you fear discovery. Keep your heads below the gunwale and none shall see you."

He nodded, "I could not do as you have done, Erik, and sailed in the dark. You are a magician."

Water Bird said, "And I will stay awake with you tonight for I need to learn how to do what you do."

I was pleased with my grandson's words. I pulled the bear's skin to completely cover me. It would also shelter me from the sun. The bobbing of our boat on the water and my exhaustion soon sent me to sleep. I woke in the early afternoon. I felt refreshed. The others were all on watch.

I said, "I need to empty my bowels. When I return then you may sleep if you wish." I slipped off my boots and breeks and entered the water. Holding on to the side I relieved myself. There would be no trace for a hunter to follow. I hauled myself on board and while I dried myself, I said, "Tell me what you saw."

Lost Wolf said, "You were right about the river. There were many boats on the water. They fished during the morning. There are none now."

I nodded as I pulled my breeks up, "The cool of the morning is the best time to catch these fish. The heat of noon drives them deeper into the river. We will leave at dusk."

Water Bird said, "If you would allow me, Grandfather, I would sleep beneath the bear's skin."

"Of course." It was good because I knew that the spirit of the bear would help him to dream.

I ate and watched the other bank. The trail that led through the forest on this side ended well to the north of where we lay. Had I asked the others they would have told me that no animals came down to the river to drink for the simple reason that there was no trail. There were easier places to get a drink.

Getting out of our anchorage was harder than getting in for we had to fight the current and it took all four of us pulling on the trees to do so. As soon as we were clear I put the steering board over and said, "Half sail, Water Bird."

Our next resting place would be the last one and it would be close to Brave Eagle's village. I was going to use the place we had hidden the snekke when the Moneton had attacked. I knew that it could not be easily reached from the land. When I had last spoken with Brave Eagle, he had told me of the division in the clan. Some supported Eagle Claws and some Brave Eagle. That had been some years earlier and I hoped that the wound was healed, but I could not be certain. I would visit with my old friends on the way back. If there was treachery then we would be minimising its effect.

Water Bird sat next to me and watched my every move. As this was relatively safer than Moneton land I whispered to him when he questioned me.

"You are sailing closer to the steerboard shore, Grandfather."

"I sailed these waters many times and I am familiar with them. The village where your father and my family were raised is behind those trees to the south of us. There are also clues that you can look for. Any white on the water is a danger."

We sailed in silence.

"You make small adjustments as you sail, why?"

"I am trying to keep the sail full. It makes for a smoother passage." I nodded to Lost Wolf and Silent Stone who were huddled together, asleep at the prow. "It lets them sleep. I did this in the Great Sea where it is harder to be smooth. It is just habit. I have been doing this since I was your age, Water Bird."

Having him awake made it easier for us to make the anchorage safely. He lowered the sail and took the way off us before Lost Wolf and Silent Stone had woken. This time we sailed beneath overhanging willows. I saw that one of the ropes we had used all those years ago was still there, attached to a tree. Vines had clambered over it and we could not use it but it gave me satisfaction to know that even in the dark I had navigated to the place I had sought.

This time Water Bird joined me in the darkness of the skin and we slept. Once again, I woke after the sun had reached its zenith but I was acutely aware of the proximity of Brave Eagle's village. I held my finger to my lips and I listened. I could tell that Lost Wolf was desperate to speak to me but I doubted that it would be important enough to risk words. Instead, Water Bird and I ate and drank ale. By the time the river began to darken, I was ready to sail. It was easier this time to push off from the shore and let the river take us. There were no sunken tree trunks to avoid.

Once on the river, I said, "And now, Lost Wolf, you can burst forth."

He smiled, "There were more boats on the river and they used the same technique that you did. They held nets between their boats. They caught many more fish than the ones we saw the previous day."

"We lived with this clan and they learned from us."

Water Bird asked, "Then why did we hide from them?"

"We lived with them before you were born. There will be friends there but there may be enemies. We will see your other grandfather on the way back but the priority is salt and now we can sail during the day. The next time that we stop will be at Salt Island."

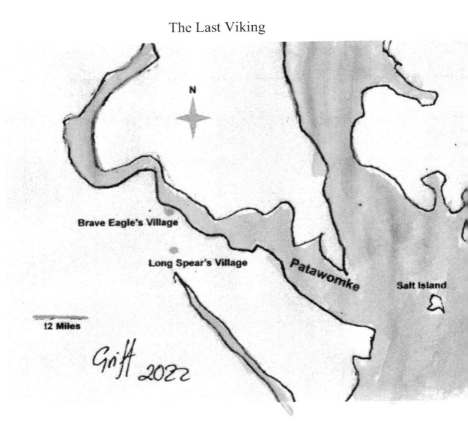

Chapter 11

The waters became choppier within a mile or two of leaving the willows that shaded our anchorage. I had Water Bird use the full sail and we flew. It was as though the snekke was eager to see the sea. Being longer and wider than my other snekke she was more powerful. Even so, some of the waves broke over the prow and Lost Wolf was soaked. He laughed like a child when that happened. He turned and said, "In a birch bark boat we would have been swamped but this fantastic beast just shrugs off the water."

When dawn broke it was a grey and murky morning but, even so, the three of them saw the vastness of the estuary. Lost Wolf put his hand to his mouth and said, "The water, it is salty. Is this the Great Sea?"

I pointed to the smudge ahead of us, "There is Salt Island and the sea begins just a mile or so from there. It is protected a little from the Great Sea by a neck of land but the water is salty enough for us to gather salt."

It did not take long to make the island which grew from a grey smudge to an island, quite quickly. I was pleased with the murk which was not quite a sea fret but murky enough to hide us. I had Water Bird lower the sail when we were just shy of the shore and I let the tide take us to grind up onto the beach. Lost Wolf and Silent Stone leapt ashore with the ropes and the stake. Lost Wolf hammered the stake into the sand and Water Bird and Silent Stone tied us securely to it. I clambered over the gunwale and looked at the camp. The tribes that had chased us away had been to the island. I saw evidence of their mischief. They had tried to destroy the three salt pans.

"Lost Wolf, rearrange those stones so that they are solid. We need three salt pans. Water Bird and Silent Stone, pile the kindling close by it. We will begin the work immediately."

I took the pot that we used to make metal and went to the other side of the island. There were no footprints. The warriors had not investigated this side. I could barely see the land ahead of us and I was confident that we would not be seen, not immediately anyway. I took off my boots and breeks and waded into the water. I sank the pot beneath it and filled it. It was heavy and I laboured back to the salt pans.

"We light a fire. Tonight we eat hot food and we will need to take turns watching until dawn. The fire must be fed. Water Bird, take Silent

Stone and see if there is any driftwood on the island. Explore it for this is our home for a few days."

Lost Wolf and I lit the fire and hung the pot from the tripod we had brought. It was not the best metal we had made but it functioned. I then went back to bring more water. I filled one of the salt pans with it. Over the next few days, the water would disappear and leave a little salt. It would not be as much as that gathered by boiling the water but it would add to our supply. We had trailed fishing lines as we had sailed and we had four large fish to eat. They were the red-fleshed fish that I enjoyed eating but they were not as big as the ones we would find beyond the headland. By the time the boys came back, the fire was blazing and the fish were cooking. The water would take time to disappear and so I went with one of the clay pots we had brought to fill with water. Lost Wolf might like to see the Great Sea but my priority was salt.

We ate as darkness fell. There would be more fish and we each enjoyed a whole fish. It was both delicious and filling. I stretched, "I will sleep first for I know what I am doing. Water Bird, you sleep too. Lost Wolf, keep the fire fed but if the water all disappears then wake me for I do not want the salt to be ruined. You can bring more water from the far side of the island. We have more pots. Wake me after three hours." We had not brought the hourglass but Lost Wolf, like me, knew how to estimate time. When he needed to make water, it would be three hours.

Water Bird and I snuggled beneath the bear's skin and we slept.

When we were woken I went straight to the pan. I could see that it would not be long until it was ready to pour into one of the remaining salt pans. I was there to teach Water Bird and I explained what we were doing. "When the salt water is like a sludge we will empty it into a salt pan. During the next few days, the sun will make the water disappear and we can begin to bag it. We will fill the pot again and tomorrow, pour that one into the second salt pan. I hope, by then, that the pan we fill this night will be dry enough to bag. Even if it is damp, we will bag it and dry it back at Eagle's Shadow."

By dawn we had begun to make the second pot of water begin to evaporate. I woke Lost Wolf and explained the process. "Water Bird and I will sail the snekke. We need more fish and I would explore the other islands while this murk surrounds us."

Lost Wolf said, "It would be better if the sun shone to help our work."

I nodded, "You are right but the murk hides us. The smoke from the fire will tell those ashore that we are here."

The Last Viking

We launched the snekke and I headed south and west towards the other islands in the estuary. Here the water was even choppier and I smiled as Water Bird gripped the gunwale. We could not see far, perhaps two hundred paces and so I kept the sail reefed a little. We neared one of the other islands, it was more of a sandbar than anything but it did rise above the water and it was there that we saw four seals basking.

Water Bird said, "Is that the great sea beast of which you spoke, Grandfather?"

I shook my head, "When you see a sea beast then you will know. No, these are a treasure and we shall hunt them for they are seals and both the flesh and the skin are useful. The seals viewed us warily and I continued towards the sea. Sometimes the sea could look inviting but this day it looked like the seas around the land of Ice and Fire, grey and perilous. I was about to turn around when I saw the distinctive fluke of a sea beast.

"There, Water Bird, there is your sea beast."

It was about a hundred paces from us and he just caught sight of the fluke. I knew he was disappointed and I waited. Sure enough, a short while later the head and body of the great sea beast appeared from the sea and I heard the gasp of astonishment.

"Now I know why the seals were basking. They feared the sea beast for it eats them. Let us return to the islands."

I turned us around and the wind caught us. We lurched alarmingly but the snekke was well made and she righted herself and then flew. As we neared the huddle of islands, I saw that there were more seals on the others. This was an opportunity not to be missed. We would hunt a couple. I doubted that Blue Feather would approve of the danger in which I was about to place her son but I had confidence in my grandson. I headed for one of the larger islands where there were a number of animals. I had Water Bird reef the sail and we approached the side of the island where the seals were absent. I ran her up onto the sand and tossed out the anchor.

I pointed to my bow and Water Bird, nodding, took it. He struggled to string it but managed it. I pointed to the metal tipped arrows and he nocked one. I took my spear and we headed across the grass-covered sand to approach them. The wind was in our faces and I knew that we were silent. The dozen or so seals basking there were oblivious to us. The danger to them lay out to sea. Sea beasts could rise from the water to take them and their sentry was watching the ocean. I spied two. I pointed my spear at the smaller one and Water Bird nodded. I held my spear ready to throw. I nodded without looking at him and then threw my spear. My spear struck true and was a mortal strike. The beast managed to slither a pace or two before dying. Water Bird's arrow had hit the other seal but it was moving.

"Loose another."

I ran to the dying seal and took my spear. As Water Bird's second arrow hit it so I managed to stab it with my spear. The other seals had escaped into the sea but it mattered not. We had our treasure.

By the time we had reached the camp, I saw that Lost Wolf was looking anxiously for us. He could not see the seals below the gunwale and he said, as we neared the two of them, "I was worried for the water is getting low and I knew not what to do."

That was my fault. I had been so anxious to explore that I had almost forgotten the purpose of our journey. "I am sorry. Water Bird, have Silent Stone help you to unload the treasure and I will show Lost Wolf what to do."

In the time it took to demonstrate how to empty the pot, the boys had brought the seals ashore. Lost Wolf shook his head, "What a strange world you have brought me to. Can this beast be eaten?"

"Not only can it be eaten but also its skin is what I wear on my feet. It stops water from penetrating. If we can hunt a couple more then all three of you will have protection for your feet and bodies. First, we need to refill the pot and then we can skin the beasts and prepare them for eating."

The pot refilled, I went to the first salt pan we had used. The salt was not quite ready but by the time the pot was ready for emptying, it would be. I returned to the seals. I took out my seax and sharpened it. "The skin is as tough as mail."

They all looked at me and Lost Wolf said, "Mail?" He struggled to get his tongue around the strange word.

"Iron made into a shirt." I sawed through the skin and then took out the guts. I threw them into the sea and the gulls flocked for the feast. "Boys, take your slings and see what you can fetch down, we can have a fine stew if you can hit them. Wait until I gut the second one."

They each chose a good stone and I sliced through the belly of the second seal. Taking the guts I hurled them in the air. The gulls swooped and the stones flew. By the time the birds had dispersed, we had three dead ones. The feathers could be used for fletch whilst the beaks and feet were used for tools.

I had forgotten how hard it was to skin and butcher a seal. It was almost dark by the time I had finished. I took the blubber and placed it in a cooking pot. I placed the pot next to the salt pot. I explained, "That will render down during the night. In the morning we will have oil and some tasty morsels to eat." I was going to say, like crackling and then realised they had never even seen a pig let alone tasted one. "Cut the meat into chunks and then put them on skewers. We can toast them by the fire. It will take time to cook but we are going nowhere." I was just pleased that the murk had gone and we were still hidden. I should have known that the Norns were spinning.

The skewered meat, eaten hot, was delicious. We put the dead gulls and the meat we had not put on skewers in the pot and, after adding sea water, put another fire on to cook the stew. It was just as easy to watch two pots as one. Water Bird and I took the second shift and when Lost Wolf woke me, I saw that he had emptied another pot of salt and a fresh one was bubbling. He smiled, "We tasted the stew. It has a strange taste but it was filling." He gestured at the sky, the moon was up. "The clouds have gone."

"Then that means we need to keep weapons to hand. You may not get to see your sea beast if enemies come."

"I know but Water Bird told me of the one you saw and it is good to know that one is so close."

After checking the stew and the boiling salt pot I went to the first salt pan. The salt was drying well but was still not yet ready to be bagged. The Norns had indeed spun and we were running out of time. We had done well but we did not have enough salt for the clan.

While we watched, Water Bird and I pegged out the seal skins. "From now on when you make water do so on the skins. It will help to preserve them."

"Will it not make them smell, Grandfather?"

"By the time we reach Eagle's Shadow then all the smell will have gone. The boots we make from its skin will keep your feet dry. It is worth the effort."

The sun appeared, red and fiery in the east and I knew that it would be a hot day. While that would dry the salt faster it would also help our enemies to find us.

I nodded to the seal oil. It was largely rendered. "Taste the chunks of rendered fat, Water Bird, they will be hot but taste them." When he did so his eyes widened. It was a delicious taste. The salt from the sea added to that tastiness. "We will leave the rest so that we can all share them but we can put the oil in this clay pot."

The clay pots we had made were crudely fired and not particularly evenly made but they worked and we poured the oil into one and rammed a stopper in it. After ensuring the salt was not yet boiled dry, we went to the snekke and, after lifting the deck, moved some ballast and secured the pot of oil in the bottom. We would not need it until we reached Eagle's Shadow and it would be one less thing to pack if we had to flee suddenly.

While we waited, I sharpened my weapons and donned my bear's skin. Water Bird asked, "Are you cold, Grandfather?"

"No, but we may have visitors today and it is as well to be prepared."

I woke Lost Wolf when the sun cleared the horizon. He and Silent Stone enjoyed their first taste of seal blubber and we all had a good breakfast. Had the day been as murky as the previous ones then I would have risked taking Lost Wolf out to sea. The sun and increasing heat of the day meant that we would have to make salt as fast as we could and keep a watch for enemies. On the previous two occasions we had collected salt we had enjoyed greater numbers than we now did. When the warriors came their birch bark boats came from every direction. It was noon when they did so and I admired their ability to coordinate their attack. It meant we had no chance to flee.

"Arm yourselves and wait for my command to loose."

Lost Wolf said, "There are many of them."

"I know."

Surprisingly they did not land but one, I took him to be the chief from the feathers he wore in his hair and the battle scars on his arms, pointed at me and spoke. I recognised his words for they were Powhatan. "I am Screaming Eagle and the chief of the Clan of the Eagle. This is our land. You are the one who comes here to steal what is ours. You are the bear in the magic boat. You have slain many of our best warriors. Who are you?"

They were going to speak to us and there was hope. The Three Sisters had been spinning, indeed. "I am Erik Shaman of the Bear and we take nothing that is yours for all that we do is to take the sea and make salt." I went to the salt pan and took a handful of salt. I let it trickle through my hand so that he could see it.

Realisation dawned, and he turned to one of his warriors, "That is why they had the magic stones placed so." He turned back to me. "I would come ashore and speak with you."

I put down my spear. I was taking a chance but we had little other choice. "Come and enjoy some of the seals we hunted." I added quietly to the others, "Lay down your weapons and we will try to talk our way out of this."

The two dozen warriors dragged their boats onto the beach. I saw that they kept well away from the snekke. They clearly feared it. We had not eaten all of the blubber and I invited them to try it. I, of course, ate a piece first to show them that it was not poisoned. Their smiles told me that they liked the taste. I gave the chief a bowl of the stew and he ate it. Water Bird was quick thinking and he used the other three wooden bowls and spoons to feed another three of the warriors.

Screaming Eagle handed his empty bowl to one of his warriors and then pointed to the sealskin, "We have seen those beasts but have yet to hunt one. Our spears and arrows cannot penetrate their skin and when we go ashore to club them then they flee."

I took out my seax. It was not one made in this new world but had come from Orkneyjar. "We make these and they can cut the skin."

I held the knife by the handle and he ran his finger along the edge. I had just sharpened it and it drew blood. He smiled and sucked the blood from the wound. "Then you are truly a Shaman. Can you show us how to make salt? We use the sun to dry the sand in pools but it takes a long time and we can never make enough."

While his men ate, I explained the process and showed him the results. "Today we will put the salt in these sacks." I took one of the bags and held it up. "When we have enough, we will sail home."

"Home?"

"We live a long way up the Patawomke. It will take many days for us to return to our families."

He nodded, "And that explains why you do not appear for long periods. My father was chief when first you came. He thought that you were magic and descended from the skies. I can see now that you are not but you are a magician." He looked from me to the snekke and back. Then he raised his hands and shouted, "I, Screaming Eagle of the Clan of the Eagle, say that Erik, Shaman of the Bear and his magic boat are now our friends. There will be no bloodshed this day." He held up his finger and smiled, "Apart from this one."

Sometimes an idea comes into your head and you do not know why. "Chief Screaming Eagle, would you like to sail in my snekke? I wanted to show Lost Wolf here, the Great Sea."

The warrior frowned.

"I swear that you will be safe and in surety of that, I will leave my grandson here, along with Silent Stone. You need not come alone. You can bring another warrior if you wish."

I could see both fear and curiosity fighting in his eyes. Eventually, he nodded. "Lost Knife, you shall come with me. The rest of you can stay here and learn from these young warriors for when they have gone, we shall use their magic to make our own salt."

I caught Water Bird's eyes and he nodded. He spoke to me in Norse, "It is *wyrd*, Grandfather, and all will be well. This is a lesson sent to me that words are often more powerful than weapons."

"Lost Wolf, you will need to do as Water Bird does. Can you manage that?"

"I have watched him and if it means that I can see the Great Sea then it will be worth it."

"Chief Screaming Eagle, if you and Lost Knife sit one behind the other before," I patted the mast as I said the word, "this mast then you will have a good view of the sea."

I put my spear in the bottom of the snekke and made certain I had my hatchet and seax. The chief and his warrior gingerly climbed aboard. Lost Wolf and I held the snekke steady until they were aboard and then we climbed in the snekke.

"Untie us Water Bird."

As soon as we were free the tide took us away from the island. Our passengers held tightly to the gunwale. "Lost Wolf, hoist the sail."

The old warrior was not as quick as Water Bird would have been but that helped for the sail came up relatively slowly. I saw Screaming Eagle turn and his eyes widened as he saw the bear on the sail. Then the wind caught us and we flew. Both men involuntarily screamed. I looked over my shoulder. We were too far from the island for the noise to carry there.

The snekke bounced over the white-capped waves. She was a lovely snekke and I realised, as we headed for the main channel, that she was the best snekke I had ever built. As we passed the islands at the mouth, I saw that there were seals basking. I shouted, "Chief Screaming Eagle, there are the seals. When we return, we can hunt one if you wish."

He shouted back, "You can stop this beast?"

"Any time that I like."

I saw his hands still gripping the gunwale. His blood would be there and that was also *wyrd*. I knew he was fearful and once we made the open sea, I turned us into the wind to slow us down and for him to see that I had the power over the snekke. I turned and tacked back and forth. I saw him peer over the side. The water was clear but he could see nothing. Then Lost Knife shouted, "Look there, Chief."

I saw where he was pointing. It was a sea beast and a big one. It was the one that was black and white. It was the hunter of seals. I headed towards it. The chief turned, "We have seen these from afar. Are you not afraid of them Shaman of the Bear?"

"When I came here from the place of the rising sun, I was on a bigger boat than this and we hunted one of those."

"A bigger boat? That cannot be."

"Yet I do not tell a lie."

We were now less than fifty paces from the sea beast and its size was clearer. It was bigger than the snekke. Lost Wolf said, "I have seen enough, Erik."

Chief Screaming Eagle looked relieved and he said, "As have I. Let us return to waters where the teeth of that sea beast will not devour us. I would tell this tale to my wife and my children."

I turned us and we tacked our way back. The waters grew calmer and I saw that the two passengers did not grip the gunwales as tightly. As we headed back, I saw a group of eight seals basking on a small island. The island had a hump upon it and, while the sentry seal kept a close eye on us, once we had passed the island, I knew that we would be unobserved. As we turned, I said, "Lost Wolf, drop the sail."

The yard and sail came down quickly and, with the tide pushing us against the sand, we stopped. I dropped the two anchors and jumped out with my spear. I held my hand out for the chief and put my finger to my lips. He nodded. Once ashore I handed him the spear. I pointed to the other two to spread out and with my hatchet and seax in my hand, we headed across the sand. The seals were watching the sea but I knew that they would know we were there soon. I hoped that the chief had both a good hand and eye. He did and he hurled the spear at a large seal that was just ten paces from us. It was a good strike but the seal still tried to follow the others as they fled. Despite my weak knee I managed to catch the seal and I brought the flat side of the hatchet down to finish him off.

The chief drew the spear from the dead seal and looked at the head, "With such a weapon as this a warrior would be invincible."

Taking it back I nodded, "Next time we come, my son will return with men to collect more salt. I will make a spear and he will bring it as a gift for you."

"Then we are friends."

We carried the dead seal to the snekke and headed back to our island. Water Bird and Silent Stone were as relieved as the Clan of the Eagle to see our safe return. They all crowded around as I slit open the seal. They gasped. When I had gutted it and the entrails thrown for the birds, I skinned it.

"This skin can be made into boots and capes." Screaming Eagle nodded. "Now we will show you how to turn the blubber into food and oil."

By the time the afternoon threatened to become night, we had butchered the seal. "If you return in the morning then the oil will be ready."

"And I will bring my sons and my wife, for today you have opened my eyes to a world I did not know existed. I am glad that we talked."

"As am I."

That night we had much to talk about. Lost Wolf had seen his sea beast and we knew that there was no rush to leave. We had the opportunity to take more salt than we would need.

Water Bird said, "When my father returns, I will have to come with him." I nodded. "You have planned all of this well, Grandfather. We are your blood and you have ensured that we will survive when you are gone. I will need to learn how to be a navigator when we sail home."

"Aye, you will. In my chest, I have the maps I made. We shall study them for you need to learn how to read them."

Moos Blood had seen my maps but he had never shown much interest in them. Perhaps he thought that I would live forever. Water Bird was more like me. I wondered if that was because I had chosen him. When Moos Blood and Brave Cub had been his age we had just been trying to survive. I had not had the time to teach. Perhaps that was the way the Allfather meant it to be. The old passed on their knowledge to the youngest generation. That night I dreamed and I saw my father and my uncle. I also saw Gytha and she was smiling.

Chapter 12

In all, we spent eight days on the island. We were visited each day and I think by the end of our time the whole of the Clan of the Eagle had visited us. We hunted more seals and I knew that even though the clan had no metal they would find a way to hunt the seals. Our coming had changed their lives. Water Bird showed his increasing maturity by giving Screaming Eagle a gift, his knife. As he said to me later, "I can always make another and this seals the friendship."

Screaming Eagle was touched by the gift and he gave Water Bird a beaded byrnie. It was I who called it a byrnie for that was what it reminded me of. It hung over Water Bird's head and would give his chest some protection in combat. It was a pretty thing and I knew that wearing it would identify Water Bird the next time he came for it had the markings of the Clan of the Eagle. We loaded the snekke with the dried salt. The hot sun had accelerated our work and we had plenty below the deck. We had seal meat and the Clan of the Eagle came in their boats to see us off.

Once we were clear of the island, I let Water Bird steer and Silent Stone acted as crew. I was able to instruct both from the stern. Our trip had shown me that Water Bird was my heir and ready to become the navigator and it would not hurt to have Silent Stone able to sail the snekke too. Lost Wolf was too old to learn such skills. As we headed north, I reflected that this was one of the few times I could remember a peaceful voyage up the Patawomke. Water Bird was a natural sailor and I had little to do to correct him. Instead, I began to make Silent Stone into a crewman. He was keen to learn. He was no longer silent, at least not with us, and I did not have to draw words from his mouth. They flowed. I saw Lost Wolf smile as the boy who had rarely spoken before we came into his life now chatted and laughed with Water Bird. Gradually, I let Water Bird become the one who instructed him. I was still needed but it would not be long before I was, like Lost Wolf, a passenger.

When we neared, towards dusk, the place I sought I took over. Brave Eagle's clan had left the river and it was empty. Flies were swarming and the birds were taking advantage of the feast. I saw the entrance we had made to the old quay and had the sail lowered. The other three used oars to take us up the narrow and overhung channel. The mast scraped on the branches that had grown since we had left. I did not approach stealthily and a young warrior appeared with flint tipped spear. He saw the snekke's prow and his eyes came to me. I did not recognise him but he knew me and the boat.

"It is the Shaman of the Bear." He shouted loudly and by the time we had tied up and climbed ashore a host was there to greet us.

Brave Eagle was now white but he still commanded, "Let our friend move. Do not crowd him." The clan obeyed. He held out his arms and I embraced him. "It is good that you return to us." He looked at the other three. "My grandson?"

"Black Feather is well and has married. You have a great-granddaughter, River's Breath."

He put his arm around my shoulders, "Come, this is not the place to talk."

"Water Bird, you and Silent Stone bring the seal meat and a sack of salt. We do not come here empty handed."

As we walked down the path he said, "And Laughing Deer, she is well?"

I shook my head, "Laughing Deer is with the spirits. She died."

"I am sad and I know that Running Antelope will weep."

It was bad luck to ask the cause and I knew that none would query the manner of her death. That was good for I did not want to relive it.

When we entered the clearing there was an outpouring of noise and I saw a white-haired Running Antelope who stood with open arms. It was good to return to the clan that had welcomed me all those years ago. I knew that we could return if we wished. With no Eagle Claws to threaten we could bring our clan back. I knew that I would not do so for as much as I liked this place, Eagle's Shadow was a better home.

Beaver's Teeth and Fighting Bird came over. They would ask about their daughters. I said, "Fighting Bird, this is your grandson, Water Bird. He is a good warrior and a navigator. Your daughters are both well and your blood continues with their children."

Fighting Bird grabbed Water Bird, "Come, let us see your grandmother. Be prepared for tears for she misses your mother."

I turned and said, "Brave Eagle, this is Lost Wolf, the chief of the Clan of the Dog and one of his warriors, Silent Stone."

"You are most welcome, Lost Wolf."

Lost Wolf shook his head, "And Erik is exaggerating, for it was my son who was chief and there are but three boys left as warriors. I am the Clan of the Bear now."

"And I can see, Erik, that there are more tales to tell. Come, sit and smoke a pipe with me. This night we will feast."

As I told our tales and all that had happened, I could not help but think that the village was now at peace and my fears that there might be discord were unfounded. All was well. Brave Eagle and the clan were hospitable and we were given a yehakin to share. There had been deaths. Brave Eagle told me the blizzard that had struck our valley when the bear had died had also struck his village. They were not as well prepared with food and some of the old had died. The clan was not as large as it had been. We had suffered no deaths yet our old home had.

The next day was spent just walking around the camp. I felt sorry for Silent Stone and Lost Wolf. It was not that they were ignored but that they could not help but see the warmth of the greeting for my grandson and me. I sat and smoked with the elders of the clan while Silent Stone and Water Bird showed off their iron weapons to the younger boys. Brave Eagle was not like Eagle Claws, he listened to his elders. I heard while they spoke, of the Moneton. They had enjoyed some respite from their raids when the blizzard had struck but I learned that in the last year, they had resumed their aggression.

Beaver's Teeth said, "We have heard that they are also being threatened by a new people from the north."

I looked at Lost Wolf and he nodded. I gestured with my pipe, "This is Lost Wolf and his clan and people were almost wiped out by a tribe from the north, the Shawnee. Tell the elders your story."

We had not spoken of it the previous night just that his clan had joined ours. Lost Wolf told the story in detail and I saw the concern on the faces of the others. At the end, Brave Eagle said, "This does not sound good, Erik. How can we fight such a people? If the Moneton warriors fear them then they must be a fierce tribe."

"I have thought of this for where we live is closer to them and we will have to face the threat ourselves." I saw Beaver's Teeth and Fighting Bird exchange a look. "We use the river as a defence. Remember the battle against the Moneton?" They all nodded, "We made the forest a fortress and the river a barrier. You can do the same. As with the time of the Moneton War, you will know when they are coming for others will suffer their attacks first and when you do hear you use the watchers in the trees and make traps. If you wish I can help you now to hunt fish in the river. An extra day or so here will not hurt. Prepare food so that you can defend. A warrior cannot fight and hunt. If these Shawnee warriors have travelled far to fight then they cannot afford a long war. Make them bleed." I shrugged, "We might bemoan our fate but we can do little about it. We can change the world of our people but not the world beyond."

"You are wise Erik and you have given good counsel. We would appreciate your help to fish and I would sail in this new snekke of yours." We agreed to go fishing the next day. Lost Wolf would stay in the camp and Brave Eagle would take his place.

After we had eaten I could tell that Brave Eagle had something on his mind and then he said, "Let us walk around the village, Erik. The walk will help my digestion."

He said nothing at first and I could tell that he was distracted when he merely smiled at the greetings we were given. He was debating how to speak his words, "Brave Eagle, unless you have a piece of meat caught in your mouth then speak and fear not my reaction. You and I have no secrets and we are as close as two men who are not of the same blood can be. You wish to ask me something and cannot form the words."

He chuckled, "I forget that you are a shaman, sometimes. You read my mind well. Here it is. You asked when you first came if the clan was happy and I said it was. That is not quite true. Last year a young maid had two suitors: Lost Squirrel and Otter's Cub. She chose Lost Squirrel. Otter's Cub did not take rejection well and he tried to fight Lost Squirrel. There is bad blood there. The elders and I have had to punish the two of them often but, in truth, it is all Otter's Cub's fault. Now that Lost Squirrel and his wife have a child they wish for peace. I was going to banish Otter's Cub and then…"

"And then we came. You would have him join my clan?" He nodded. "Yet he sounds like trouble. Why should we bring a thorn into our harmonious home?"

"There is no reason why you should but if anyone can work the miracle it is you."

We walked in silence. "Bring this troublemaker with you tomorrow and he can help on the snekke. I will see how he fits in with Silent Stone and Water Bird."

The Norns were still spinning.

While we prepared the snekke and the clan launched their birch bark boats, I spoke to my two crewmen. "Try to speak to Otter's Cub. I want to know his heart and you two have shown me that you have eyes and ears."

Water Bird nodded, "We will, Grandfather, for we know that the Clan of the Bear is special but as Lost Wolf and Silent Stone have shown us, sometimes newcomers can make a clan stronger."

Water Bird would make a good leader when he came into his inheritance,

Otter's Cub was younger than Golden Bear. I did not remember him from the Moneton War. He was nervous as he approached the snekke and that confirmed, in my mind, that he had been too young when we had left to have either known me or seen the snekke.

"Welcome, Otter's Cub. Water Bird and Silent Stone will tell you what to do. I am honoured that you travel in my snekke."

"I need to tell you, Erik, Shaman of the Bear, that I am frightened beyond words. This seems like magic."

Silent Stone said, "And that is what it is, magic, but not all magic is to be feared."

Water Bird added, "Aye, Silent Stone will sit at the prow with you for I must work the sail."

"And you, Brave Eagle, shall sit close by me." While they arranged themselves Lost Wolf prepared to loose us from the moorings. "Let go. Push us off, boys. Otter's Cub, help them." I knew that by giving him something to do would take his mind off the strangeness.

As we emerged into the river I said, "Hoist the sail." As soon as the wind caught us, we flew across the river. The rest of the fishermen were there already and when they saw the bear, they all cried out in joy.

"You have built an even better boat, Erik."

I nodded, "*__Laughing Deer__*' is the last boat I shall build but she is the best."

We had a job to do and we headed downstream to the narrowest part of the river before the estuary. When I was satisfied with our position, I turned the snekke and Silent Stone and Water Bird dropped our anchors. The birch bark boats fanned out alongside us and we strung the nets that they had brought. They were not as big as the ones we used on the Shenandoah but that did not matter. The crews of the boats had twice the work that we had as they were forced to paddle to keep their boats in position whilst hauling on their nets. Two boats, commanded by White Fox, would act as transports to bring the fish to us. We hauled the nets aboard and the fish were scattered on my deck. White Fox's two boats collected a smaller number of fish from the others and we spent a hard two hours hunting fish. Eventually, I called a halt.

"We have enough fish now and your warriors in the boats must be exhausted."

Brave Eagle nodded and, making his way to the mast, stood, "We have enough fish. Return to the village and have the women meet us at the quay."

The winds and the current were against us and it took us longer to reach our mooring than when we had left that morning. I said, "Brave Eagle, send Otter's Cub to me. I would speak to him."

I smiled as a terrified warrior made his way down the snekke to join me. He shook his head, "How can you smile, Shaman? This is terrifying."

"Others have said the same but in time you will come to enjoy it."

His face registered that he had understood my words.

"Brave Eagle tells me that you are unhappy in the village."

He was silent for a moment and then nodded, "I will kill Lost Squirrel one day."

"And will that make Birch Leaf love you?" He stared at me. I said, "She has made her choice and it was not you."

"Every day that I see her makes my heart ache and I cannot sleep. If I do not do this then the ache will eat me from the inside, like a worm."

We were nearing the mooring and I said, "There is another choice. You can come with me to Eagle's Shadow. Life may not be any easier there but at least you will not see Birch Leaf every day. Your life will go on and you do not know what is in your future."

He shook his head, "I am not certain."

"I understand. When I leave, if you wish a berth with me then bring your belongings and say your goodbyes for I will return here no more."

"I will consider your words and I thank you for the offer. All that the clan has offered me are threats of retribution."

"And that is to be understood for you are like the one bird that does not sing harmoniously with the others. You stand out and your voice marks you as different. You need another flock where you can learn to sing."

We landed and spent an hour unloading the fish. It was a fine harvest but when they had all gone, Brave Eagle and Otter's Cub included, the four of us had a deck to clean. While we did so I asked Water Bird about Otter's Cub.

"He is an angry young warrior, Grandfather, but I did not fear him. He was respectful towards us and seemed to fear you. He resents Brave Eagle and White Fox. They have made it quite clear that he will be banished if he continues his path. He sees it as unfair."

"And you, Water Bird, do you see it as unfair?"

"Brave Eagle has the clan to think of but I feel sorry for Otter's Cub. He fell in love with the wrong woman. He is being punished by all."

"And do you think he would cause the same trouble at Eagle's Shadow?"

It was Silent Stone who answered, "Eagle's Shadow has power, Shaman, and it soothes a warrior's soul. The spirits that guard it give comfort when you sleep. If anything can heal Otter's Cub it is Eagle's Shadow."

I had already decided to take the boy if he wished to come but Silent Stone's advice confirmed it.

We stayed for another few days while the fish were prepared for preservation. Our gift of salt had proved to be timely. Brave Eagle and his warriors also went hunting and we were given meat to take with us on the voyage back. Otter's Cub did not speak to me but spent all his time with his family.

The night before we left, I spoke at length to Brave Eagle, "I have made the offer to Otter's Cub. We will leave tomorrow no matter what. If he comes then he comes but if not…"

"White Fox has said that if I do not banish the boy he will." He shrugged, "I am getting old, Erik and White Fox will be the leader. I will bow to his wishes."

"And this, Brave Eagle, will be the last time I visit the clan. Others will make this voyage but I will not be on the snekke. When we say farewell, it will be for the last time."

He nodded and tapped his chest and head, "Yet you can never leave here. You plucked me from the sea and gave me life. You helped to rescue my family. You showed us how to fight the Moneton. You are embedded in my clan and in me, Erik. When next we meet, in your Otherworld, we will not have the pains that plague old men. We shall be young and lithe once more. We will spend eternity speaking and that is good."

"And your words are my words, Brave Eagle. All is well."

We did not leave early for I knew that my old friends from the village would wish to speak to me and besides I wanted an empty river when we left so that we could sail as far upstream in the dark as we could. I was given many gifts. All were handmade and as precious to me as gold. I hugged Running Antelope and felt her tears. Brave Eagle and I had the warrior's clasp that was our bond.

When I saw Otter's Cub with his bow, spear, shield and sleeping blanket then I knew we had another member of our clan. *Wyrd.*

Chapter 13

We had to rebalance the snekke. Water Bird came next to me and Otter's Cub joined Silent Stone at the mast. "Silent Stone, tell Otter's Cub what it is that you do and in the fullness of time he might become a sailor."

"Aye, Shaman." I wanted our new member of the clan to be occupied and not worrying about the motion of the snekke.

"Lost Wolf, you need the eyes of your youth today. Once we pass the place where we slept, we are in the land of the Moneton."

"Will we not stop there again, Erik?"

"No, for we will sail through the night. I hope to be where the two rivers meet soon after dawn."

I had intended to stop but when the wind came from the south and east, I knew we had to take advantage of it. The current was against us but it was a sluggish one. We could make good time and with the help of Ran and the Allfather, we might make the Shenandoah before the Moneton realised that we were back on the river. Having fished for Brave Eagle's clan the previous days there were no boats on the first part of the voyage and it felt as though we had the river to ourselves. Perhaps the empty river helped us to focus our eyes for, as the sun set to the west, Lost Wolf called out, "On the other bank," he pointed to steerboard, "I see warriors. There are three of them."

I looked to where he pointed and saw, on the bluffs overlooking the Patawomke, three Moneton warriors. They were on the wrong side of the river to be a real threat and we were far from Fears Water's village. The Monetons' home was also on our side of the river but I did not like it. Word would spread or they might be able to send a boat across. We would travel, I hoped, faster than the news that the magic boat had been seen on the river once more but it was a warning that we had to sail as quickly as we could.

"I will take over now, Water Bird. You sleep while you can. If I need assistance, I will wake you."

"Thank you for trusting me, Grandfather."

"You have it in your blood." He pulled the bearskin over him. "You three can also sleep."

Otter's Cub said, "I do not wish to sleep. Could I sit where Water Bird sat?"

"Move down the snekke on your hands, knees, and feet. Keep to the centre and sit exactly where Water Bird sat."

He obeyed my words precisely and I was pleased. He was not arrogant nor was he reckless. I had wondered if his actions and attitude towards Lost Squirrel suggested a flaw in him that might hurt my clan. He sat with his arms on the gunwale and the stern as I had done. He had observed well.

"This boat seems like a bird that swims across the water. It appears effortless."

I nodded to the billowing sail, "The wind does the work for us."

"And if the wind is against you?"

"Then we can still sail but not in a straight line. The Patawomke is not a straight river. There are loops and turns where we will slow but most of the river heads north and we can use that."

We sailed in silence as darkness fell. I was confident in my ability as a navigator but I kept the snekke in the centre of the river. It was a wide one and we had room to tack when the river changed direction. Otter's Cub succumbed to sleep although it was well into the night when he did so. I was left alone. This would be the last time I would sail up the Patawomke. There were no more reasons for me to voyage south again. Brave Cub and Water Bird were both navigators. Golden Bear was also skilled. The next time the snekke went for salt they could take both snekke and have more warriors. We would not need salt for another year or two. Thanks to my words with Screaming Eagle we had made more salt than I had expected. I wondered what might have happened had we talked before and then I realised that was a waste of thought. We could not change the past and we had been caught in the web woven by the Norns.

I stroked the wood of the snekke. She was a beautiful boat. I would still sail her on the Shenandoah, but this would be my last night watch. I smiled as I remembered the ones on the Great Sea. Had I known that we would find such a home, I might not have fretted and worried as we had sailed south to a land we did not know. I shook my head, I was not remembering it as I should have. I had the whole clan in the drekar and even if I had known how beautiful Bear Island and the bay were, I would still have been terrified that I might make a mistake. It was always dangerous when you looked back for you forgot the bad things and just remembered the good.

I saw the false dawn in the east. I nudged Otter's Cub, "Wake the others and take your place by the mast. Now is the time to make water, eat and drink. The most dangerous part of our voyage is to come."

I realised that we should have stopped for the night but the trouble was it would have meant camping close to where the Moneton village lay and I had not wished to risk it. The Norns had spun. Otter's Cub woke Water Bird and then crabbed his way to Silent Stone and Lost Wolf. He would do.

Water Bird rubbed his eyes, "Where are we, Grandfather?"

"In perilous waters. Here, take the steering board while I make water." The others were all doing the same. When I had finished, I drank some ale and then ate a dried fish we had been given in Brave Eagle's village. The salty taste was fresh and the fish was delicious. That done I said, "Now prepare weapons. Tell the others that there may be danger ahead. Bring my spear and bow here. Have your sling ready and warn the others. The Norns have spun and while we are tantalisingly close to the Shenandoah, I fear that we will be seen."

He smiled, "I have come to realise, Grandfather, that you can never predict the effect of the threads. We had a friend in Screaming Eagle and thus far Otter's Cub is doing well."

I nodded. Water Bird had the optimism of youth. I had the pessimism of age. When he returned, I let him steer while I strung my bow. I took four arrows and placed them next to my chest along with the bow. I had the spear so that I could reach it easily. "Now eat and drink. You will stay by me and you can take over the steering when I tell you."

We watched the sun rise from the steerboard shore. Its light bathed the other bank in a bluish light. Fears Water's village was not far away. I could nearly see the place where the Moneton arrow had struck my knee and almost killed me. I touched my Hammer of Thor and said a silent invocation to Gytha and Laughing Deer to watch over us.

"There, Shaman."

I looked to where Silent Stone pointed. It was to larboard and there were Moneton warriors. This time it was clear to me that they had seen us for there was agitation and noise. I could not make out any words but I guessed that they were summoning warriors to fetch boats. They would hunt us.

"Keep as still as you can for movement slows us. The wind is with us but they will launch boats and pursue us."

Water Bird had heard the tales from his father of our previous voyages. "Will you head beyond our river and try to lose them?"

I shook my head, "No, Water Bird. That worked once and it will not work a second time. We will risk the rocks and the tumbling waters. We are stronger than the birch bark boats and we have weapons that we can use. It is hard to paddle and loose an arrow." He nodded. I called out, "When we are pursued do not waste arrows. They are too valuable. Use your slings and aim for the men at the front of the boats."

Lost Wolf nodded and shouted, "But they may not catch us."

I pointed. Ahead of us, they were launching boats. There were five of them. "Believe me, Lost Wolf, they will do all in their power to destroy us and I will not underestimate this enemy who has hurt me once before."

There were five men in each boat. If they caught us, we would die. If we survived it would be because of the skill of the navigator. Did I still have those skills? I looked at Water Bird. My grandson's life depended on my skills. I would draw on every memory and every battle to save him and the others. They were my clan.

We managed to pass them before they launched all the boats and, as I had expected, one boat was faster than the others. They would be like an arrow pursuing us. I knew that the stories of my snekke would have been shared in their camp. I was the spectre that had thwarted their ambitions. They would hunt me like a stag. The five boats would be ready to cut us off if I tried to deviate from a straight line and they would rely on the power of their paddles to catch us. I knew that I would have to turn when we neared the Shenandoah and that was when they would have us.

I peered beyond the mast and the sail. The Shenandoah lay just a thousand paces or so ahead. In the time we had lived here, I had seen a slight change in the course that the river took. By the time Water Bird was a grandfather it might be different again. The river was a living thing.

"Water Bird, I am going to take us over the rocks. I may have to use my bow. If I do then sail where there is no white water. *'Laughing Deer'* will respond well to your touch. If you steer then keep your eyes ahead. We will do any fighting that is necessary."

"I will do my best, Grandfather."

"Keep watching astern and when the nearest boat is ten lengths from us let me know. I will watch for the turn."

I planned on sailing beyond the mouth so that when we turned, we would have the widest part of the river to aim at. As the wind was coming from that quarter, we would have even more speed. The birch bark boats would struggle against the current and the turbulent water.

"Otter's Cub and Silent Stone, stand close to the mast when you use your stones and sit to refill them."

They both waved their acknowledgement. We were as prepared as we could be. Now it was down to my skill as well as more than a good piece of luck. Good for us and bad for the Moneton.

The turn was just a hundred paces away when Water Bird said, "Now, Grandfather."

Reaching for my bow and my arrow I said, "Keep her straight. If you need to turn then I will tell you."

I turned and stood. Even that slight movement made the snekke shift a little. We did not lose much way but enough to encourage the warrior at the stern of the leading boat to shout something. I had always had skills as an archer. It was partly the strength of rowing when I was young but I also had an understanding of wind and angles. I saw the nearest boat and it was drawing closer. With two hands on the paddle, the warrior had no protection. The beaded chest protector he wore might be useful against flint and bone but I chose a metal arrow. I drew back and released in one motion. Even as the arrow was in the air, I reached for a second one, a flint one this time. The arrow had just thirty paces to travel and it slammed into the warrior's chest. His lifeless hands dropped the paddle and the boat began to slew around. I nocked and released my second one. This one had more than an element of luck. It struck the middle warrior in the neck and made the boat become beam on. The current and the unbalanced boat meant the other three were thrown into the water as the boat capsized. I nocked a third arrow. This one also had a flint tip. The range was long but I had confidence I could hit a warrior. The arrow hit the leading Moneton at the prow of the next boat in the shoulder. He held on to his paddle but I knew that his strokes would be less powerful.

Dropping my bow I said, as I took the steering board from Water Bird, "Slings. Hold on for we are about to turn." The last arrow had delayed me enough so that I had but moments to make the turn. "Silent Stone, haul on the larboard stay."

Otter's Cub would have had no idea what I meant but Silent Stone was a quick learner and he pulled on the stay as I put the steering board over. It allowed Water Bird and Otter's Cub to hurl their stones while Lost Wolf sent an arrow. There were mixed results. Warriors were struck but not wounded badly enough to stop them. What they did do was to slow down the pursuit as the remaining four boats closed up. Our turn had brought them closer and if they had more crew then they might have been able to use bows and stones in return. What they did do was to paddle even harder knowing that they were within touching distance of us.

"Keep sending the stones and arrows." I knew that it would, at the very least, distract the warriors and a distraction when crossing the stones at the mouth of the river could be disastrous.

I saw, ahead, the white water and I turned the steering board a little. "Silent Stone, Otter's Cub, sit down so that I may see ahead." As the four boats were astern of us there was really only Water Bird who could harm them. Had he had a bow he might have been able to do more damage but a well-struck stone smacked into a warrior knocking him back. That boat slowed. I might have risked reefing the sail a little but the more speed we had the better the chance to fly over the shallows. I saw a gap of darker water to steerboard and I put the steering board over. It was the slightest of touches but the snekke responded as though she was a horse and I had pulled the reins.

"That confused them, Grandfather." Water Bird could see what I could not and knew that the move, slight though it was, had forced them to try to turn. Their boats were not as nimble as the snekke and they began to lose way. I dared not look around and I had to rely on Water Bird and his reactions. The other three were spectators.

"Hold on tightly, for this will become rough."

Even as I spoke a rush of water hit the side of the snekke, threatening to swamp us. The younger ones held on to the mast whilst Lost Wolf clung to the gunwales as though his life depended on it. The experience in the Great Sea had been a foretaste of what might happen. The rock that struck us was not marked by white water but I felt it grind along the keel. I prayed it had not damaged us but it slowed us slightly and the Moneton took advantage.

"One of them is gaining, Grandfather."

I looked ahead and saw some flatter water before the next shallows. "Take the steering board."

My grandson dropped his sling and sat with his arm on the steering board. I picked up my bow and grabbed an arrow. I stood and saw that they had gained and one boat, with a full crew of five, was just two lengths from us. One thing I knew how to do was to stand on a deck that was tilting and rising as though it was a sea beast. I balanced myself and drew back. I timed the arrow so that our stern had just hit the river. The arrow slammed into the warrior's chest. It was a flint arrow but it still drove through his bead vest. I had another arrow nocked before he slid backwards. The second paddler found his dead companion's head on his lap as my second arrow hit him in the head. With two of them dead and the weight at the back of the boat it slewed around and then capsized.

The other two boats were too close to avoid it although they did try. The last two boats were also upset and their crews had to fight for their lives in the teeming water. My crew all cheered. Dropping my bow I sat and took the steering board. The last of the rocks were ahead but this passage was more familiar to me and I sailed a safe course between the white water.

"Reef the sail, Silent Stone."

Otter's Cub shook his head, "I would not have believed that we could defeat twenty-five Moneton. You are truly a magician, Shaman of the Bear."

"But it was at a cost."

Water Bird said, "Cost?"

"We may have damaged the hull but, more importantly, we have told the Moneton that we live down this river. Now our vigilance will need to be constant."

"Will they risk the rocks?"

"They do not need to. They can carry their boats around them. They will have lost good warriors this day as well as five boats. I am guessing that their shaman will need to make magic to try to restore the confidence of his clan but one day, perhaps next year, they will come."

We sailed slowly up the river and I kept a good watch for signs of a cracked strake. No water entered the snekke but I was still cautious.

"Water Bird, keep a watch astern. If any Moneton survive and try to follow along the bank I would know."

"They will be in the river, Grandfather."

"I know and the current should take them to the Patawomke but all it will cost you to know that is a stiff neck for a while."

He grinned, "Yes, Grandfather."

"The rest of you, watch for water by the deck. That was a hard grounding and we cannot afford all our work at Salt Island to be undone by being soaked in river water."

I sailed as carefully up the river as I had ever done before. Otter's Cub was right, we had done far better than we might have hoped but we had been seen and, whilst until that moment we had been hidden at Eagle's Shadow, now the cloak of invisibility was gone. They knew not how far up the river we lived but they knew the direction in which to search.

It took until late afternoon for us to see the spiral of smoke from our fires. It would be a beacon attracting our enemies when they came, knowing that the Moneton would see all that I was now seeing. I had another reef to put in the sail and I handed the steering board to Water

Bird. After reefing the sail I made my way to the prow where I sat with Lost Wolf.

My action was so unusual that Lost Wolf commented, "What is wrong, Erik?"

"Until the attack, the Moneton did not know for sure where we lived. Now they do and they will come. It will not be soon and we will probably have another winter to prepare, but they will come. I would see what they would see."

"They will all have perished in the water."

I shook my head, "There will be survivors. I have plucked enough from both the Great Sea and the river to know that." I peered at the bank. The smoke clearly came from a camp on the south bank. I pointed to an open area of beach. "There, they will see that and land."

"How can you know that?"

I shook my head, "I cannot know but I can guess. It is flat and we can both see the smoke more clearly. They will know that the camp must be close. I know that we have another large loop of the river but they will not. They will land here, out of sight of the village and scout it out."

Sure enough, the river began its large loop to the west just a thousand paces later. The ditch we had dug would afford us some protection from the Moneton. It was then that the idea for the sluice gates game to me. If we deepened the channel and built a gate at each end then if an attack came, we would open the gates and the river would flood the ditch. We would be surrounded by water. The flooded ditch would not stop them but it would slow them and give them problems they had not foreseen. It was a plan.

We were seen from the camp and I was grateful that Moos Blood had the foresight to keep a watch for us. This would now have to become a permanent duty, Brave Eagle's camp no longer kept such a watch. Had we been enemies who landed then we would have been upon them before they knew. It was painful to have to think in such a way but the Moneton and the Shawnee were not like the Powhatans. They were warlike and aggressive. We would have to be as strong in our defence.

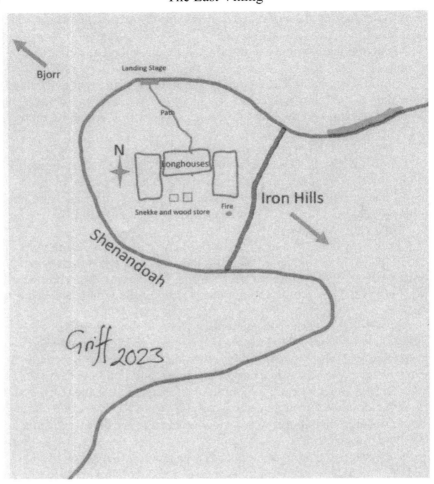

Chapter 14

As soon as we landed and had taken everything from the deck, I had the planks removed. By the time Moos Blood and the warriors reached us we were unloading the snekke's hold.

"You have done well, Father."

I pulled myself from the hold by his outstretched arm and gave him the dire news without any preamble, "The Moneton know that we are here. They saw us cross the rocks."

"You did not use the rollers?"

I shook my head, "The Norns were spinning, Moos Blood, and we did not have any choice. The Moneton were too close to us. The river took their boats but there will be survivors."

He nodded, "But you are all alive and brought back my son."

I pulled Water Bird from the snekke so that he could embrace his father, "And he is now a navigator. I need to go to the sea no more."

My son beamed and after releasing his son said, "And I see we have another warrior."

I helped the young warrior from the snekke, "He is Otter's Cub and is of Brave Eagle's clan." My son cocked his head to one side and I said, "Let us empty the snekke and then I can check the hull. Tomorrow we will have to take her from the water. She hit the rocks."

With many hands helping it did not take long to carry all the bags of salt and dried seal meat to the village. I stayed alone and unloaded the ballast stone by stone. I thanked the Allfather that there was not a trace of water within. Of course that did not mean that the keel was not cracked but whatever the damage was, we now had the opportunity to repair it. My chest and weapons had already been carried up the hill and I took my walking stick. It was a sign of the times that I needed the stick to help me up the slope. I had done nothing especially strenuous on the voyage but each day my weakened knee seemed worse. I kept the pain to myself for I knew there was nothing that could be done. I still had a purpose and until I had finished my work, then I could not be the invalid who sat and watched as others worked.

When I reached the village, I was pleased that Otter's Cub was not alone. Silent Stone, Red Wing and Blue Jay were showing him the layout of the village. Everyone stopped what they were doing when I reached the open area between the longhouses.

Brave Cub led the clapping of the hands of the whole clan as I approached. My second son came over to hug me, "I hear we now have friends at Salt Island."

"Perhaps. They are not enemies, but when next we send a snekke for salt we also need to send gifts. We need to trade. We will need more iron ore."

He nodded, "Lost Wolf told us that war will come. You seem to see further into the future than we can. What are your thoughts, Father?"

"We have two enemies now. One, the Moneton, will come sooner than the Shawnee and we know that they will come down the river. I know where they will land." He looked surprised and so I explained. "Not far from the narrow neck of land where we have our ditch is the small beach downriver of us. If they do not land and pass around the bend then we can spy them and that means the only other place they can land is the quay. I have plans for I believe we will have the winter, at least, to prepare. It is now almost harvest time and the Moneton lost warriors. How many I do not know but I do know that they were brave men and they are always the hardest to replace. We have more work ahead of us."

"But we have another warrior and if boys like Water Bird can learn to be navigators, then who knows what we can achieve."

He was right. Little White Dove and Willow Leaf took me away from the men and into my longhouse. My daughter said, "My brothers seem to forget your age, Father. You do too much. Let us tend to you while you tell us the tale of Otter's Cub." My look of surprise made her laugh. "It is the women of this clan who need to know the stories of the people you bring. We are the ones who make them welcome. Otter's Cub may well fight alongside my brothers but we will be the ones who feed him and take care of his hurts."

As they took off my seal skins boots and washed my feet, I drank the mead they offered and told them the tale of Otter's Cub. Willow Leaf shook her head, "His poor mother. Imagine her son having to leave the village. Love is a wicked weapon sometimes, Shaman. We will make him welcome and this is meant to be. Moon Calf and my son are happy and now Doe's Milk can have a husband."

I could not help snorting, "How can you say that they will be wed? They have just met."

It was Little White Dove who, having put salve on my feet stood and with her hands on her hips said, "Have you not eyes, Father? Doe's Milk is a woman and she needs a husband. Water Bird, Silent Stone and the others are too young. Otter's Cub was sent here. Doe's Milk is soft and gentle. She will be perfect for Otter's Cub."

Willow Leaf said, "Grey Shadow will watch them for we have put him in Lost Wolf's longhouse. You need to do nothing, Shaman. You have enough to think about with the clan. It is we women who ensure that all runs smoothly within our homes."

Little White Dove said, "Running Antelope must have been distracted not to have seen the conflict coming. Is she old now, Father?"

I was still stunned by the women's words and I nodded, distractedly, "I suppose. She has white hair and…"

"We would not let such a thing happen here. Now, tonight we eat here in the longhouse but tomorrow we will have a feast to celebrate your return. We will cook something special with the seal meat. Most of the clan have never tasted it. Cooked with some of the squash and ground-up maize we can make a meal that all will remember."

Willow Leaf made to leave and I said, "Before you go and as you appear, along with Grey Shadow, to be three spinners of threads, you should know that the Moneton know where we live. They will come."

Willow Leaf said, "And before you found me that would have terrified me but you have taught my family that you can only run for so long and then you stand and fight. They will come and they may hurt us but we will survive because we are the Clan of the Bear and, like our leader, we are strong."

After she had gone, I said, "Willow Leaf has changed since she came here."

"Her marriage to Black Feather brought her two things, a fine young husband and a second family. It was almost as though she was reborn here at Eagle's Shadow. Grey Shadow has also grown younger since she came here. Both women now have grandchildren and see hope for their families where there was none." She held my hand, "That is down to you, Father." She closed her eyes and said, softly, "And my mother. When you came from Bear Island you made a clan from nothing."

I squeezed her hand, "I would not say nothing, daughter. We made four fine young people and they are the foundations of the clan."

Any further conversation was ended as the younger ones entered to swarm over me. I was still their grandfather. I could not evade their attention even if I wished it, and I did not. I loved it.

"Tell us of the Great Sea, Grandfather. Water Bird said you saw the sea beast."

I smiled and said, "Aye, I did, and when you are old enough you will sail to Salt Island and see it for yourself. Until then you will have to make do with my inadequate words." I spent the time until the food was ready telling them of the sea beast and how we had hunted it. They enjoyed the story and were wrapt in it but inside I was sad, for in the telling I was reminded of all those who hunted with me and then died at the hands of the Penobscot. Their lives had been snuffed out too soon.

I walked, the next day, with Moos Blood and Brave Cub to see how our home looked to an attacker, while Golden Bear sailed the snekke downstream to fetch back the rollers we had left there. They could be used and I wanted no further signs to aid the Moneton.

My walk with my sons was depressing. My heart sank as I saw the places where we were now vulnerable. The clearing of the fields next to the river had left an open space on either side of the small quay. There was nothing to stop an enemy from simply landing and heading up to the longhouses. It was Brave Cub who inadvertently gave me the idea. He pointed to the long green plants that trailed along the ground. They were a crop which, if left untended, would grow very large and a little bitter. We tended to harvest them when they were young. I was never keen on the taste which seemed a little bland to me but they bulked out soups and stews and grew easily. They also had a bright yellow flower that could be eaten and which the women liked.

"Watch, Father, that you do not tread on the fruits."

I looked down and saw them sprawling towards the water. They had vines and clung to anything. That gave me the idea. "If we cut saplings and planted them here then what would these plants do?"

They both looked at me as though I had lost my mind. Brave Cub humoured me, "They would climb, Father. What is in your mind?"

"We need a barrier here next to the river. We have to slow down an enemy if we can. If we put stakes in and leave some of the plants to rot down and seed themselves then come the spring, instead of spreading out along the ground, they will climb up the wood. It will look more substantial than it is but even if an enemy tried to destroy it then they would make such a noise that we would hear."

Brave Cub nodded, "And that would give us a bigger harvest. It is a job for the boys to forage the stakes."

We walked to the dock, "And here is our greatest weakness. Come the spring we need a night watch here. Ulla and a young warrior. The warrior will have to lose sleep. During the day we can see the approach of an enemy but at night…"

Moos Blood said, "But the Moneton will land before here, you said that yourself. They will land at the beach and that is why we built the ditch that we can flood."

"But the Shawnee may come from the north and west. If it is the west and they use the land then they might be slowed by the ditch, but if they come from the north or use the river then they will strike here."

Moos Blood asked, "Should we not send warriors out each day to look for signs of our enemies?"

"That would waste the effort we might put into our new defences. Better that the warriors make us strong and we gather all that we can before the winter comes." I could see that my son was not convinced. Perhaps he thought that I was getting old and making mistakes. I was getting old but my mind still worked as sharply as ever. We had reached a patch of cleared earth close to the quay and I took the old spear shaft I used as a stick. I made marks on the ground as I spoke. "The Moneton know that we are somewhere here." I made a large circle around the cross I had placed in the centre. "They have never explored this far upstream and they will come warily. They will also come in numbers and as we hurt both their men and boats that will not be until after the winter."

They both took in my words and Moos Blood nodded, "But the Shawnee."

"Are even less likely to come before the new grass. They do not know us. They will know that Lost Wolf and the last of his clan are gone and may seek them but," I made a mark a long way from the cross, "This is Lost Wolf's village and the Shawnee would have to search this area."

The circle I made was so large that Brave Cub laughed, "It would be like searching the Great Sea for one sea beast."

I used the stick to push me to my feet, "Do not forget the Norns. I know I have not. We will, Moos Blood, send out patrols as soon as we can after winter. We will have warriors watching but between now and that time we work on the defences and then gather food. Last winter was mild but remember the winter of the bear." They both nodded and with a clear plan in our heads we set to organise the work.

We put Otter's Cub to work with Bjorr Tooth. Now that he had become a father and had sailed with me the young warrior understood my mind better than any. He was good for Otter's Cub. Of course, Doe's Milk found every opportunity to be on hand to help the two of them. Little White Dove had been right that the Powhatan warrior had been sent to us. He responded well to the attention and even an old man like me could see that soon they would be wed. As Willow Leaf also encouraged the match then it was as certain as the rising of the sun each day.

The young boys loved the responsibility of cutting down the saplings, especially as they got to use the hand axes. I do not think I ever saw weapons sharpened as much as they were. The hardest and dirtiest task was deepening the ditch and making the sluice gates. I worked with Water Bird and Silent Stone on the sluices. I had seen such things before. I had to dredge my memory for the shape and construction but if I closed my eyes and threw my mind back to my childhood then it came to me. I remembered the monastery close to Larswick where the monks had diverted the river to feed the fishpond they used for food. The monks had been clever men.

I had the boys split planks which we nailed together to make the actual gate. That was easy. The harder part was to make the runners that would have to be smooth and endure water. We shaped the wood as smoothly as we could and then soaked the timbers in pine tar. We made both gates at the same time. When I was happy with the protection afforded to the wood, we dug the holes for the first gate. I say we but it was the two boys who gambolled in the mud. When the holes were deep enough, we hammered in the runners. I used a vine with a weight attached to ensure that the posts were vertical and I had made marks on my spear shaft so that they were the right distance. We finished one gate and the boys were anxious to see if it worked.

Shaking my head I said, "We put the other one in place and then help the warriors on the ditch. The last thing we will need to do is to break through to the river on each side. That will be the crucial time. If I have miscalculated then the village will become an island."

Silent Stone had found his voice and that had freed his mind, "What would we do then, Shaman?"

"Build a bridge."

He smiled, "Your people are as clever as the bjorr, Shaman. They too are great builders. You are better because you can build boats to move along the river."

I smiled at his words but I realised the one place for which we had no protection was the quay. Would an enemy attack our boats? I resolved to put my mind to that problem.

Sometimes you see things that you do not expect. As I walked around the village and spoke to the men whilst inspecting the land, I detected unhappiness. Little White Dove was the one who was attuned to the mood of the clan. Her mother had enjoyed that gift and it had passed down to Little White Dove. When I found her alone, I asked her the question that had been on my mind, "Daughter, why is Long Nose unhappy? Is he ill?"

She smiled but it was a sad smile, "Not unless an empty heart is an illness. He sees the other warriors with wives and children. Even Otter's Cub has found a wife and he is but recently arrived."

"There will be other maidens who become women."

"It is not as easy as that. You dreamt of our mother before you had even met her. That does not happen to everyone. Do not worry about this, Father, you have other problems to wrestle with. He will not leave the clan for he has friends like Black Feather, but he will have a face like one who has eaten an unripe fruit until he finds a woman and he will find one."

"How do you know?"

She tapped her head, "Mother comes to me and speaks in here at night when I sleep. She has told me that the clan will grow and be happy. I trust to her. This sadness is temporary and will pass."

My daughter's words were of comfort to me not least because I knew that when my time was done, she would still have my dead wife's counsel.

We had the harvest gathered by the time the palisade, as I referred to it, was finished. This time some fruits, large ones, were left on the vines to rot down. They would grow quickly when the winter was over and we would see if they could climb as well as I hoped. What I did know was that their tendrils would creep through the gaps and make a bond to create a stronger wall. That done and before we hunted, we used the whole village to break through to the river. We had two groups as we had to break through at the same time. While the soil was removed and made into a barrier on our side of the ditch, I went with my two helpers to grease the sluice gates. I hoped we had made them strong enough. They were certainly heavy enough. I used the best ropes we could make to help us to lift them.

It was late afternoon when the cry went up from both ends and the breach was almost complete. I had given Water Bird my horn and I nodded to him to blow three blasts. I was with Brave Cub and his half of the clan. Moos Blood had the rest. As the last blast echoed, Brave Cub dug his wooden spade into the bottom of the hole he had made. The water began to trickle immediately. We had judged the moment well. The force of the river was so strong that had Golden Bear and Black Feather not been on hand then my son might have been dashed against the sluice gates. As it was, he was hauled, laughing, from the racing Shenandoah.

I was relieved but then the focus of my attention shifted to the gate. Would it hold? Water seeped through the bottom but not enough to worry me. The water would swell the wood and seal the leaks. The water that did come through would help us embed stakes. The warriors and the women all cheered when the gate held.

"I will walk to Moos Blood now."

With my two boys in tow, I walked the length of the ditch. "Tomorrow, we embed stakes in the bottom. When we have to flood the ditch, they will be the weapon that weakens the enemy."

The other gate had held and as we went back up to the village, I told Moos Blood what was needed. He nodded, "But we also need meat. The boys can make the stakes and I will take the rest to hunt." He pointed at the trees. "The trees know that winter is coming. The village is secure now. Let us make sure that none die of hunger."

My son would make a good chief. He planned for the future.

That night I was tired but I still found that sleep eluded me. The problem of the boats was like a piece of meat lodged between my teeth. It would not go away. I rose and went outside. Lighting a pipe with the leaves that helped me to dream and made me calmer, I smoked until the bowl was empty. I was yawning before I even entered the longhouse and slipped beneath the bear's skin. I fell asleep immediately. I did dream but it was not a dream I had enjoyed before.

I was back in the land of ice and fire. It was wintertime and the ground was frozen hard. I saw men slipping and sliding as they tried to walk along the slippery slope. A log that was not secured suddenly took off, seemingly of its own volition and hurtled down the ice to crash into the icy sea.

I woke and it was dawn but I had my answer.

It was left to me and the children of the clan to cut and plant stakes. The ground was soft enough for us to hammer them in and then I let them sharpen the tips. It was good that they did the work for when we flooded the ditch, they would be well aware of the hidden danger below the water. It was as I watched them sharpen the stakes that I realised we would need more iron to make more weapons. The problem was that we could ill afford to have warriors away from the village for any length of time. We had salt but we could only get iron from the cave of the bear. The soil we had removed was now placed a short distance from the ditch and the rollers we had brought back from the river, along with others we had cut to clear the forest, were made into a barricade. The ditch was a good defence but I wanted a second one to allow warriors to ascend the paths and get to the village if we were attacked.

The men spent three days hunting. They worked well together. None of them were trying to outdo the others. That had sometimes happened with the Clan of the Fox. Some young warriors in my former clan saw it as an opportunity to show off. My clan worked for each other and that was good. When they fought, they would fight as one and as I had learned, a clan that did that had a better chance of winning and surviving. The work on the defences was now largely finished and so the whole clan spent the next days preserving the meat. The weather was changing and so I made the decision that we would spend the next few days fishing while we could. I was still refining the plan I had to make our snekke safe from an attack.

I took Water Bird and Silent Stone with me. They worked well together and that was more important than their age. My grandson had shown that he was a sailor and a navigator. In the time I had left, I would make him as skilled as he could be. I had learned from many navigators and I was merely passing on their knowledge to the next generation. Their weakness was their lack of strength. For their age both were strong but if the net became too heavy then they might struggle to lift it aboard.

We headed upstream. It did not matter now which direction we took. There might be enemies in both directions. For that reason, we took weapons in case we had a fight. In the event, it was a peaceful few days that we enjoyed. We gathered more than enough fish to preserve and we now had plenty of salt. Little White Dove knew how to make vinegar and that also helped with the preservation. A by-product of beer, vinegar was as useful to us as salt. It preserved and it cleaned wounds better than water alone. During the summer the women had made more pots from the river clay and we stored both the salt and the vinegar in those. We were far more organised than we had been even in Brave Eagle's village. That was thanks to Laughing Deer. Before she died, she had passed her skills on to our daughter and she had done the same with the new women as well as all the girls. When I was gone the clan would survive. Even as I thought it, I clutched my hammer of Thor. It did not do to provoke the sisters, even in my head.

By the time the weather took a wintery turn we had finished fishing and the preservation was well underway. If the warriors thought that they could enjoy a few days of rest before hewing wood for the winter they were in for a shock.

I gathered them, not in the open space before the longhouses but at the top of the steep slope that led directly to the river. We had contemplated making it into terraces to enable us to farm it but had never got around to it. Now I had a plan to use nature and save our snekke. "We are going to make a slide here to launch the snekke." I saw the confusion on all of their faces. Brave Cub, Golden Bear and Water

Bird looked confused but also had interest written all over them. "If we leave our snekke by the water then an enemy could come and destroy them. We could not leave enough men to guard them and we have few enough warriors as it is. I propose to lay wooden rails down to the river. They will be narrow but high enough from the ground so that the keel does not snag." I turned and pointed to the nearest longhouse, "We fix a wooden ring there and pass a rope through it. We can let the weight of the snekke slide them down to the water." I smiled and shrugged, "I know that it will take all of us to haul them back up, but the effort will mean we have a better chance of saving the snekke and we can launch them quickly. Carrying them up the slope by hand is not easy. This slipway will save effort." I looked at them as they each took in what I had said. Some nodded and looked positive. Others needed convincing. "We keep the boats up here during winter." I pointed to *'Gytha'*. We do not use the snekke every day. Keeping them out of the water will ensure that they last longer. Weed and the worm will not get to them."

I let them turn and speak to one another. I heard some positive comments and some negative ones. When I deemed that they had spoken long enough, I said, "Has anyone a better idea to keep our boats safe?" There was no answer. "Then tomorrow we cut the timbers for the rails. What we do not use we can keep as firewood. There will be no wasted labour. We take the wood from the forest beyond the ditch. We need to remove anywhere an enemy can hide."

Brave Cub and Golden Bear came to speak to me when the others returned to their longhouse. "This is a good idea, Father, but will not our enemies see the rails and the bare hillside?"

I smiled, "Golden Bear, after my words can you see, in your mind, what I have planned?"

He smiled, "A rough idea but it is something I have never seen before."

"Nor have I and that is the point. If we, who know ships and how they work, do not understand the wooden slipway then what chance will our enemies have? They will see it but it will not help them. We left this slope alone for it was too steep to use. They will seek another, less exposed path and those paths, as at Brave Eagle's village, will become death traps. What we learned there we will use here."

Brave Cub put his arm around my shoulder. He was now taller than I was. "Father, what will we do without your mind when you are with Mother?"

"You will use your minds and come up with things you have yet to even dream of. I have wrestled with this problem for some time. Let the dreamworld be your guide. There is no problem that we cannot solve."

We were helped as the weather, which had been becoming colder, suddenly warmed up and the next few days saw clear skies with little wind and, mercifully, no rain. It was as though the Allfather was doing his best to help us.

The idea was a sound one but it was harder to put into practice than I expected. Clearing the slope of vegetation was hard enough but it was the planting of the wood that taxed me. While the warriors hewed timber, I worked with the youths. The girls also helped. They scrambled about the slope and used stone knives to hack out the plants that grew where I intended the rails to go. Inevitably there were accidents and sometimes one of them would tumble down the slope and into the river. The laughter from the others made it more like a game but I saw how hard it would be for an enemy to scale the slope and the difficulty I faced. The solution, when it came to me, was not a dignified one but it worked. While we still waited for the timber, I had Water Bird and Silent Stone run a rope around a tree which we greased. I tied one end around my waist and they went to the river with the other. I had the other youths above me to help me keep straight. I had a stone hatchet and I used that, as I was lowered, to make the slope as clear as possible. Then I had to climb back up and dig the holes for the posts.

It was Water Bird who suddenly realised we could halve the time it was taking, "Grandfather, you now have the line. Let the others tether me the same way and then the two of us could come down next to each other."

I looked at the boy who was rapidly growing, "You can do this?"

He smiled, "I have watched you and I am of your blood. I can copy you."

He was right and it did halve the time. In fact, it helped for we were able to communicate what we were learning as we were lowered. By the end of the day, we had holes dug for the posts that would keep the rails where I wanted them to be.

The warriors arrived back with the timber before we had finished and while they were trimmed, they watched Water Bird and I as we dug the last of the post holes.

Golden Bear laughed, "You are like two spiders hanging from your threads!"

"And if we build half as well as spiders then I will be a happy man, Golden Bear."

One thing I was realising was that I could not do everything myself. I let Brave Cub and Golden Bear oversee the making of the rails while Moos Blood and I, tethered like spiders, embedded the posts along the line of the trackway. We used stones to pack it. They were a mixture of large and small ones with river sand mixed in. It took another day and I was weary beyond words when we eventually finished. My waist was chafed from the rope and my knee screamed at me in agony.

Water Bird told my daughter of my pain. He watched my every move and Little White Dove reprimanded me when she saw my face, "Father, you are no longer a young man. Let others do this work and you supervise."

"This is my idea. I should be the one to shoulder the burden of work."

She sighed, "When our mother died, I became the one tasked with caring for you. Mother would have stopped you before now. Do you not trust your sons? My husband? The young warriors?" My silence seemed to shout the answer but no words came. She began to rub salve on the red flesh. "Water Bird is like a young version of you, Father. My nephew follows you around and emulates you in every way. He wears his hair like you and he has copied the way you walk. Use him to give your commands, tomorrow. Sit at the top of the slope and be patient. The men of the clan are not yet Erik, Shaman of the Bear but if you do not give them the opportunity then how will they learn?" She cocked her head to one side and gave me a cheeky smile, "You made no mistakes?"

I laughed, "Very well. You have worn me down and my ears burn with the questions you have hurled at me. I will watch."

The next day was a rarity for me. I sat on the stump of a tree and shouted orders. It was hard not to jump up and try to help but I knew that Little White Dove was right. The men, my sons and grandson especially, went out of their way to get things right. Everyone worked as one and by the end of the day, we had the timbers in place. They were all eager to try it out but I shook my head.

"You have worked well today but tomorrow will be even harder. We will haul *'Laughing Deer'* up the slope and then try a launch. That may well take all day and while I have watched this day, tomorrow I will sit at the steering board when my snekke takes the ride of the Valkyrie."

Golden Bear asked, "Valkyrie?"

I smiled, "That is another tale I will tell you. It is a pleasant evening and we will eat outside so that the whole clan may hear the tale."

The three longhouses meant that meals were taken apart and eating outside proved to be important. The men were able to share the work of the day with the women who had been busy preparing food as well as making winter preparations. I stood to tell the story of the Valkyrie. There were many tales and as the Norns were three of the Valkyrie then they had heard some of them already. When I told them the volva's words, *'Ladies of the War Lord, ready to ride, Valkyries, over the earth'* they were confused and I had to explain to them what a horse was. When I had finished the tales, I told them of the things we had across the sea that were not here. The idea of coins was confusing for them. I had lost the last of my coins in the bay close to Bear Island, or else I might have been able to show them one. I could see the disbelief on the faces of some. Otter's Cub kept shaking his head.

Brave Cub said to the newest member of the clan, "It seems fantastical, Otter's Cub, but," he took out his seax, "this is all the evidence we need to know that my father speaks the truth."

"I do not question Erik, Shaman of the Bear, but I cannot conceive of a beast with four legs that can be tamed and ridden."

I smiled, "Some of them are only as big as a deer and they are used to carry goods and pull carts." I knew I had made a mistake when I said the word *'cart'*, once more I had to explain. It was as wearying explaining to them as working on the rails but it was necessary. They would pass the stories on long after I was dead. I might be the last Viking in this new world but his story would live on. It might become a legend, like the Valkyrie, but that would not make it any less true.

I allowed my sons to grease the rails but I went to tie the rope to the stern of the snekke. Before I did that, I removed the steering board and laid it on the quay and then used a paddle to head for the slipway. Water Bird and Silent Stone waited there for me with the rope. They passed it to me and I tied a good knot in the centre of the snekke's stern. I slipped out of the boat and waved to my sons.

"Come boys, we will move to the side. I hope that the rope is strong enough but if it is not then we do not want to be in the way of a snekke hurtling down the rails."

With every warrior hauling on the rope the snekke made its way up the greased wood. Even though I was not directly beneath the slipway I could see that my calculations had been good and the keel cleared the ground.

"We are secure!" Brave Cub's voice was a relief.

"Come, we shall make our way up to the snekke."

I picked up the steering board at the quay and we climbed the path to the village. Everyone was gathered around the snekke. Golden Bear asked, "When we bring them up for real, where do we store them?"

It was a good question. The old snekke and wood store was too vulnerable to attack. I pointed to the space between the longhouses. "We will put them there. We can make a roof over the top from wood and that will protect them."

Moos Blood nodded, "And also protect the longhouses too."

I had not foreseen that but he was right. *Wyrd.*

"Now let us see if we can launch a boat as easily as we haul it up."

I began to climb into the snekke. "Are you sure this is wise, Father?"

"This is my snekke, Brave Cub, and I trust my sons and the warriors to ensure that they will safely lower me down." I climbed in and placed the steering board on the deck. I held on to the gunwales and said, "Lower me gently."

The snekke started to slide down the rails. Being this close I heard and felt the groans from wood rubbing on wood. I realised we should have greased the snekke too. I made sedate progress down the slope as the warriors strained on the rope. Perhaps it was my extra weight or a flaw in the rope but when the rope suddenly snapped, the snekke sped down the rails as though the Allfather was pushing her. I heard the shouts and cries of alarm from above me but I just concentrated on the patch of river I would hit. I gripped the gunwale. The snekke was out of control and the Norns had spun. I did not fear the water but I feared that the snekke might be destroyed. The prow of the snekke hit the water and disappeared into the river. Water showered over me. It crashed into the bottom of the snekke. For a brief moment, I wondered if we would sink to the bottom of the river but she was well made and fought for life. She rose like a sea beast and righted herself. The prow, the carving of my wife, rose majestically and seemed to shake the water from her. She was not destroyed, at least not yet. I had to work quickly for the current began to take us. Even though the water in the bottom was ankle-deep, I ignored it as I used the paddle as a steering board. I knew then that only I could do this. I had more experience than any man alive in sailing snekke and I had made this one. I worked carefully to make the improvised steering board work. I did not panic as the river took me away from the slipway and towards the Patawomke. I had to work hard to move the snekke but this was my boat and she responded well to me. My sons and the warriors had slipped and slid down the slope and they made their way to me. I saw the relief on their faces.

I beamed, "It works!"

Moos Blood shook his head, "You could have been killed."

I shook my head, "I will not die in a snekke. It was the rope that gave way. We need two ropes and I do not think we need one aboard. The less weight we have the better. We can now protect our two snekke. We will need to make more grease." I smiled, "Now, who wants to sail back to the landing stage with me?"

I was a happy man.

Chapter 15

We had gathered in the harvest and it was stored. We had hunted and fished and all was preserved. We had wood in the wood store and we had one more major task to undertake. We had to haul the snekke from the river and prepare them for winter. I think that after my experience Moos Blood would have preferred to carry them up the slope as we had done in years gone by. I was adamant that we had to use the slipway.

When winter finally came and the leaves had all fallen, we hauled the two snekke up the slipway and they were placed with *'Gytha'* between the longhouses. With a simple roof made of saplings and branches, they would be protected from the worst of the winter weather.

"The accident when we launched it the last time was a gift for it showed us where I had made a mistake. We can rectify that mistake." I smiled at my son and added, quietly, "This will make the whole clan closer for we can use all but the nursing mothers to pull on the rope." I took out the deer's bone I had carved and smoothed while the ropes were being made. "I have made this to make the hauling easier. If we attach this to the tree then the rope can pass through. The bone is strong for the stag was a powerful beast and I have used sand to make it as smooth as Iron Blade's bottom."

He smiled and nodded, "You are still the Shaman, Father, and we will do as you say. What we shall do when you are in the Otherworld I know not."

"You will learn as I did. I followed others until the battle by the falls when the Penobscot took my friends. We started small, your mother and I, and I learned how to lead. You have a clan which is united. Your brothers can help advise you and your sister is as wise as any. Learn to listen and never act rashly. Better to let your mind make decisions. As my brother discovered, when your heart rules it blinds the mind."

Remembering what had happened the first time, every member of the clan was there to help haul the snekke up the slipway. We had removed the masts and steering boards already and the ballast lay piled at the quay. It made the snekke more buoyant and lighter. I waited in the river with Water Bird. We secured the ropes and then stood well off to the side. It helped as I was able to see the snekke better and my grandson and I were both safe should the rope snap. I was confident that this time the better ropes would hold. We had two of them. The second rope was a safety rope, if the first one broke the second would hold the snekke until a new one could be fitted. This time we had used even more grease on the rails and *'Laughing Deer'* slid, seemingly effortlessly up the slipway. I waited until the rope was brought down to us by Silent Stone before I took my hand from my hammer of Thor. The second snekke was smaller and lighter. She almost flew up the slipway. By the time my grandson and I reached the village, the snekke were already upturned as the clan waited for me to supervise the cleaning of the hulls. The women had gone back to the preparation of food and just the warriors awaited me.

I smiled, "Let me watch what you do. If I think you need my advice then I will offer it."

My sons looked at each other. They were being given the freedom to do what they thought was right but there was a great responsibility. I was not worried. If anything they were over careful. They cleaned every piece of weed from the hulls and then used stones to smooth over any rough areas. I heated the pine tar for them. I knew that having my eyes on them would only make them more nervous. I took Water Bird and Silent Stone with me. I was able to show them how to judge when the tar was ready.

Golden Bear came over, "I think we are ready for the pine tar, Father."

"Here it is. I will go to make water."

He stared at me, "You do not wish to inspect the hulls?"

"Why, have you not made a good job?"

"No, but…"

"All will be well." I left them and headed into the forest to make water.

The day after we had placed the snekke together the younger warriors clambered up on the top to add more branches to protect them in the winter. It was not a day too soon for that night a wind came from the north. Winter was coming.

The most important asset having been secured, we made our normal preparations for winter. We had more mouths to feed for the clan was growing. Willow Leaf, Grey Shadow and Little White Dove apart, every wife in the village had given birth. Otter's Cub had married and would be a father but his child would not be born until the new grass. The longhouses were filled, once more, with the sound of babies wailing and mothers singing lullabies. I remembered warriors back in the Land of Ice and Fire who had not liked such a noise. For me, it was reassuring as it meant that life went on. I now had even more grandchildren. In a way, all of the young members of the clan felt like my grandchildren but the child of Corn Tassel and Golden Bear, Iron Blade, was a boy born of my blood.

We spent the days outside when we could and an urgent task was to make ropes. The Moos we had hunted close to Bear Island had provided the best material to make rope but we used whatever we could. We even incorporated our own hair when we could. I knew that would only help to strengthen the rope for they were like the volva's spells. The children and women were best suited to the work for they had the smallest fingers but we all toiled together. Songs would be sung and stories told. Lost Wolf and Grey Shadow told stories of their people and Willow Leaf of hers. They became the lifeblood of the new clan as they bonded us together. The forge caught my eye and I realised that my clan was like a sword. We had taken metal from four peoples and forged them together. I knew from weaponsmiths that weapons made in that way were always stronger than swords made from just iron.

Lost Wolf, Grey Shadow and I were the elders of the clan but as Grey Shadow rarely ventured beyond the door of the longhouse, she did not feel the cold as much as Lost Wolf and I did. I did not feel in the least self-conscious when I donned my bear's skin and bjorr hat to wander outside. Lost Wolf had a bjorr skin cape too. Often, we would be shooed out of the longhouse by the women who wanted to clean or just talk without us being in the longhouse. Now that winter was here the warriors frequently went hunting. We did not need much extra food but looking for animals would also tell us if there were enemies close by. They knew where they had walked and any footprints that they did not recognise would be a sign of danger. It meant that Lost Wolf and I were often the only warriors left in the village. When we were outside, we carried our weapons. Had an enemy managed to evade our warriors I am not sure if the two of us would have been able to do anything other than slow an attacker down.

We had a routine when we left the longhouse. We would head to the sluice gates to see if they had been damaged by rain or falling trees. We would inspect the ditch and the stakes. It was important that we knew where they were. Then we would head down the path to the quay. Now that it was no longer needed for the snekke most of the birch bark boats lay upside down with vines tying them together. Coniferous branches covered them. We would stare across the river. Our warriors would be there but watching for danger was always a good habit.

"You know, Erik, I thought I was a good leader but I can see now that I was not. My son and I felt too safe and we were not vigilant."

"I have learned, Lost Wolf, that a lack of vigilance can be fatal."

"As my son and most of my clan discovered. If you had not found us then I fear my people would have died out and Iron Will would be the last of the Clan of the Dogs." I noticed that without thinking he had stroked Ulla's head. The dog was now old and did not go with the warriors. He and Lost Wolf were together when Ulla was not watching over Iron Will.

"That is why I think we were sent. My sons feared that my voyage might bring danger. You cannot hide from danger. Brave Eagle and his people thought that they were safe and the Moneton came. Warriors are meant to protect their clans and that is what we do." I suddenly realised what I had said, "I am sorry, Lost Wolf, I did not mean any insult."

He shook his head, "No, you are right and a man cannot cause offence if he speaks the truth. The truth might hurt but we cannot change the past. We learn from our mistakes. If we hide them or bury them here," he tapped his head, "then that will make us repeat them. Our new clan now has the blood of many clans and that can only be good. This will always be your clan, Erik and there can be no other like it anywhere. When I saw the sea and the sea beast, I understood for the first time the magic that is within you. I could not understand before I saw it, the idea of sailing beyond land. It would have terrified me to do that and yet you say that you went many days without any sight of land."

I nodded, "Often I went for days without sleep. I did not nor do not see that as magic. It is just a skill I have but I can understand why you might think so. I think that none of my clan will ever return east but one day some of my people may return and I hope that they are greeted warmly and not attacked as we were."

"Our bones will be dust by then."

"Aye, but our spirits will still walk the land and I hope our descendants heed our words."

Each day that the warriors returned I questioned them about what they had seen. In my heart, I did not believe that we were under threat until the new grass began to grow but it did not do to make assumptions.

The days grew shorter and the warriors were away for just a few hours each day. Lost Wolf, Ulla and I were at the wooden quay when we saw the birch bark boat heading towards us. I might have been worried had Long Nose and Black Feather not been paddling.

"All the rest of our boats are here, Erik, what does this mean?"

"I know not but I fear the Norns have been weaving their spells once more."

As the boat came close, I saw that there was something covered by Long Nose's deer cloak. As we held the boat to allow the two men to disembark, he said, "Shaman, we found this boat floating along the river. I dived in and found this." He pulled back the cloak and there was a young woman. I took her to be about fifteen summers old but she was pale and thin.

Lost Wolf said, "Does she live?"

Long Nose nodded.

"Then let us take her to the women. You and Black Feather take her. Lost Wolf and I will see to the boat."

They used the deer skin cloak to carry her as gently as they could up the path to the village. As we lifted the boat from the water we studied the vessel and Lost Wolf said, "This is Shawnee-made."

I had not recognised the designs on the side but Lost Wolf had. "How do you know?"

"They use the mark of the hawk. See it is here at the prow and again at the stern. This is also how they make their boats. She has come from the Shawnee."

"Is she a Shawnee maid?"

"She did not look like one and she has the look of our tribe but the markings she wore I did not recognise."

"Let us go to the village. Perhaps this is the work of the Norns or it could be the Allfather sending us a warning."

As we climbed the path, I noticed how slippery it was becoming. A frost was already forming. I would have to use my seal-skin boots soon. By the time we reached the village the rest of the warriors had returned and it was almost dark. The warriors were all gathered around Long Nose and Black Feather. Golden Bear smiled, "My sister sent us hence and said they would see to the woman. They will tell us when we may enter."

I nodded and told them what Lost Wolf had said to me. Long Nose said, "The boat came from upstream and that is where we believe that the Shawnee live."

Black Feather said, "The woman was awake when we found her. She grabbed Long Nose's hand and said, '*Save me*' before she fell into a stupor."

Long Nose nodded, "When she touched me it was like the shock of falling into an icy river or stepping into a steam hut. It was as though my hair stood on end. I have never felt anything like it before."

I smiled, "I know of what you speak. When I met Laughing Deer even before we spoke, I had the same shock."

"I do not understand."

"You will. You were meant to find her. Why did you jump in the river? Could you see the woman?"

Black Feather said, "We just saw the boat. I had no intention of getting wet." He turned to his friend, "Why did you jump in?"

Long Nose shook his head, "I heard a woman in my head say, '*Save the bo*at' and I obeyed." He looked at me, "She sounded like you, Shaman."

"That was Gytha. She was a volva in my clan and she is the spirit who guided me here. You and the woman are connected, Long Nose."

When we were allowed in it was just Long Nose, Lost Wolf and me who were admitted. The woman was still asleep and swathed in blankets but Grey Shadow, Willow Leaf and my daughter seemed confident that she would recover. "We added honey to some ale and fed her that. Her breathing became easier and she slept."

"Did she speak?"

"No, Shaman." Grey Shadow nodded to her husband, "She is of our tribe but I do not know the clan."

Long Nose said, "She was in a Shawnee boat."

The three women all looked at Long Nose and then at me. Little White Dove said, "Then they are coming, as you said, Father."

"But this does not mean we sleep with knives close to us. It is winter and if they were foolish enough to come then the land would destroy them." I pointed to the path. "When Lost Wolf and I came up the path it was difficult. Soon it will need footwear that will not slide."

I saw relief on their faces, I had been a warrior for so long that I took for granted much that they could not comprehend. I knew the problems of attacking an enemy and we had prepared well.

The next morning, when I awoke, I heard Little White Dove speaking. The woman was awake and I went over to her. "This is my father, Erik, Shaman of the Bear. He is chief, Whispering Leaf."

She tried to rise and I said, "You must rest until the women say you can rise. You are safe now, Whispering Leaf. Can you tell me your story?"

"I was," she looked over to where Blue Eyes, Little White Dove's youngest was playing with a wooden rattle, "the age of the boy when I was taken by the Shawnee. We lived far to the west, beyond this river. We were the Clan of the Chipmunk and few in number. Eight of us were taken and the rest were killed. I am the only one who managed to become a woman. The others died when..." she shook her head, "I cannot speak of it. The chief of the Shawnee, Red Eyes, wanted me to be his third wife. He had allowed me to remain a maiden until I became a woman and was old enough to bear children. I was due to be married to him when the days are at their shortest. I escaped and ran to take a boat. I know not how long I was on the river." I saw Lost Wolf's eyes widen when she said, 'Red Eyes'. He knew the name.

"You took no food with you?"

"The warriors who watched me were inattentive for a short time and I knew that I had to make my escape while I could."

"How far away is the village of Red Eyes?"

She shook her head, "At least three days from here, perhaps more. I was awake for two days and then I woke to see my saviour. I must thank him."

I smiled, "He will see you soon enough. You are welcome to the protection of the clan. None shall harm you while you are here. You have my word."

She smiled, "I feel safe even though you look like no man I have ever seen."

Little White Dove said, proudly, "My father comes from a land beyond the Great Sea. He sailed on the ocean for almost a month."

"The Great Sea?"

Little White Dove laughed, "We have much to tell you. For now, you must rest and recover. You have eaten a little porridge. Grey Shadow will ensure that you are healed."

After I had eaten, I went with Moos Blood and Lost Wolf to speak to the other warriors. "From the words of Whispering Leaf, the Shawnee might be just three days away."

Brave Cub said, "That is closer than we thought."

I nodded, "And as she was the intended bride of the chief, I think we can expect that he will try to hunt for her. She told us that her family lived well to the west and so he may look there first."

Fears Water said, "She will bring disaster to us all."

Long Nose growled, "She will be part of our clan. We protect our own."

I wanted to avoid conflict and I said, "Fears Water, you of all people should know that we cannot abandon anyone. The Shawnee would come in any case. As my son said, they are closer than we thought. They were moving in our direction. I still believe we are safe until the new grass but from now on we have three men walk as far west as they can and look for signs." They all nodded.

"Can I see her now, Shaman?"

"Of course, Long Nose and she wishes to thank you."

"For what? We never leave any that we find alone."

He glared at Fears Water who had the good grace to say, "I am sorry, Long Nose, and you are right, Shaman."

I was left with my sons and Lost Wolf, "When I am gone you will have to deal with problems like this. We are lucky that we all get on but you can see how one minor problem can cause conflict."

"Fears Water was wrong, Father."

I nodded, "I know, Moos Blood, but he now has a family and he was thinking of them and not the whole clan. We keep the warriors busy. Have them make more arrows and put their minds to the placing of traps. I had intended to do so when the new grass comes but perhaps we should do it now, as a precaution."

The warriors were happy to be given the work and when not making arrows we placed traps on the paths that led to the longhouses. We ensured that the whole clan knew where they were. They were easy to avoid but only if you knew where they were placed. Most of them were traps that would make a noise and warn us but there were others like the ones we had made at Brave Eagle's village. Lost Wolf and I left the traps to the others and we gathered spare weapons. Those that could be sharpened were and new flint heads were added to axes and knives.

While we performed these vital tasks Whispering Leaf recovered and, as I had expected, she and Long Nose became closer. He had saved her and she was indebted to him but there was something else. The Norns had spun their threads and they were bound for life. When they announced that they would wed it came as no surprise to any of us. When the Shawnee had not arrived by the winter solstice, I knew that we were safe until the new grass. We had another Bear Winter but this time we did not need to hunt the bear. We could plan for war.

Chapter 16

We had peace but I had pain. The cold seemed to aggravate my wounded knee and I found myself using the steam hut and the soothing leaves in my pipe more frequently. I knew that drinking mead would also help but we had a limited amount of that and I would not take it all. That was not my way. The aromatic leaves, however, were plentiful and, along with the steam hut eased some of the pain. Lost Wolf would often join me. He had no wound but he had aching bones and joints. It was whilst we sat in there that we spoke of our hopes and dreams for the future. We looked beyond the Shawnee and the Moneton. When the savage sea beasts came in packs to devour the seals they passed through and then were gone. We were not helpless seals; we were warriors and we knew how to defend our land. We saw our grandchildren prospering and taming more of the forest. It was Lost Wolf who suggested that sometime in the future we might be able to colonise the opposite bank. It was flatter than our knoll but more open to an attack.

"There will always be enemies, Lost Wolf."

"But you are thinking of our small clan with just eleven warriors. By then Water Bird, Silent Stone, Blue Jay, Red Wing, Brown Feather and Otter's Teeth will be warriors. Then there will be others like Iron Blade. With the weapons you have and the snekke, you can rule this part of the river. Our enemies will learn to fear us."

I shook my head, "That was always my brother's flaw. He wanted to rule. I do not."

"I am sorry, Erik, my words were badly judged. I meant the clan would keep peace along the river close by here. We are a haven for all lost people. You gather them like our nets take fish."

I remained silent. We had tried to live like that in Orkneyjar but Sweyn Forkbeard had decided that he wanted more land and we would take it. What if there was a Shawnee version of the Dane? The leaves took effect and soothed my mind. I would be in the Otherworld when that day came and could do nothing about it. My task was to make the clan as safe and strong as I could while I lived.

As the winter dragged on, and it seemed to last forever, so the tension in the village grew. The Bear Winter had not been as snowy as the last one but it had been cold and wet. The bottom of our defensive ditch was now ankle-deep in water. That had kept the village a little drier but the women still complained about the mud in the longhouses. Whilst the food was not running short yet our supplies were dwindling. The new grass was still some time away. When the days were as long as the nights and the new shoots appeared at the recently erected palisade, I made the decision to launch the snekke.

I gathered the men around me, "The new grass is almost upon us and we need food. We will launch the snekke and the birch bark boats. Lost Wolf will stay with the women while the rest of us explore up and downstream. We will fish as we do so but it is the sighting of tracks that is the most important. Brave Cub will take one snekke and half the boats downstream. I will take the other snekke and Moos Blood will lead the boats. We go armed for war."

The preparation and launching of the boats would take some time and so we planned on leaving the next day. We inspected *'Laughing Deer'* first. She was sound and we had prepared her well. I waited in the river with Water Bird and she slid gently down to us, barely making a ripple when she touched the water. While *'Doe'* was prepared, Water Bird and I fitted the steering board and raised the mast. We paddled her to the quay and then waded through the shallows back to the slipway. *'Doe'* landed in the water even more gently. By the time the warriors reached the quay we had sailed the second snekke around.

Our first task was to load the ballast. We had used the ballast to protect the birch bark boats. This time there was a little damage to the boats and two needed to be repaired. It was dusk by the time the boats and snekke were prepared.

As the warriors prepared to walk up to the village I stopped them, "It is now the time of the new grass. Each night we will have to watch here and at the two ends of the river. There are nineteen of us. We divide the warriors and boys into three watches. Each watch covers the hours of darkness but only two need to be on duty at any one time."

Brave Cub frowned, "There are eighteen of us, Father."

"I am number nineteen and I will not be in one place but will visit each of the three watches."

Moos Blood said, "You are the Shaman, you need not do a watch."

I smiled, "I choose to. Moos Blood, you will have the watch by the upstream gate. Golden Bear, the downstream and Brave Cub, the quay. Choose your own warriors but make sure the young are not left to watch alone. This is as much about teaching them as keeping a watch."

Some of the younger watchers would be barely eight summers old but with such a small clan everyone had to grow up quickly.

As we headed up the trail Lost Wolf asked, "And you are leaving me to watch the village?"

I nodded, "I would stay but I am needed to sail the snekke. Your presence will be reassuring."

"It is not because you think I would be of little use."

I laughed, "You and I have forgotten more about being a warrior than the others have learned."

He smiled, "Good."

My crew were self-chosen. Water Bird and Silent Stone would be with me. They would not need to haul nets, we would be using lines run astern. I wanted their sharp eyes. I planned on getting as far upstream as I could. I did not mention it to Moos Blood but I intended to sail to the fork in the river. That would be too far for the birch bark boats but my skills as a navigator would make it an easy journey for us. The two boys were armed with bows and slings. I had my spear, seax and bow.

As we headed upstream, I shouted, "Moos Blood, land and inspect the banks on both sides of the river. It will stop you from being exhausted and we need to know if there are footprints."

"And you?"

"I am too old to get in and out of the snekke. We will sail as far upstream as we can and then return."

"No heroics, Father."

I smiled, "Of course not."

I tacked upstream but as I did so I told my two crew members what I was doing and why. Each voyage might be my last and I needed to pass on my skills. We soon left the boats behind and sailed up the empty river. Birds took flight as we silently rounded bends. We startled a herd of white-tailed deer. Everything suggested that there were no other men close by. It was noon when we reached the confluence of the rivers. I headed for the northern branch and pulled into the bank.

"I want you two to land and inspect the ground as far as the path takes you. I will make the call of the loon three times when you are to return. Look for the signs of feet and fires. Keep an arrow nocked."

Water Bird nodded, "We will not let you down, Grandfather, and this is Silent Stone's land. All will be well."

As they slipped ashore, I felt as nervous as at any other time in my life. I was used to risking my life but now I was risking my blood and that was harder. They vanished and silence surrounded me. The lapping of the water on the snekke was the only disturbance in this empty land. In my head, I was counting. When I deemed they had been gone long enough, I made the sound of the loon by cupping my hands around my mouth. Then I waited. It seemed like an age but I felt relief when the two youths appeared.

They clambered aboard, "There were no footprints and the fires we found were last year's."

That was a warning. When we had last been here there had been no fires.

"Good, now let us do the same on the main branch. This time you will look at the southern shore. We have seen no evidence of any on that side of the river so any signs, prints or fires will be a warning."

The current took us to the confluence and I headed upstream. We travelled just five hundred paces before we stopped. I dropped the anchor and we ate some of the fish we had caught. It was raw but it was so fresh that it was delicious. "Now slip ashore and listen for my call."

When the two of them returned before I had made the call then I knew they had found signs. Silent Stone pointed behind us, "Shaman, we found a fire and prints. The fire was this year's and the prints told us that there were four men."

Water Bird added, "They had a boat. We could see where it was drawn up."

That told me it had been recent. "Now let us return home. Catch as many fish as you can."

I wanted the two of them occupied so that they did not dwell on the potential danger. This all made sense to me. Whispering Leaf had fled before winter. They would not have been able to search for her. They would have looked across the river from their home. Whispering Leaf had told me that their village lay on the northern shore of the river. Red Eyes would send scouts out. That they had found nothing, for we had not landed before this day, was now clear to me. Now, of course, if they returned, they would see signs that Water Bird and Silent Stone had been ashore. I could not expect them to hide their tracks. What would confuse them would be the lack of signs of a boat being dragged onto the bank. The snekke would be unknown to the Shawnee.

We had travelled further than any other and were the last to return. Lost Wolf and Brave Cub stood on the quay to watch for our return. The sun was setting behind us when we did so. "You had us worried, Father."

"There was little point in scouting if we did not do a proper job. Boys, when you have secured the snekke take the catch to the longhouse. I will walk up the slope." Using my spear shaft I headed up the hill. I said, simply, "They have sent scouts and are closer than I expected them to be."

"And we found signs of the Moneton too."

I stopped, partly to catch my breath and also to clarify what I knew, "Do the women know?"

Lost Wolf nodded, "Some of the younger men could not wait to tell their wives." He shook his head, "Some gossip like old women."

"Then we smile and say that all is well and our preparations will stand us in good stead. Speak to your warriors this night while you eat. We must begin to keep a good watch tonight although I do not think that they will be here any time soon. Tomorrow I will speak with all the warriors." We were nearing the lights of the longhouses and I said, "Now we smile and show confidence to the clan."

The food was good for the dried food and stored beans were augmented by the fresh fish brought in earlier. Even so, there was an apprehensive atmosphere in the longhouse. I sat between my two sons, Moos Blood and Golden Bear.

"We saw no signs on the banks after you left us, Father."

I nodded, "That is good for it means the fires we found are the extent of their exploration. When they return, they may see the footprints of Water Bird and Silent Stone but I do not think Red Eyes would worry about the two boys. What did you find, Golden Bear?"

"The Moneton have crossed the rapids. We found the signs of their feet on the northern bank of the Shenandoah."

"But not on the south?" He shook his head. "Good, then as with the Shawnee, we have time." I lowered my voice, "We will speak more openly tomorrow but from now on we make sure that none of the clan leaves sight of the village without armed warriors to watch for them. When the water is fetched, they will be protected. When they wash the clothes there will be watchers. Our families are both a strength and a weakness. We must not let them be taken and they must be guarded."

Moos Blood shook his head, "Do not be too sure, Father. My mother told them all about her capture and enslavement. Willow Leaf did the same and since Whispering Leaf has come the women are all determined to carry a weapon and defend themselves. If the Shawnee and Moneton warriors think they will have an easy victory the knives and hatchets the women all carry will tell them otherwise."

Moos Blood looked over to where Water Bird was animatedly speaking to Brown Feather, "My son grows in confidence each time he travels with you. You are good for him."

I wondered if he resented the bond between us. My father had never been happy about the relationship I had with Gytha. It was as well to bring such matters into the light. "Does that make you unhappy, Moos Blood? He is a good sailor and a clever warrior."

149

Moos Blood smiled, "Why should I be sad if my son is close to his grandfather? You are teaching him things that will make the clan stronger." He nodded to his youngest son, Blue Jay, "I know that Blue Jay will want to enjoy the company of his grandfather too."

I said nothing for I knew, in my heart, that Water Bird and I would be closer than I would be with any other grandchild. The reason would not be my choice but I knew that I was living on borrowed time. The walk up the hill had shown me the pain in my knee would slow me down. When it came to a fight then, this time, I would be too slow. When Eagle's Claws had attacked us, I had been lucky and able to use the night and the bear's skin to hide from the enemy. The next time would not be so easy. I was happy that I had spoken for I heard the sincerity in my son's words. He would lead the clan well when I was in the Otherworld.

That night was our first real watch and I went out to see if they were all vigilant. They were and heard me coming. I returned to my bed where I slept for an hour or so and then went out a second time. In all, I made four visits to the sentries. The next morning Little White Dove and Sings Softly took me to task. Water Bird was smiling as his aunt and Fears Water's wife chastised me.

"What were you thinking?"

"Aye, Shaman, we have other warriors who are younger and can go without sleep. We do not need you to risk your health."

"Not to mention disturbing the babies. You should know better, Father."

"Then perhaps I should sleep outside the longhouse for this will be my routine from now on. I cannot change my nature, Little White Dove. I have spent a lifetime losing sleep to watch over those that I love. I am an old man now and this is who I am."

Their faces showed that my words had touched them, "It is because we care for you, Father. Losing our mother was hard enough but you are the heart of the clan."

"And I will always be here, even when I am in the Otherworld. I still feel the spirit of your mother, Little White Dove. I am part of this clan and of this land. The body I have is old and weary. My spirit still feels young and alive. My spirit will live on."

Water Bird was no longer a little boy but he was like one as he hurled himself to hug me, "Do not die, Grandfather. I need you."

I put my gnarled hands and arms around him, "And I will stay alive as long as I can but the Norns spin, Water Bird, you know that." I held him from me, "When I am no longer here close your eyes and hear my words. When you sail the snekke see me at the steering board. When you sing the songs then think of me but I have not yet dreamed my death. My watches of the night are there to make sure that I do not die by a blade in the blackness."

The atmosphere in the longhouse was sombre and I knew it was my fault. I went outside and sat on the old stump to smoke a pipe. It calmed me and Lost Wolf came to join me. He said nothing for that was how it was sometimes. Words were unnecessary and simple companionship was all that was needed. Gradually the other warriors joined us. I saw that all wore their knives and hatchets on their belts. That was good. When they all arrived, I stood and went to the open area where they gathered around me.

"As we thought the Moneton and Shawnee have come. It is sooner than we thought but the Norns spin and we are caught in their threads. This is like hunting for the sea beast in the Great Sea. The two enemies know we exist and that we live but they have a huge area to search. They will send scouts. If we see any scouts then we must kill them and hide their bodies. We need to keep them in the dark as long as we can. We still hunt and fish but the difference will be that half of the warriors who do so will be watching for enemies. It means we work harder to gather less food." I held up my empty pipe, "The times when we can sit and smoke, watch the children play and enjoy each other's words will be fewer from now on."

Moos Blood asked, "Do we flood the ditch?"

He made a good point and while I walked the perimeter and the night watch I wrestled with the problem. "Not yet but soon. When we do flood it then our night watches will change. We will no longer need to watch the sluice gates but we will have a new beck to walk. Today we head across the land to hunt and search. We will do as we did yesterday but without boats. This day we walk our side of the river and head east and west as far as we can." I looked at their faces, "We are the Clan of the Bear and our enemies will learn to fear us."

I had already decided that from now on I would wear the bear's skin. It was a symbol of who we were. I went to the longhouse and fetched it and my iron-headed spear. I held it up to point to the west. After laying the wooden bridges we had made we headed across the ditch and into the forest. Lost Wolf would be our only guardian for the women and children. I saw that he had painted his face with charcoal and held his bow. He nodded as I passed. Words were not needed. He would die to protect the clan.

We found animals and brought back a deer but we saw no signs of men. We walked until noon in a long line that spread out across a forest that we had not fully explored. This was a huge land. I could walk across the whole of Orkneyjar in a day. Three days would have seen me cross the Land of Ice and Fire but as I had found it was many days to the ridge that lay beyond the Iron Hills and we had barely explored the land close to the village. We sat and ate.

Moos Blood pointed back to Eagle's Shadow, "One thing we cannot hide is the smoke from our fire. The enemy will see it and once they do then they will know where we live."

I nodded, "And yet they will not know until they reach it if it is to the south or north of the river. The loop in the river is confusing. If they come by boat, in either direction, then we use our boats like weapons. Remember when we encountered the warriors near Salt Island, Moos Blood?"

He nodded, "Aye, the snekke cut through them as though they were nothing."

"That is why we will, from tomorrow, have a snekke sailing upstream and one sailing downstream. We will keep pace with the men on the shore. Tomorrow, we need to look north of the river." I smiled, "We have not hunted there. The animals are in for a surprise." I sounded more confident than I was. Moos Blood was right. The smoke from the fires that fed us might be the thread that trapped us.

Chapter 17

Our new routine did bring us more food and for the next week, we saw no signs of any enemy. I sailed, *'Laughing Deer'* with my crew. The two youths were now skilled enough to sail the snekke without comment from me although Water Bird was the more natural of the two. He always looked at ease while Silent Stone kept one eye on me to ensure he was doing it right. I was the one who ran out the fishing lines whilst watching the warriors who were ashore. Each night, when we returned weary but content, we would stand in the open area sharing what we had seen. We were exploring our land and I had instilled in each of my family the need for maps. We used one map to mark what we saw. Lost Wolf was amused by it all for he saw just trees. I pointed out that I had used maps of the sea which had little or no land. Trees could be identified as could the rocky outcrops and patches of water. My sons and Water Bird were the only ones who truly understood how to read the map I made.

The weather was warming when we saw the first of the Shawnee. It was Moos Blood and the warriors on the land who found them. We were heading upstream and Moos Blood was on the northern shore. I heard the cries of alarm from the north and I had the snekke stopped and turned with the sail reefed. I nocked an arrow and nodded to Water Bird, "Be ready to heed any command I make. Silent Stone, nock an arrow."

The sounds of cries grew and I realised that they were heading for us. The shaven-headed Shawnee with the painted face and holding a stone-tipped spear suddenly appeared before me and stopped in horror and shock when he saw the boat with the bear-skinned warrior. It was the last thing he saw. He was so close that I could not miss and my arrow struck him in the chest.

Moos Blood appeared behind him. My old sword ran red with blood. He nodded at the dead warrior, "There were four of them. We slew three quickly but this one evaded us and headed not back into the forest but came to the river." He turned, "Fetch the bodies." As the others headed back north, he said, "Do we give them to the river?"

I nodded, "But not here. Load them in the snekke and we will take them beyond the loop. I would not distress the women with the sight of bodies floating by."

We moved the catch closer to the stern and put the body on the deck. The other three bodies made us almost overloaded and I had Silent Stone step ashore to return with the hunters. I took the steering board as we headed downstream. Water Bird stared at the bodies. He was closer to death than he had ever been.

"This is for the clan, Water Bird. Better that they die than we."

"I know but it seemed such a quick death. One moment he was alive and then your arrow killed him." He snapped his fingers, "He was dead like that. When he woke this morning, he did not think he would die."

"If he had any sense, he might think that he was taking a risk, heading into an unknown land and seeking enemies. When I was young, I went on raids and we knew that if the Saxons we sought were alert, then men might die."

"And you think the same now."

"I do. The Shawnee had a spear and if he had not been shocked by the sight that greeted him then he could have sent the spear at me and I might have died. Of course, he was doomed from the moment that your father saw him. We were lucky and this is a warning. We flood the ditch."

There was no one at the quay when we passed and for that I was grateful. I saw *'Doe'* appear and we reefed the sail.

Brave Cub nodded as he saw the bodies, "Then it begins."

"Aye, the Shawnee scouts are within a day of Eagle's Shadow. We will slip the bodies into the river. Tomorrow, we flood the ditch. The war has begun."

That night there was a buzz of conversation about the Shawnee and the Moneton but my mind was focused on the problems at hand. When I had suggested sending the bodies downstream it had not been a thoughtless act. I wanted the Moneton to see the bodies. They might have heard of the Shawnee and they might not but the bodies did not look Powhatan and it would give them a problem. The Shawnee, too, would realise that their scouts had been killed and they might even know where but as the path they had taken led to a river where there was no sign of a boat landing, they would probably continue along the northern shore.

I slept little that night. I was not afraid, my mind would not let me sleep. It raced like a drekar before an east wind. I spoke with all the sentries. Wearing my bear's skin made them start but was also reassuring. Silent Stone and Water Bird had told the whole village of the reaction of the Shawnee. He had been terrified. The legend of the Ulfheonar was a powerful one and one was now in this new world. *Wyrd*.

The whole clan came to see the opening of the gates. I ensured that all but a handful were well up the slope. I did not use the horn. We did not know how close our enemies were but, instead, I used my grandson, Blue Jay to run and tell his father to open the western one. I hoped that my gates would work. Brave Cub was with me and I nodded as a signal. Blue Jay sprinted away and we hauled on the rope. It was hard work because of the pressure of the water but as it rose the pressure lessened and the water flooded the stake-filled ditch. It raced down the ditch, the muddy water's top flecked with white like racing horses. By the time the gate had cleared its runners, the ditch was filled. Reassuringly we had to move back as it began to seep over the top of the ditch. When Moos Blood and Golden Bear opened the other gate, we knew immediately for as the waters met, someway between us, it caused the water to spill back and rise even higher. I wondered if I had miscalculated. We had made four bridges from the rollers we had brought back from the rapids but I was not sure if they would bridge the new stream. I stayed watching long after most of the women and children had returned to the village.

Brave Cub nodded, "We are now surrounded by a river, Father. If nothing else our enemies will have to endure wet feet."

"Aye, but unless the level drops then we are trapped."

Lost Wolf said, "Not so, Erik. We have the boats."

He was right, of course, and I was guilty of seeing the drinking horn half empty. Eventually, the river found its own level and when Brave Cub and Humming Bird tried the bridge, to my relief, it bridged the gap. We could cross while an enemy could not.

That day we could not sail or scout as far as the previous day as we had waited to see the new river. It was not a surprise when we saw no new signs. The next day, however, I sent the boats and scouts out before dawn. I knew that I was tiring out my warriors but if we were not vigilant then the whole clan would have an eternity of sleep.

We sailed upstream with reefed sails and Moos Blood and the warriors moved as though hunting deer. We pulled into the bank close to where we had killed the warrior. Moos Blood and the warriors ghosted up to me. "We have seen their signs, Father, there were more of them this time but their tracks headed north and west."

"Let us return to the village."

When we reached the village Brave Cub and the others had not yet returned. I waited with Moos Blood and was relieved when the snekke and birch bark boats appeared.

Brave Cub stepped out, "We have seen more signs but none closer than the last time."

"Tomorrow, you must be even more cautious."

The tension was beginning to get to everyone. Each time we neared Eagle's Shadow I saw the spiral of smoke from the fires and knew that it was a beacon that would be seen and soon. When we had killed the Shawnee, I had looked back and could see nothing. The Allfather had helped us by sending a breeze that moved the snekke and dispersed the smoke. If we had a still day then it would be disastrous.

It was two more days before we had news and it was of the Moneton.

"We ambushed three of their scouts." I gave Brave Cub a questioning look and he shook his head, "We lost none and no one escaped. We sent their bodies down the river."

"And that means the noose is tightening." Moos Blood was with me and I said, "Tomorrow we have half of the warriors in the snekke and birch bark boats and the other half ashore. If they have been searching along the northern shore and not found us then they might switch to the south. I want the flexibility to tackle them whichever side they are on. We will leave the boys and youths with Lost Wolf. We cannot be sure that we have spotted every sign of our enemy."

"Even Water Bird?"

I shook my head, "He is the one who will sail the snekke while I use this old nose."

Silent Stone was unhappy to be parted from both Water Bird and me but he accepted that he was needed to guard the village. We had established a new routine so that when the water was fetched then all those in the village did so and the same when washing was being completed. The rest of the time saw the clan in the open space between the longhouses where they could be protected.

We sailed along the river. Bjorr Tooth, Otter's Cub and Long Nose were in my snekke and Moos Blood led the two birch bark boats that accompanied. We were just turning the bend to the place we now called Shawnee Point when Bjorr Tooth hissed, "Birch bark boats."

Water Bird was at the steering board. "Do all that I say." He nodded. I turned and said, "Moos Blood, danger. Bjorr Tooth, full sail!"

I wanted the same shock as we had enjoyed before. I could not see the boats and for all that I knew they might outnumber us but I knew that our best hope lay in shock and surprise. *'Laughing Deer'* leapt forward as the wind caught us. I knew that Moos Blood would struggle to keep up with us but there were four of us with bows. *'Laughing Deer'* was also a weapon and that day proved to be our most powerful one.

As we turned the bend, I saw that the eight boats had all stopped. They were in three loose lines. The sight of the top of our mast must have made them wary. Two warriors leapt overboard as the carved prow of our snekke raced at them. We rode over one boat and smashed through a second. I loosed an arrow at the nearest warrior. It was like hitting fish in a small pond. We could not miss. With two bowmen on each side, we ploughed through the Shawnee fleet.

"Turn us around, Water Bird." I did not cease sending arrows as we heeled, the gunwale perilously close to the river. I saw behind us Moos Blood and his men spearing those who floundered in the water. A warrior cannot swim and fight at the same time. It was carnage. It took Water Bird some moments to regain complete control of the snekke but in that time I saw that we had destroyed three boats and the others had all capsized. Survivors of our attack were clambering ashore but even as they did so the others sent arrows into them. Not all were mortal but we had stopped the attack and hurt them. It was a victory.

"Back home!"

With the current with us, Moos Blood was easily able to keep up with us and we spoke as we headed the few miles back to Eagle's Shadow.

"Will that stop them, Father?"

I shook my head, "They want Red Eyes' woman and we have hurt them. From what Lost Wolf said the Shawnee have not yet suffered a defeat. They will not like this but we must have killed good warriors this day. They will return to their chief and the next time that they come it will be with every warrior that they have. We explore this side of the river no more. They will find us." I pointed at the smoke from the fires. We could see it and that meant so could the Shawnee.

Brave Cub had found nothing but that did not mean we were safe. "The Moneton would not be surprised and shocked by the snekke. Tomorrow, we draw them up the slipway and carry the birch bark boats to the village. They can be made into a barrier. We are now about to see if our defences are good enough.

There was too much to do for anxiety to make us nervous. "Leave the ballast in the hulls. I have plans."

"It will make the snekke harder to haul."

"Trust me, Golden Bear."

He was right, it was hard but we managed it. Once the snekke were at the top I had the ballast taken out but instead of being stored for the winter, I made a stone trap. I used a couple of saplings buried in the ground to make a store for them. It took some time but by the time we had finished the rocks were behind a barrier of wood. By the simple expedient of hitting the key branch with my hammer, the whole pile of rocks would fall and sweep an enemy who might be trying to ascend the slipway. "If they try to ascend the slope then we simply release the rocks and the avalanche will clear the slipway."

Moos Blood shook his head, "A clever idea, how did you come to think of it?"

I shrugged, "The spirits?"

When the boats were brought up, I had them made into a barrier to complete the fourth wall of the longhouses. It would not stop an enemy but it would afford protection from spears, stones and arrows whilst also slowing down those trying to get over it. I had fire-hardened javelins stacked behind it and bags of arrows were placed along the perimeter. I wanted us to be as prepared as we could be.

The attacks had done one thing, they had made our night watches even more important. None of the clan had objected to the duty but now there was a reluctance to return to their longhouses. The warriors were protecting their families and nothing was more important than that.

We gathered before dawn in the enclosed space between the longhouses. We had eaten, a night duty ensured hot food for all, before dawn. I looked at Water Bird and the youths, "You will all be under the gaze of Lost Wolf and the women today. Your job is to keep watch from here for the enemy." I pointed to the roof of the longhouses, "One of you will watch from up there. It is an important job and one that a warrior cannot do. You will patrol the river and the ditch. If there is danger and we come back quickly then you will have to be on hand at the bridges to lower them for us."

Fears Water asked, as the young men nodded, "We will be beyond the ditch?"

"Aye, Fears Water, we are few in number and have to use surprise to defeat our enemies. We know the land and they do not. Their scouts will have a poor picture of the land."

"But is that not dangerous, Shaman? Should we not remain hidden?"

I laughed, "Look around you, Fears Water. We have tamed the land around Eagle's Shadow. Even a blind man could tell that it has people living here. They will leave the land that is untouched by man and find our trails. They might cross the trail to the Iron Hills or the one to the Bjorr Water. They are clearly not animal trails. We use ambush and our skills to hurt them. We whittle them down as we would a branch we wished to make into an arrow." Not only Fears Water but all the other warriors nodded at my words. They now understood. "We will divide into two groups. I will lead one with Brave Cub, Bjorr Tooth, Otter's Cub and Long Nose. Moos Blood will lead the others. I will take my warband towards the Patawomke and Moos Blood towards the Shawnee. We walk until noon. It is important that we keep one eye on the river in case they come by boat."

Golden Bear said, shrewdly, "But you do not think that they will."

I shook my head. They might use the boats to bring them closer to Eagle's Shadow but both of our snekke have hurt both bands of warriors. I cannot see them risking disaster by fighting a weapon that has destroyed so many boats and killed so many warriors. They will trust to the spear and tomahawk." Again, they nodded. "We wait for an hour and then return. I will have my horn and Moos Blood his. If we are discovered, and only if we are discovered, then three blasts will be a warning to everyone." I took out my seax, which glinted as the first rays of the sun appeared in the east, "Kill as many as you can and do so without taking a wound. We are few and they are many. Now, go!"

I slung my bow over my back and grasped my spear. I knew that the skin I wore would make me hot but that slight discomfort was worth the shock when a warrior saw me.

I led my band down the slope to the bridge that lay close to the eastern sluice gate. We watched the river and seeing waterfowl swimming along it, I ordered the bridge to be lowered. In my mind, I had planned on making them like a drawbridge that could be raised and lowered but the early arrival of our enemies meant we had not yet implemented that plan.

"We leave this one here for us to use."

"Is that wise, Father? What if the Moneton get behind us? Did you not ask the boys to be ready to lower the bridges?"

"I did," pointing along the ditch I added, "But it may be we are deeper in the forest. We aim for this one but we know that if we have to take another route there will be a bridge for us to use. The last thing we need is to be forced to cross a deadly ditch."

I hurried across and once on the other side, I waved my spear so that we made a longer line. It meant we were not walking along our path and had to negotiate the trees and bushes but that was no bad thing. It would disguise our presence. Birds and animals fled at our approach. That could not be helped. A hawk, circling high in the sky would be able to detect our movement from above but an enemy would only see birds rising somewhere ahead of them. The bear's skin also afforded me some protection from thorns and branches, I felt that it made me part of the forest. Man was not natural here but the bear was. I was aware of the others as we moved along but my senses were attuned ahead. One thing I knew from my youth was that you could smell other men when you were raiding. The breeze was in our faces and that would carry any Moneton smell towards us. I could smell nothing. We moved steadily eastwards. Every so often I would hold up my spear and we would stop and listen.

By the time the sun was high in the sky we needed a break and to have food and ale. I needed to make water. We spread out on either side of the trail that animals used to come to the river for water. I signalled for silence and, after I had relieved myself, laid my weapons down next to the bole of a tree. With my back to it, I ate the pickled fish and the spring berries. I washed them down with my ale and then listened. I calculated that we had travelled five Roman miles from our home. That was based on the speed we had moved and the time it had taken. We would have run that far in a couple of hours but our cautious movement made it take us longer. The silence meant that I heard the two birch bark boats as the paddles dipped into the water. I hissed a warning. Had anyone been close it would have sounded like a snake's warning. I grabbed my bow and kneeling, drew an arrow. I felt Brave Cub slip next to me and we watched. The two boats had just three warriors in each one. They were scouts. I saw that the warrior in the middle was scanning both banks. I sensed Brave Cub nocking an arrow and I shook my head. These men were not a danger to us for there were too few of them. In addition, I had heard another noise in the distance, men were moving through the forest.

As the second boat passed us, I turned to Brave Cub and spoke in his ear, "There are men in the forest. Warn the others. We ambush them. Listen for my words. I will speak in Norse."

I had taught the warriors some Norse. They were all command words. Their use would confuse an enemy.

He nodded and slipped away. As he passed the other three he spoke in their ears and they nodded. Each one nocked an arrow. These were flint arrows but they were well made and our bows were, I knew, stronger than those used by the Moneton. For one thing, they were longer and took more strength to draw.

We waited and I heard the Moneton as they moved through the forest. They were using the animal trail which was the easiest way to move. I heard them because they were speaking. Their words were too muffled to hear them precisely but they marked the progress of the men. I knew that as Bjorr Tooth and Otter's Cub were closest to the path, they would have a clear sight of the leading two warriors. We could not afford any wasted arrows. I nocked an arrow but did not draw it.

I saw the flash of colour from the dyed feathers worn in the hair of the Moneton warriors. I had seen them before and knew that the different colours signified something but I knew not what. I counted eight. They were still scouting and seeking us. I wondered if they had a camp along the Shenandoah or had they just sent this handful? I could clearly smell them. They had covered their bodies in grease. Every clan had their own salve to keep away the biting insects. I raised my bow. I could now see, through the trees, the line of men. They were moving as slowly as we had done and were examining the ground for our signs. My caution had been well justified. I am not an arrogant man but I did know my own skill. I knew I could hit the man at the rear of the line, even though he was more than a hundred paces from me. I would have to wait until I had a clear line of sight but I tracked him.

Because I was waiting for it, I heard the sounds of the first two arrows and I drew back. The cries of the two warriors at the front of their line who were hit made the other warriors stop, and then they raised their weapons. They stared around. My target seemed to stare at me but I knew that it was an illusion. I was too still. I did see his eyes widen as my bow snapped and released the arrow at him. I did not take my eyes from him but drew a second arrow. He was struck in the chest and fell. I traversed my bow as the next warrior raced towards our line. He could not see us but he had seen the flight of arrows. He moved like a startled white-tailed deer and jinked through the trees. I waited patiently and when he was just ten paces from me drew back and released. The arrow slammed into him so hard he was knocked from his feet.

There was silence. I slung my bow and, taking my spear headed towards the trail. I had killed two and I had enough confidence in the others, whose targets were closer, to believe that they had succeeded too. My spear was there to finish off any wounded warrior. When I reached the first man, I saw that he was as old as Moos Blood. He was a veteran. I had wondered if they would send their younger untried warriors. I drew my arrow from his body. The head would be ruined but I could reuse the shaft and the flight. I picked up his weapons. I broke his bow and I took his bag of arrows. I rammed his stone knife into the tree close to him. It broke the blade. I did the same with the first warrior I had killed. The others saw what I was doing and emulated me. I waved them close. "Hang the bodies from the trees."

Brave Cub asked, "Why, Father?"

"They will send men to search for these eight. Finding their bodies hanging in the trees will worry them and make them more cautious when they come next time. We need to slow them down."

When it was done, I led my warband down the river trail. "If we can we will ambush the boats."

I had been a scout when I had been a young warrior. The boats would have been given orders to coordinate with the foot patrol. Eventually, they would close with the bank. We had travelled, perhaps a thousand paces when I heard the distinctive sound of paddles driving into the river. I nocked an arrow and took shelter behind a tree. The others did the same. The two boats had closed with our side of the river and I saw the leading warrior peering into the undergrowth. I knew that I could hit him. Suddenly an arrow flew from my right and an arrow hit, not the warrior but the boat. He shouted and the man at the rear used his paddle to take the boat further from the shore. My arrow hit the leading warrior but it was in the shoulder. He was a tough man and kept paddling. Brave Cub's arrow took the man in the centre but the steersman was not harmed. I nocked a second arrow. The boat that followed was not as lucky. Five arrows slammed into the three men. One man was not killed instantly but the capsized boat ensured that he would struggle to survive.

I turned as the capsized boat, bodies and the other boat headed downstream. Otter's Cub held his head in shame, "I am sorry, Shaman, I released too early."

I nodded, "There is no shame in missing, Otter's Cub, but just as I allowed you and Bjorr Tooth to take the men closest to you on the path so you should have waited for me to release." I smiled, "It is a lesson and you have all done well."

He asked, "Is that it? Have we defeated them?"

Brave Cub put his arm around the young warrior, "We have poked the nest of snakes and hurt them but they will come and the next time it will be in numbers." He looked at me, "We will wait for them closer to Eagle's Shadow tomorrow?"

I nodded, "And we make traps to make them fear the forest. Let us use nature to help us."

Chapter 18

Moos Blood and his warriors had found just four scouts and they had been killed. As we spoke of the skirmishes I said, "The Moneton are closer and we have hurt their scouts twice. They sent greater numbers but we use the same precautions for both. We take the boys with us tomorrow and Lost Wolf. We make traps for them."

Golden Bear smiled, "As we did at Brave Eagle's village."

"Aye, and we know that they worked. We will keep two sentries further out to watch for enemies."

That night I could not sleep. It was not nerves but pain from my knee. I had walked further on my wounded leg than I had since I had been to the Iron Hills. It woke me constantly. It was not a problem for me to rise and ensure that all were on duty. I just did not wander far from the longhouses. I did not risk the slope, I just counted the men sleeping in the longhouses and knew that the duties had been changed. As I lay in my bed, my knee slavered in the salve that brought some relief, I wondered how it would hold up in a battle that promised to be fought at close quarters. The Moneton warriors we had slain had been fit warriors. Taking them in an ambush was one thing but hand-to-hand fighting was quite another. I was the first awake, thanks to my poor night of sleep. I made water and added wood to the fire. The wood was dry and the smoke it created was thin. It would be seen, of course, but the enemy would be within sight of the ditch and the quay when they did so. Hot food would sustain the clan. As I mixed the maize and water to make the porridge, I wondered how the Moneton and Shawnee warriors were being fed. When we had raided in our drekar we had endured cold, dry rations. It was always an incentive to take a settlement where we could enjoy hot food. The men seeking to take our village would be the same. We might have full bellies but they would be hungry.

Grey Shadow left her longhouse to join me. She smiled, "Getting old is a chastening experience is it not, Shaman? The need to make water is more frequent and the aches and pains that accompany movement are unwelcome."

"I know but old age has blessings. We can watch the young and see their hopes and dreams."

She nodded, "I have lived longer than my sons and that is sad, but now I have grandchildren and I would see them become adults."

Lost Wolf came from his longhouse and I could not help but laugh, "So the three elders are the first to rise and prepare the food for the young."

Grey Shadow smiled, "And I for one do not mind. We are useful and not baggage to be carried. When I was young some of the elders seemed to think that the young had to wait upon them."

Lost Wolf took a wooden spoon to help us to stir, "You forget, wife, that we apart, some of the other elders of our clan did so before they were slain by the Shawnee. It was we two who fought and escaped with our family and Silent Stone."

"You are right, husband, perhaps we were meant to join this clan, Shaman, for here I feel that we are not strangers but part of a family."

"And over the next days, the fate of that family will be decided. We either defeat two powerful enemies or the Clan of the Bear dies out here on the Shenandoah."

I know not what the others thought as they emerged, in the light of a new day, when the three of us had such reflective looks on our faces. We did not explain and they could deduce what they would.

Lost Wolf, Water Bird and Silent Stone came with my warriors as we headed into the forest to the east of us. I stopped just one thousand paces from the water-filled ditch. Brave Cub knew what we intended and both Long Nose and Otter's Cub had a vague idea for they had been in Brave Eagle's village but I explained it carefully so that all knew my plan. "Our aim is to channel them into the traps. I want them moved away from the river into the forest. We add to their journey. We put briars and brambles to bar their way and force them to head for our traps. Our traps do not need to kill but if we can then so much the better. We want to hurt and demoralise them. We need them to make a noise. This is the furthest point we will make traps. We work our way backwards and none head any further east." We had spoken the previous night about how to make traps and no further words were needed.

Using our axes we hacked saplings, buried them in the ground and sharpened their points. We disguised the points with undergrowth. I had worked out that at this point they would know where Eagle's Shadow lay and would be eager to join with us. We then dug pits and embedded sharpened branches, like natural arrows, in the bottom and then covered them with brush. I knew that this time the warriors would be coming this way in daylight and would be able to examine the land. They might spot some of the traps but the slower they came the more of them could be killed as we waited for them. It took until the middle of the afternoon for us to complete our work. We had not seen or heard any signs of the enemy but I guessed that they were still some miles away. Our ambushes the previous days would have made them wary. They would have started at innocent movements in the forest. I knew that the next day would be the bloody one.

We reached the cleared area close to the ditch. The making of the rails and the hewing of firewood had cleared the land for fifteen paces. It would not hold up our enemies but there was no cover there and we would have a clear line of sight. The last twenty paces of the forest were left without traps for that would be where we would wait. I turned to Brave Cub, "Use the spare timbers to make a barrier here. I want it as high as Iron Will."

"Aye, Father. It will be a last stand before the ditch."

When the warriors had all crossed back I said, "And now one last trap. For this, we need good swimmers."

I saw some of the newer members of the clan frown but my sons merely smiled and Moos Blood said, "The mind of the Shaman is like a snapping turtle's jaws. It works faster than a man can blink. Let us go and see what he has conjured."

When we reached the river, I pointed to the two ropes I had placed there after breakfast, "We will tether this rope just below the surface and secure it to the other bank. If they bring their birch bark boats along the river then they will be stopped. They will be able to cut the rope but they will be slowed and we will be warned. Attach some pieces of bone to this end and they will rattle when the rope is moved."

It took until darkness to complete our tasks but we were, in my mind, as secure as we could be. I knew that the Norns might spin but that was out of our hands. I had done all that I could to keep the clan safe.

We had taken to eating outside the longhouses as the weather had improved. We could all see each other and that, somehow, made us closer. I thought back to the halls we had built where the whole clan could eat and talk. I would have built a mead hall but I knew that it would take too much effort and I was not sure that I had the skills. Ships I could build but large buildings were another matter. The conversations went from the mundane to the meaningful. Young couples like Otter's Cub and Doe's Milk had their heads together as they spoke of their unborn child and their eyes sparkled love. Others, like Willow Leaf and Little White Dove, talked together about planting new crops. The warriors discussed the ambushes and the fight to come. I was, largely silent.

I was surprised when all went quiet and Little White Dove said, "You still plan, Father, on leaving Lost Wolf and the young warriors here to guard the ditch?"

"We need to have someone watching the ditch and be ready to lower the bridges to allow us to cross the ditch when we fall back."

"And why cannot the women and the girls do that?"

I was lost for words.

Grey Shadow smiled, she had lost some of her teeth over the years and it gave her a strange smile, "You will need every man and boy that you can get, Erik. We can move a wooden bridge."

Willow Leaf nodded, "Aye, and hurl a dart."

We had made darts. They were simple enough and used sharpened bone set into baked clay. With feathers at the back they could be thrown by any of the clan. I doubted that they would kill but they could hurt, they would distract and they were a weapon that our enemies would never have seen for they were my copy of a weapon the Saxons had used against us.

Lost Wolf chuckled, "Aye, and I would not like to face our women at close range." His face became serious, "And I will be happier, Erik, Shaman of the Bear, if I am fighting alongside you."

There was a murmur of approval from the other warriors.

Moos Blood nodded, "It makes sense to me, Father. It almost doubles those who can fight. My sons can hurl stones and send arrows. They can guard our backs. This is a battle for the survival of the clan."

I knew that I was defeated. The women could fight but I feared for them. Some might die. A warrior expected to fight but it was not right that women should have to. Moos Blood was perfectly correct. This was a battle for the survival of the clan.

"Then let us use the whole clan and show our enemies that the Clan of the Bear has teeth and we know how to use them."

After that it became a sort of celebration. The sentries were relieved and when they joined us were told of the new plan. Lost Wolf and I enjoyed a pipe of the dream leaf and I found myself actually smiling.

That night I did sleep and the dream leaf worked for I dreamed.

It was dark and the night was filled with twinkling lights that I saw were eyes. Dawn broke and the lights became warriors. The warriors were in two long lines and the lines gradually joined to become a huge snake. To my shock and surprise the snake began to eat its own tail and all went black. In the darkness I heard Laughing Deer's voice, 'Soon you will join us, husband. Watch for help where none is expected and save our blood.' She disappeared and I saw flashes of faces, my brother Arne, Siggi, my father all appeared and disappeared in an instant and then all went black. Suddenly I saw a glow and I headed towards it. I found a door with a handle. I put my hand on it. 'Now is not your time, Erik the Navigator.' It was Gytha. I pulled my hand back. All went black.

When I opened my eyes, I was in the longhouse. People were moving around and it was day. I had not checked the sentries. Why had I slept so long? I leapt from my bed, "Moos Blood, you should not have let me sleep so long."

Laughing Deer gave me a strange smile, "It was as though you were in another place, Father. We tried to wake you but could not. We knew you were alive but you seemed not to be in your body."

I nodded. I had been not only in the land of dreams but I had glimpsed the Otherworld. I knew then that this would be the day. The enemies were coming.

"Arm yourselves and take your positions. The snakes are coming and we must be vigilant if we are to survive. Listen for my horn."

"You have not eaten."

"Daughter, I will eat when this day is done."

I donned my bear's skin and fastened my old leather belt around my waist. I no longer needed the scabbard for Moos Blood had my sword but I had a sheath for my seax and a loop for my hatchet. I tied the bag of arrows to the belt and then put my bjorr skin hat upon my head. It would add to the illusion that I was an animal. Taking my bow I first strung it and then slung it over my shoulder. Before I left the longhouse, I took my spear and then looked around. Everyone was busy and did not see my eyes as I watched them. I saw my son and daughter and their children as they prepared for war. I had done a good job in raising them. I smiled, we had, it was not just me who had done that, Laughing Deer had more than a hand in raising them for they showed the care that she had lavished upon them. The others, too, were almost as close as my own family. The Norns had spun and we now had a clan that was like a huge family. Sometimes the Norns spun and good came of it. Perhaps they had felt I deserved something. I was just grateful for the time I had enjoyed with all of them.

Brave Cub entered, "We are ready, Father, and wait for you."

I nodded, "I am old and need more time."

"Lost Wolf is there already. He is eager to go to war again."

I wondered if Lost Wolf had experienced the same dream as I had.

Outside the warriors were waiting. Golden Bear had a small pot of crushed beetles. He came to me and smeared it around my eyes and nose, "If you are going to be an Ulfheonar then you should look like one." He stepped back, "Now you have a face for war."

My three sons and my grandsons were all before me and I said, "I never say it and I should. I am proud of all of you. You are not just warriors you are good men and that is not always the same thing. Your mother would be proud."

They looked at each other, not knowing what to say. Lost Wolf had been watching and he said, "We should be in the trees before our enemies."

"You are right. Lead on, Water Bird."

The Clan of the Bear went to war.

Chapter 19

Erik, Shaman of the Bear

The sentries had already laid down the bridges and we crossed them. I had the line of warriors, youths and boys move together as one so that the path to the bridge was not clearly marked by fresh footprints. We had spoken of our plan. Lost Wolf, Water Bird and Silent Stone would join me and be the middle of the line. Brave Cub would anchor one end of the line and Bjorr Tooth the other. Long Nose would be between Brave Cub and Silent Stone. I laid my spear next to the tree I had selected and then took out three arrows. I laid two of them on one of the branches before me and loosely nocked the other. That done I turned around. Lost Wolf was just a couple of paces from my left. Water Bird was to my right and Silent Stone was next to Lost Wolf. I spoke quietly, "Remember, you two, as soon as the enemy come close, then you will stand behind us both. Your job is to watch our backs and to make certain that the path is clear."

Water Bird said, "We can still send arrows and stones, Grandfather?"

"Of course, but as soon as I tell you then you will both race back to the ditch. I cannot be worrying about you two."

Silent Stone was nervous, "Perhaps they will not come."

"They will, or the Moneton, at least. They lost too many men yesterday. As for the Shawnee, I do not know. I confess that I am not confident about how this Red Eyes will act."

"You were right to speak of a snake, Erik, for that is what he is. I had heard of him before Whispering Leaf came to us. He is the war chief of the Shawnee. He cannot afford to have his men slain and for him not to retaliate. It may not be today but he will come."

I nodded. That did not help us. If I knew for certain that he was not coming then I would have the whole clan waiting to ambush the Moneton. Then I remembered the dream. It was snake that was coming. Lost Wolf called the chief a snake. They were coming. We had two battles to fight.

It was the birds taking flight just four hundred paces from us that alerted us to the Moneton. I drew back the bow a little. I made a hissing noise and the two boys turned. I nodded towards the forest and raised my bow. They each nocked an arrow. Now it would begin. The last Viking in this new world was going into battle once more. Would it be my last fight? I put those thoughts from me as I watched the undergrowth move. Then I heard a cry from further away in the forest. Someone had tripped one of our traps. There was a flurry of movement and there were more cries. The trap had panicked them. If my plan had worked then they would be heading down the trail to Lost Wolf and to me. It meant the warriors, youths and boys would be able to make a flank attack. As some of the Moneton would have a shield that meant a greater chance of a hit, for the shield would protect their front and not their sides. The advance slowed and I heard moaning from the forest. We had hurt at least one of the Moneton and the others would be warier.

They discovered more of our traps. One crash and terrified scream of pain told us that a warrior had fallen into a stake filled pit. He would take no further part in the attack. We were whittling them down. A voice shouted out an order. The snapping of branches and the crashing of falling men marked their progress but we heard fewer cries. The tension was getting to our men. I saw Water Bird and Silent Stone look around for reassurance. I smiled when they did so. It seemed to satisfy them. This would be their first real battle. The skirmish against the Moneton in the birch bark boats would be as nothing compared with this.

The first warrior that I saw fall was not hit by me but by Bjorr Tooth. The young warrior had a powerful arm and a good eye. He must have had a good line of sight to hit the warrior for when he fell he was at least one hundred paces or more from me and Bjorr Tooth was almost at the river. The involuntary cry of the warrior and the crash of his body made the advancing warriors halt and look around. They had moved stealthily through the undergrowth but when they stopped and peered around, I took my chance. I drew and released in one motion and the flint tipped arrow slammed into the side of the Moneton warrior's head. That precipitated a rush from the Moneton. Our arrows flew and kept on flying as we sent missile after missile at faces and bodies marked by feathers and bone. It was then that I heard a cry from behind me. I did not turn as Silent Stone did for I knew it was the Shawnee. Moos Blood and his warriors were engaged. We had a battle on two fronts.

Our advantage was that we were protected by trees and by branches jammed between trees and bound with vines and brambles. Our hands had been cut about when we had made the barriers but they were as effective as a wall. There were still traps and pitfalls before the Moneton and I doubted that they had yet seen their attackers. We wore no feathers and the painting of our faces with red cochineal from the dead beetles merely made our features harder to discern against the shadows of the forest. Still they came and I wondered just how many had they brought. In a way the more they brought the safer we would be in the future... if we won.

I had used half of my arrows when the warriors halted. I guessed they were evaluating their choices. When arrows began to rain blindly down from the sky, I knew what that choice had been. They were hoping for lucky strikes. Had we been packed together then they might have enjoyed some success but we had all chosen trees with thick branches above us and there was at least four paces between each of us. They must have sent sixty or more arrows before they stopped. Silence filled the forest. The moaning of the Moneton wounded had ceased and I guessed that they had either died or been taken to safety.

Suddenly a cry rent the air and twenty or more Moneton burst from their places of concealment. There were still traps and we also had our barrier. I said, more for Water Bird and Silent Stone than anything, "Be strong and trust to our defences."

It was easier than I had expected and more men were dropped than I had anticipated. Even so eight warriors made it close to me and Lost Wolf. I sent an arrow into the face of one. He was so close that the feathers sprouted from his forehead. As Water Bird and Silent Stone ran behind me to protect my back, I dropped my bow and picked up my spear. It was then that I was seen and the first Moneton I saw stopped, his eyes widening as he took in the bear's skin, bjorr hat and red eyes. He hesitated and, as I had learned, hesitation was fatal. The metal spear head drove into his body and I felt the head grate off his backbone. His death was a merciful one. Water Bird and Silent Stone had switched to slings and at the close range that they were used they were deadly. When our defences were finally breached it was an accident. Two huge warriors ran at the barrier and they must have used the body of the man I had speared as a board upon which to leap. As they came in the air above us, Lost Wolf and I stabbed at the same time. The men died but their bodies straddled the barrier and made a bridge. The Moneton did not immediately take advantage of it for they fell back.

Lost Wolf said, "Is it over?"

I shook my head, "They are regrouping."

The noise from the battle with the Shawnee was worrying. I was tempted to leave this battle and go to Moos Blood's aid. I knew I had to trust to my son and the spirits who had told me to *'look for help where none is expected*. I still did not know what it meant but we would stick to the original plan.

I took a decision, "Fall back to the ditch."

I waited until I sensed movement from my left and right and then Lost Wolf and I moved back. I saw that his forearm had been cut. It must have been when the warrior launched himself at us. If that was our only wound then the Allfather was truly smiling upon us. When we reached the ditch the women and children all stared at us. I smiled, reassuringly, "We are all whole and we have hurt them. Little White Dove, take the women and children up to the longhouses. Defend the barrier. We will hide behind our wall of wood and give them a surprise."

She nodded, "Let us obey the Shaman."

Grey Shadow strode up to Lost Wolf, "First I will tend to this old fool's arm."

"It is a scratch."

"Let me be the judge of that."

While his wound was tended, we pulled back the bridges. Of Moos Blood there was no sign and so I left one for him. I assigned Water Bird and Silent Stone to hide and stay close to it.

I placed my spear on the ground and then nocked an arrow. There were four bags of arrows behind the barricade. We could all replenish the ones we had used. Grey Shadow bound her husband's arm and, after kissing him, headed up the path to the longhouses. She had to force Ulla to accompany her. The dog was attached to Lost Wolf. For an old woman, Grey Shadow was remarkably spry and almost ran up the path. I waved the warriors, youths, and boys to shelter behind the log barricade. We would hear the Moneton as they came. Our traps had brought them to this crossing place. Of course, they could try to cross the ditch anywhere but if they did then the cries of their warriors as they found the stakes would tell us that. I deduced that they would follow our path, mainly because it was the safest one. When I heard voices from the trees, beyond the open space, then I knew the Moneton had followed. Our ambushes and attacks had made them cautious. They did not attack directly. I risked peering over the top of the logs. My hat would look like an animal and not a man. With just my eyes level with the top log I looked over and saw that there were at least forty warriors. They had, indeed, emptied their land of warriors. I consoled myself with the thought that no matter what happened to us the rest of the Patawomke Valley would be safe from their predations.

I saw a leader, he wore more feathers than the rest, pointing his spear at the ditch. I hissed, "Be ready." I began to raise my bow. I had already chosen my target, the leader. He did not use a verbal signal but a visual one. He jabbed his spear at us and they ran towards us.

"Now!"

I stood and released as they covered the short distance to the ditch. A warrior cannot run and loose an arrow, at least not accurately, nor can he throw a spear. We were relatively safe from their missiles but if they reached the log barricade then it would be a different story. The handful of warriors we had to face them would be outnumbered. My arrow struck the leader in the right shoulder. The arrow was a good one and drove deeply into the flesh. I saw that half of the shaft was embedded. He kept coming but I knew that his right hand, the one that held the spear, would be weak. Their speed of movement meant that only one of the warriors we hit suffered a mortal wound and they hurled themselves at the ditch. It was invitingly narrow and did not look particularly deep. The younger ones, the warriors who reached the stake filled stream, screamed as they found the wooden spikes. Some fell forward, to be impaled upon them. Others tried to pull spiked feet and legs from the water. It was then that our arrows and stones began to reap the living and turn them into the dead.

Moos Blood and his warriors also chose that moment to return and I knew that the Shawnee had to be close. He and his warriors fell upon the left flank of the Moneton. I shouted, "Water Bird, bridge the water."

The sudden attack and the trap filled water was more than enough for the Moneton and they retreated. However, their leader lived and there was still order. My son and the rest of our warriors crossed. I saw that Fears Water was hurt. As soon as they had all crossed, I said, "Pull back the bridge. Fears Water, get to the longhouses."

Moos Blood smiled, "We have done well but the Shawnee are like fleas on a dog."

"Then let us hide once more."

They took their places along the barricade as Water Bird and Silent Stone rejoined Lost Wolf and me. I felt better about the defence for we now had almost double the number of defenders. The path behind us wound between trees and would be a channel that we could block. Our defence would be to hurt them and then fall back to our next line of defence. The last one would be the longhouses. We waited and we listened. It seemed an age before we heard anything and when we did then even I was surprised. It was the sound of fighting and dying in the forest. I looked down the line. None of the warriors in Moos Blood's band were missing. I risked looking over the barricade and saw that the Shawnee were fighting the Moneton. My dream came back to me. It was the snake eating itself. The help was our enemies. *Wyrd.* Perhaps they each thought that the other band was one of our allies. I cared not for they were killing each other.

We had hurt the Moneton already and as my son had said, the Shawnee were as numerous as fleas. The Moneton broke and fled. Thankfully some of the Shawnee followed them. I looked at the sky and saw that the sun had passed its zenith. I took the opportunity to drink some ale. I passed the skin to Lost Wolf who murmured, "I did not think I would live to see the afternoon. Your Norns have, indeed, spun."

"It is not over and the tunnel is still dark but I spy a light at the end of it." My hand went to my Hammer of Thor as I spoke some of the dream I had dreamt.

The Shawnee, now reorganised, began to bang their shields. I had not heard any do that on this side of the Great Sea but I had heard it when I had fought Saxons. They chanted and I said, quietly, "They will come when they stop the chanting. Pass it on." The whisper slid down the line. I chose a metal tipped arrow for I wanted my next missile to be a deadly one. I tried to picture what the Shawnee would see. They would spy the Moneton dead in the water but they could not know that they had been killed by stakes. They would assume arrows. They would see the logs and know where we waited. Having driven off the Moneton then they would assume we were weakened and see victory was within their grasp. If we could hurt them and do so quickly then we had a chance.

The Norns were spinning.

As soon as the banging stopped, the air was rent by a shrieking scream as the Shawnee hurtled towards the ditch.

"Now!"

We rose as one and sent arrows and stones at the wave of warriors. My heart sank for they outnumbered us more than the Moneton had. The battle between the two tribes had hurt the Shawnee but not enough. My arrow slammed into the chest of the leading warrior. He was a huge, shaven headed creature who wore bones in his ears. His eyes widened when he saw the bear and then, as the iron tip drove through the bones he wore across his chest, through the flesh to crack open his breast bone and slice into his heart, the life went from them. I loosed another and another as they reached the ditch. The dead Moneton became their allies for some of their bodies afforded a bridge.

Bird Song's voice from behind me, told me that the Three Sisters had not yet done with me, "Father, Grandfather! The Shawnee have crossed the river!"

We were now attacked from two sides. I took the only decision I could, "Moos Blood, take your warriors and get back to the longhouses.

We will hold them as long as we can." My son was torn, I could see that. I nodded, "Go, it is the right thing to do,"

"You are right, may the Allfather be with you. On me!"

"Water Bird, follow your father."

"No, Grandfather, I was told to guard your back and I will do so," I remembered the dream.

Lost Wolf laughed as he sent another arrow into a Shawnee, "This is a good day to die, Erik, and my sons shall be avenged."

My men, it seemed, all had the death wish while I was not yet ready to go to the Otherworld. I would fight until the last, as my brother Arne had done.

The enemy reached our side of the ditch as there were fewer arrows flying at them. I looked and saw that my bag of arrows was empty. I grabbed my spear and shouted, "Make your way back up the hill. The barricade will slow them." The warriors hesitated but obeyed me, "Good and use your slings and arrows over my head."

Lost Wolf gave an ear piercing war scream that made the Shawnee pause, "And I will fight at your side. We will show them!"

Some of my warriors still had arrows and they used them to great effect. The boys used their slings but the Shawnee kept coming. I saw Red Eyes. He was not leading his men but commanding them. He had a shield upon which were painted two red eyes. If I still had an arrow then I could have killed him and the battle would be over. *Wyrd.* He had with him what looked like bodyguards. I thought back to the three killers sent by Eagle Claws to kill me all those years ago. I held my spear in two hands. Lost Wolf and I backed together. Our spears jabbed and poked at wild warriors who saw a bear and an old man before them. The two boys stepped from our sides to throw their stones and the focus of the attack became we four. The others were slightly above us as they moved up the slope. There they were able to aim their arrows and to find flesh. We four would be the blockage that slowed up the attack. I needed to buy the time to let Moos Blood deal with the other attack. We were backing up between trees. The Shawnee were forced to make a frontal attack.

I remembered then, the fight at the falls when the Penobscot had driven our warband to its doom. Arne and the others had made the Penobscot come to them and they had slain many of them. Eventually, the savage warriors killed all but me, however, they had paid a great price. We had to do the same with the Shawnee.

My spear darted like a snake's tongue. It knocked aside the Shawnee stone tipped spear and slid effortlessly into the warrior's middle. I pulled it out, throwing the dead man to the side to impede the advance of the rest. An arrow flew from behind me to smack into the head of a Shawnee who tried to leap over his dead companion. It was then that the arrows came from the Shawnee. Red Eyes saw that we were the blockage and tried to remove it. I was saved by my bear's skin. The stone arrows, sent from inferior bows, could not penetrate but Lost Wolf had no such protection. One arrow found his leg and another his arm. He dropped to one knee.

"Get Lost Wolf to safety."

To enable the two boys to do so I advanced towards the Shawnee. It was then that Red Eyes saw his opportunity. He raced forward with his three bodyguards. Lost Wolf shrugged off the attempt by Water Bird and Silent Stone to help him. He raised his spear and raced to join me. Red Eyes and his three men were still some paces from us as Lost Wolf and I stabbed and slashed at the Shawnee who were before us. He was bleeding heavily and I knew he was weakening.

As one of the bodyguards ran towards us, he said, "Thank you, Erik! I will see you in the Otherworld." He ran at the bodyguard and rammed his spear into the man. The Shawnee was mortally wounded but he had enough strength to smash his stone club into the side of Lost Wolf's head.

Silent Stone's scream of anger filled the air. He and Water Bird moved towards Lost Wolf, "Get back!" I did not look behind me but I must have been distracted for one of the other bodyguards seized his chance and rammed his spear at me. I reacted but not quickly enough. The stone spear gouged into my leg. I brought my spear head back and it raked across his throat. Blood spurted.

"Water Bird, get up the hill and warn your father. Go!"

I did not turn but I heard him say, "Come, Silent Stone, for my grandfather is right. Farewell, Grandfather. I will seek you in my dreams."

I nodded as I struck my spear at the next bodyguard. Red Eyes had a stone tomahawk and his shield. He shouted, "The bear is mine."

His bodyguard nodded and brought his own axe down to smash through the shaft of my spear. It fell to the ground. I drew my seax and my hatchet. I would have preferred my sword and shield but I would do all that I could to stop the enemy from getting to my family. The path ran red with Shawnee blood but there were still enough of them to hurt. My death might delay them long enough to organise a defence.

If I thought there would be honour from Red Eyes, I was wrong. He intended to kill me but fairness did not enter into it. His remaining bodyguard flanked him as he advanced and he would try to hurt me and ensure that his chief had a victory. The blood oozing from my leg would weaken me but not for a while. I had time to slow them. The more of them that I killed the more chance my family and clan had of survival.

Red Eyes was a powerful warrior and when he brought his tomahawk over to strike at my head, he must have thought he had an easy kill. He had never fought someone who was wielding an iron weapon and when the hatchet bit into the wooden handle of his weapon his eyes widened. I stopped the blow and he pulled it back. His bodyguard chose that moment to swing his axe at my side. I had my seax in my left hand and he must have thought it was my weak side. I used the seax as I would my shield, had I carried one. I swung it up and across. I slowed the axe but the stone still raked my side and blood flowed. I whipped my seax up and across. It slashed his neck and the blood spurted, showering both Red Eyes and me. As the man fell, Red Eyes stepped back. His easy victory was not so assured. He shouted, "Kill him."

I took the opportunity to head back up the trail. The longer I could hold them then the better chance the clan had of survival. Red Eyes hung back and allowed three younger warriors to try to kill the bear. I could not move back quickly for I had a wound in my leg and the other knee still carried a wound. The three caught me but paid for their success. Being above them allowed me to swing my metal hatchet. The warrior who held up his shield thought he had protection. The metal, still sharp enough to shave with, sliced through the hide and into the side of his head. The second was spattered with blood and brains. The distraction was enough for me to slice the seax across his throat. The third one enjoyed success. His spear hit my side. The bear's skin took some of the power from the blow but it still dug into my flesh, rasping along my ribs. My hatchet split his head in two. The other warriors decided that I was too great a threat and they left the path to head up through the trees. It left Red Eyes to face me alone.

He came warily. His tomahawk was weakened and he feared my two metal weapons. I felt the blood dripping down both my leg and my side. Soon I would succumb to the loss of blood and then I would die. I had to end the battle and do so quickly. I surprised him by not retreating and, instead, advancing towards him. I swung my hatchet and he tried to block it with his shield. This time the hatchet did not strike his head but it cut through the hide and into his arm. I felt is slide across the bone. He reacted by swinging his tomahawk at me. This time I met it with the seax. He was strong and his power threatened to drive the stone weapon into my head. The Norns were spinning. The knee wounded by the Moneton arrow all those years ago chose that moment to give way. It

simply buckled and I fell. The tomahawk struck fresh air. I had the wit
to slash as I fell and the seax sliced into the back of his calf. He too fell.
The slope was steep and there was nothing to stop us as we rolled down
the hill. I looked up and saw the sky. I was now in even more peril for
there were Shawnee warriors who had been wounded and they were
gathered at the bottom. Red Eyes was still alive but wounded. I would
be outnumbered. I remembered the fight at the falls and my brother
facing many enemies.

Using the hatchet I pushed myself to my feet. My wounds and my
knee screamed in pain. The first warrior who came at me had a stone
axe. I had longer arms, and my seax sliced across his belly before the
stone could connect. A second came on my blind side and he stabbed
me in the side with a bone knife. I swung the hatchet and it connected.
Red Eyes saw his chance. He rose to his feet and grabbing a spear in
both hands he ran at me. I could not move. If I had tried, I would have
fallen. I flailed with my hatchet and deflected the stone spear a little but
it still drove at me and entered my left side. His arms pushed harder and
it sank into my body. I knew it was a mortal wound. I used the last of
my strength to slash the seax across his throat. I watched the light leave
his eyes.

My wounds had weakened me and my body would not support me
any longer. I sank to my knees. I screamed in pain. The scream came
not from my lips but from my body. I rolled onto my back and the spear
broke. The wounded Shawnee gathered above me to finish me off. I still
held my weapons before me but there would be too many of them. Then
I heard another scream. It came from Water Bird. He led the boys down
the slope and they screamed and shouted like eagles. I smiled as I saw
his hatchet hack into the neck of a warrior and then all went black.

Moos Blood

I did not want to leave my father but I knew that we had to save the
clan. His sacrifice would not be in vain. When I reached the top of the
slope I saw that Grey Shadow had raced down the slipway to the
advancing Shawnee warriors. There were more than thirty of them and
they were finding it hard to climb, as my father had predicted. When
Grey Shadow lost her footing she slid down the slope. Her weight
knocked three warriors into the river and her slashing knife hacked into
the leg of another Shawnee warrior. Even as he screamed his
companions speared the brave wife of Lost Wolf. Like my father and

her husband, she would not die in vain. I took the hammer that lay next to the rock pile and with one blow broke the timber that held it in place. The rocks rolled and crashed down the slope.

"With me!"

Taking my father's sword I slid on my backside down the slipway. Grey Shadow's death had shown me that this was the most effective method of descending. I watched the stones as they bounced and rolled down the slipway. Some smashed and broke legs. Others flew into the air to crack and crush skulls. It effectively ended their attack but there were so many of them that we had to finish them off. Sliding down I sliced into the neck of one warrior with the Viking sword. My feet smashed into the face of a Shawnee who had miraculously avoided the stones, as he hurtled backwards his skull smashed into a stone. By the time I reached the river they were all either dead or trying to swim across the river.

I turned. Water Bird and the young warriors were at the top of the slope. "Go and help your grandfather." We struggled but managed to make the top however, it took longer than I wanted. When we did reach the longhouses we ran to the aid of my father. I was just in time to see three Shawnee stab at him with spears, knives and stone hatchets. Water Bird and the others fell upon the Shawnee with such ferocity that they brought to mind the Viking warriors my father had called berserkers. We hurtled down the path to aid them but to be truthful the attack of the young bloods was more than enough to destroy the will of the Shawnee. Their leader and best warriors dead, the young ones who were left fled, but we were in no mood for mercy and we pursued them all the way back to the neck of the river where they had beached their boats. The survivors packed into two and headed upstream. They would tell a tale, no doubt, of a more numerous foe than the one which had defeated them. It was a victory but the cost was too high. Erik, Shaman of the Bear should not have had to sacrifice his life for the clan and yet I knew that, given the choice, he would not have had it any other way.

As we walked wearily back to Eagle's Shadow, I knew that we had much work to do the next day. The enemy dead would need to be burned. That was not out of any sense of responsibility, we did not need the carrion. Even as we neared the village we heard the howling of Ulla as she mourned Lost Wolf. It was an eerie moment and it sent shivers up my spine. By the time we reached the place my father had died, he and Lost Wolf had been taken by the women up to the village. They and Grey Shadow would be given funerals to match their sacrifice. Ulla lay on top of the butchered body of Lost Wolf. He and Grey Shadow would be buried in the way that their clan wished but I knew my father's wishes. As we reached the top I saw the old snekke, *'Gytha'*. The last Viking would have a Viking funeral.

Epilogue

Moos Blood

When Erik the Navigator, Erik the Bear, Erik the Shaman died it was as though our world had ended. He had built a clan from nothing and held it together against all enemies. It was not only me who wept, nor just his family, it was everyone in the clan who knew just what he had done for us. Lost Wolf and Grey Shadow were laid to rest amidst tears for they had saved their clan and now had helped to save their new one. Ulla, the faithful dog and guardian of the clan, laid himself down on their graves. He died the night they were buried. He was faithful until the end.

When we had burned the bodies of the Moneton and Shawnee we had counted them. More than sixty warriors had died and there had been others who had managed to reach the river and we knew not their fate.

We prepared the snekke and placed my father's body in the bottom. We placed his sword in his hands and his seax was in his belt. His hair and beard were combed and oiled.

Willow Leaf shook her head, "He was such a handsome man."

Little White Dove said, "To us, he was our father and I will mourn him until the end of my days."

We placed his compass by the steering board and then covered him with his bear's skin. Finally, we laid kindling around his body. Brave Cub fastened the steering board so that it was central and Silent Stone held the sail ready to hoist it. Each of his children and grandchildren kissed his forehead for the last time. The women had done a fine job and not a wound was to be seen. My son wept uncontrollably. He was not unmanned for others did so, but Water Bird and Erik, Shaman of the Bear had enjoyed a relationship that ran deep. I finally had to take him from the snekke. Golden Bear and Brave Cub held the torches and I said, "Now, Silent Stone."

The young warrior hoisted the sail and both the current and the wind took her as the torches were thrown into the snekke. I should have known that the Norns had a last trick to play. The clouds had been gathering all morning and suddenly they unleashed a rainstorm that made it hard to see your hand before your face.

We had planned the funeral and we stood, sodden and soaked watching the snekke sail down the Shenandoah. We waited for it to burst into flames and sink but it did not. The rain was so hard that it must have doused the fires for the snekke with its old sail continued downstream to the Patawomke and the sea. We still saw the odd flame flickering in the gloom of the rain but the sight of a snekke and sail burning were hidden from us. We could do nothing about the rain but we could continue to honour our leader and we carried on with the funeral rites as we had planned them.

Water Bird had known him the best in the last years and had been close to his grandfather. It was he who sang the song of Erik the Navigator as the snekke, with sail billowing and flames sparking, left the quay and headed down the Shenandoah for the last time. He had changed some of the words and that told me that Water Bird had more Viking in him than any other.

The Norns had spun, their spell was cast
The clan's enemies came at last
The Moneton came by river and land
A vengeful tribe, a fierce warband
The clan prepared to fight for life
In a land of peace free from strife
Erik's clan was by the water
The Moneton they would slaughter

With Viking sword and sharp seax
Erik's clan sent the Moneton to hel
Erik's clan was like a Norseman's axe
Their hearts were true they fought as one
The clan of the bear that day was born
Golden Bear and Brave Cub
Fears Water and Moos Blood
With Erik the Bear together they stood

The walls were made, the five they waited
To see the traps that they had baited
The Moneton found death and pain
Still they came again and again
The arrows flew, stones found bone
But the five of them were alone

The Last Viking

With Viking sword and sharp seax
Erik's clan sent the Moneton to hel
Erik's clan was like a Norseman's axe
Their hearts were true they fought as one
The clan of the bear that day was born
Golden Bear and Brave Cub
Fears Water and Moos Blood
With Erik the Bear together they stood

Golden Bear was but a bairn
With the slingers he did return
The stones they threw and arrows sent
Broke the charge the Moneton were spent
Brave Eagle and his doughty clan
Defeated the Moneton as was their plan
Warriors were made on that bloody day
They held the Moneton carrion at bay
With the blood of Lars the clan fought well

With Viking sword and sharp seax
Erik's clan sent the Moneton to hel
Erik's clan was like a Norseman's axe
Their hearts were true they fought as one
The clan of the bear that day was born
Golden Bear and Brave Cub
Fears Water and Moos Blood
With Erik the Bear together they stood

Though Erik has gone to a better place
And we all mourn him in our earthly home.
We still see his Viking face
And know the sailor still will roam
We sail his boat made with his hands
We touch the skin of the bear he slew
We walk each day through Erik's lands
And smile at the places Erik knew

The clan of the bear that day was born
Golden Bear and Brave Cub
Fears Water and Moos Blood
With Erik the Bear together they stood

The clan of the bear that day was born
Golden Bear and Brave Cub
Fears Water and Moos Blood
With Erik the Bear together they stood

As we watched I kept expecting to see the sail catch fire but the snekke did not want to die yet. She was sailing with the man who had made her. We kept watching long after the snekke, still unburnt, had disappeared.

It took a year for us to learn the fate of the snekke and my father. When we sailed to Brave Eagle's village to trade and to head to Salt Island, we were told a tale that still makes the hairs on the back of my neck prickle. They had seen the snekke, seemingly empty, sailing down the river. It was dawn and the birch bark boats were fishing. They said that the snekke looked to be without a helmsman but still sailed a true course. When we visited Salt Island the warriors from Screaming Eagle's clan confirmed that the snekke had made the Great Sea. **'Gytha'** had sailed into the rising sun and was headed east when last they saw it. We knew not its fate but the story made us content. The last Viking in the land to the west of the Great Sea had died and would now be in Valhalla with his oar brothers. It was, as he would have said, '*wyrd*'.

Erik

All was black and I found myself floating above the earth. I watched as Water Bird hacked his hatchet into the skull of a Shawnee and I heard the cheers as my clan celebrated the victory. All went black again and I searched for the door that would take me to Valhalla. I was floating once more and this time I was aboard a boat. It was a snekke and I saw, flashing before me, images of the Shenandoah, Patawomke, Bear Island until the snekke became a drekar and I was at the steering board but alone. I spied the Land of Ice and Fire and then Seal Island. When I saw Orkneyjar I knew that my journey was almost done. The drekar disappeared but I did not drown. Instead, I rose as though lifted on ghostly hands. Gytha appeared next to me and held her hand for me. I took it and I walked on clouds. Laughing Deer materialised on my right hand side and took my other hand. I saw the door to Valhalla and this time it was open. When I looked down, I saw Arne, Siggi, Dreng and Ebbe. They were carrying the

*shield upon which I stood. We walked into Valhalla and I saw my
father and uncle with golden horns of mead in their hands.
Arne said, "Here we have the last hero from the New World. He has
sailed for the last time and Erik the Navigator can take his place
amongst the greatest of warriors." He held up a hand to help me to
the ground, "You were the greatest of warriors brother. Welcome."
The cold was gone, the wounds were healed and I was with my family.
I had come home.*

The End

Glossary

Alesstkatek-River Androscoggin, Maine
Aroughcun -Raccoon (Powhatan)
Beck- a stream
Blót – a blood sacrifice made by a jarl.
Bjorr – Norse for beaver
Byrnie - a mail or leather shirt reaching down to the knees.
Chesepiooc - Chesapeake
Cohongarooton- The Potomac River above Great Falls
Fret - a sea mist
Galdramenn - wizard
Gingoteague - Chincoteague Virginia
Lenni Lenape - Delaware- the tribe and the land
Mamanatowick - High chief of the Powhatans
Mockasin - Algonquin for moccasin
Muhheakantuck - The Hudson River
Natocke – Nantucket
Njörðr - God of the sea
Noepe -Martha's Vineyard
Odin - The 'All Father' God of war, also associated with wisdom, poetry, and magic (The Ruler of the gods).
Onguiaahra - Niagara (It means the straits)
Østersøen – The Baltic
Pamunkey River -York River, Virginia
Patawomke – The Potomac River below Great Falls.
Pânsâwân - Cree for dried meat
Pimîhkân – Pemmican
Ran - Goddess of the sea
Skræling -Barbarian
Smoky Bay - Reykjavik
Snekke - a small warship
Tarn - small lake (Norse)
Wapapyaki - Wampum
Wyrd - Fate
Yehakin – Powhatan lodge

Historical references

I use my vivid imagination to tell my stories. I am a writer of fiction and a storyteller, and this book is very much a 'what if' sort of book. We now know that the Vikings reached further south in mainland America than we thought. Just how far is debatable. The evidence we have is from the sagas. Vinland was named after a fruit that was discovered by the first Norse settlers. It does not necessarily mean grapes. King Harald Finehair did drive many Vikings west, but I cannot believe that they would choose to live on a volcanic island if they thought there might be better lands to the south and west of them. My books in this series are my speculation of what might have happened had Vikings spent a longer time in America than we assume.

Pinus echinate or shortleaf pine is native to Virginia and grows both in swamp plains and mountains. For the purposes of this story, I have the Powhatans call it the shortleaf pine.

The name, Shenandoah, was not, as history might tell us created by George Washington. The name of the river existed before George Washington undertook his expeditions. I am assuming that in the one thousand years since the time of Erik, the river will have changed its course but I have tried, wherever possible to use the river as it is now. I have canoed down the river and can attest to the shallowness in places. The snekke would, indeed, have had to be carried over them.

Seals are found in the Atlantic as far south as Georgia although they are less common there than in the colder waters further north. I am writing about a time a thousand years ago and so I am using my imagination to conjure a world although a world based on the facts that I know.

This is the last in the series. There will be no bridging novel as there was with Dragonheart. Erik's family in the Shenandoah Valley might have stories to tell but I will not be telling them. The three-novel series I began all those years ago has become a little more. Stories will do that sometime. I breathe life into them and like Frankenstein's monster, they have a life of their own. I liked Erik and I hope I gave him the death I think he would have wanted. (Yes, to me, all my characters are real). I am grateful to all the readers who contacted me about the stories: the archaeologist who told me he had excavated a stratified 10th-century Danish coin from the bay in which I placed Bear Island, to Ron who sent me the scholarly paper, published in 1936 which described a tribe of blue-eyed and blond-haired Sioux Indians who were made extinct in the 1850s by disease. As I say I am a storyteller but the emails I have received tell me that my story is not as fantastical as I first thought when I began writing about Erik and his family.

I hope you enjoyed reading the series as much as I enjoyed writing it.

I used the following books for research:

- Vikings- Life and Legends -British Museum
- Saxon, Norman and Viking by Terence Wise (Osprey)
- The Vikings (Osprey) -Ian Heath
- Viking Longship (Osprey) - Keith Durham
- The Vikings in England Anglo-Danish Project
- Anglo Saxon Thegn AD 449-1066- Mark Harrison (Osprey)
- Viking Hersir- 793-1066 AD - Mark Harrison (Osprey)
- National Geographic- March 2017
- Time Life Seafarers-The Vikings Robert Wernick

Griff Hosker
May 2023

Other books by Griff Hosker

If you enjoyed reading this book, then why not read another one
by the author?

Ancient History

The Sword of Cartimandua Series
(Germania and Britannia 50 A.D. – 128 A.D.)
Ulpius Felix- Roman Warrior (prequel)
The Sword of Cartimandua
The Horse Warriors
Invasion Caledonia
Roman Retreat
Revolt of the Red Witch
Druid's Gold
Trajan's Hunters
The Last Frontier
Hero of Rome
Roman Hawk
Roman Treachery
Roman Wall
Roman Courage

The Wolf Warrior series
(Britain in the late 6th Century)
Saxon Dawn
Saxon Revenge
Saxon England
Saxon Blood
Saxon Slayer
Saxon Slaughter
Saxon Bane
Saxon Fall: Rise of the Warlord
Saxon Throne
Saxon Sword

Medieval History

The Dragon Heart Series
Viking Slave *
Viking Warrior *
Viking Jarl *
Viking Kingdom *
Viking Wolf *
Viking War
Viking Sword
Viking Wrath
Viking Raid
Viking Legend
Viking Vengeance
Viking Dragon
Viking Treasure
Viking Enemy
Viking Witch
Viking Blood
Viking Weregeld
Viking Storm
Viking Warband
Viking Shadow
Viking Legacy
Viking Clan
Viking Bravery

The Norman Genesis Series
Hrolf the Viking *
Horseman *
The Battle for a Home *
Revenge of the Franks *
The Land of the Northmen
Ragnvald Hrolfsson
Brothers in Blood
Lord of Rouen
Drekar in the Seine
Duke of Normandy

190

The Last Viking

The Duke and the King

Danelaw
(England and Denmark in the 11th Century)
Dragon Sword *
Oathsword *
Bloodsword *
Danish Sword

New World Series
Blood on the Blade *
Across the Seas *
The Savage Wilderness *
The Bear and the Wolf *
Erik The Navigator *
Erik's Clan *
The Last Viking

The Vengeance Trail *

The Conquest Series
(Normandy and England 1050-1100)
Hastings

The Aelfraed Series
(Britain and Byzantium 1050 A.D. - 1085 A.D.)
Housecarl *
Outlaw *
Varangian *

The Reconquista Chronicles
Castilian Knight *
El Campeador *
The Lord of Valencia *

The Anarchy Series England
1120-1180
English Knight *

191

The Last Viking

Knight of the Empress *
Northern Knight *
Baron of the North *
Earl *
King Henry's Champion *
The King is Dead
Warlord of the North
Enemy at the Gate
The Fallen Crown
Warlord's War
Kingmaker
Henry II
Crusader
The Welsh Marches
Irish War
Poisonous Plots
The Princes' Revolt
Earl Marshal
The Perfect Knight

Border Knight
1182-1300
Sword for Hire *
Return of the Knight *
Baron's War *
Magna Carta *
Welsh Wars *
Henry III *
The Bloody Border
Baron's Crusade
Sentinel of the North
War in the West
Debt of Honour
The Blood of the Warlord
The Fettered King
de Montfort's Crown

Sir John Hawkwood Series

The Last Viking

France and Italy 1339- 1387
Crécy: The Age of the Archer *
Man At Arms *
The White Company *
Leader of Men *
Tuscan Warlord
Condottiere

Lord Edward's Archer
Lord Edward's Archer *
King in Waiting *
An Archer's Crusade *
Targets of Treachery *
The Great Cause *
Wallace's War *
The Hunt

**Struggle for a Crown
1360- 1485**
Blood on the Crown *
To Murder a King *
The Throne *
King Henry IV *
The Road to Agincourt *
St Crispin's Day *
The Battle for France *
The Last Knight *
Queen's Knight *

Tales from the Sword I
(Short stories from the Medieval period)

**Tudor Warrior series
England and Scotland in the late 15th and early 16th century**
Tudor Warrior *
Tudor Spy *
Flodden

The Last Viking

Conquistador
England and America in the 16ᵗʰ Century
Conquistador *
The English Adventurer *

Modern History

The Napoleonic Horseman Series
Chasseur à Cheval
Napoleon's Guard
British Light Dragoon
Soldier Spy
1808: The Road to Coruña
Talavera
The Lines of Torres Vedras
Bloody Badajoz
The Road to France
Waterloo

The Lucky Jack American Civil War series
Rebel Raiders
Confederate Rangers
The Road to Gettysburg

Soldier of the Queen series
Soldier of the Queen
Redcoat's Rifle

The British Ace Series
1914
1915 Fokker Scourge
1916 Angels over the Somme
1917 Eagles Fall
1918 We will remember them
From Arctic Snow to Desert Sand
Wings over Persia

Combined Operations series

The Last Viking

1940-1945
Commando *
Raider *
Behind Enemy Lines
Dieppe
Toehold in Europe
Sword Beach
Breakout
The Battle for Antwerp
King Tiger
Beyond the Rhine
Korea
Korean Winter

Tales from the Sword II
(Short stories from the Modern period)

Books marked thus *, are also available in the audio format. For more information on all of the books then please visit the author's website at www.griffhosker.com where there is a link to contact him or visit his Facebook page: GriffHosker at Sword Books or follow him on Twitter: @HoskerGriff

Printed in Great Britain
by Amazon

27261311R00116